By TEMPESTE O'RILEY

Caged Sanctuary
Dreamers' Destiny
Grand Adventures (Dreamspinner Anthology)
Whiskers of a Chance

DESIRES ENTWINED
Designs of Desire
Bound by Desire
Desires' Guardian • Desires' Pride
Temptations of Desire
Truth in Lace

Published by DREAMSPINNER PRESS
www.dreamspinnerpress.com

Dreamers' DESTINY

Tempeste O'Riley

DREAMSPINNER PRESS

Published by

DREAMSPINNER PRESS

5032 Capital Circle SW, Suite 2, PMB# 279, Tallahassee, FL 32305-7886 USA
www.dreamspinnerpress.com

Dreamers' Destiny
© 2016 Tempeste O'Riley.

Cover Art
© 2016 Reese Dante.
http://www.reesedante.com
Cover content is for illustrative purposes only and any person depicted on the cover is a model.

ISBN: 978-1-63477-212-9
Digital ISBN: 978-1-63477-213-6
Library of Congress Control Number: 2016900161
Published May 2016
v. 1.1

Printed in the United States of America
∞
This paper meets the requirements of
ANSI/NISO Z39.48-1992 (Permanence of Paper).

ACKNOWLEDGMENTS

THANK YOU to Peter and Katy for your faith and encouragement. Peter, without you, Cam and Liam would never have been. You challenged me to truly write what I know, to take Wicca and give it a place in the stories where it's as positive and loving as it is in real life. I hope you're happy (said with both sass and love always).

A special and heartfelt thanks to Dianne for not only the help and pushes along the journey but for the inspiration of your namesake within these pages. I hope I did you justice.

And as always, much appreciation to DSP for your continued support for me and my insanity—I mean writings.

I wouldn't be here without all of you!

Life may not be "a dream within a dream," but this story both begins and ends with one. Always remember to make the most of each moment.

CHAPTER 1

LIAM SHIFTED his weight as he straddled Cameron's hips and positioned himself so his hard cock settled in the valley of Cam's tight little butt. He loved how Cam's ass rounded, how there were those prominent little divots near the top that begged for his tongue to dip into them. As he looked down at his lover, his gaze automatically traced the tattoo that covered his back and cheeks. He loved the sensual way the wings arched and curled over his shoulder blades and trailed down the sides of his back, the last bit cupping his firm ass. The Celtic knot in the center framed the slight bumps down his spine in such a way he couldn't help but trace them on his way down. The gold and silver ink contrasted beautifully against Liam's creamy, pale skin.

He caressed Cam's neck and shoulders before he moved down Cameron's back again. Liam molded a palm over one bare buttock. With the other hand, he stroked up and down Cam's back. Up and down. His fingers paused on different spots of the tattoo and then started again. Liam bent forward, tracing the intricate design with the tip of his tongue. The hint of sweet skin and musk burst across his taste buds, drawing a groan from deep within him. He never could get enough of this man.

Cameron squirmed, pushing up against Liam. "Lee, please don't tease."

He chuckled, loving how ready for his touch Cam always was. "Just taking my time, baby. Can't get enough of your taste... of you," he added and nipped Cameron's side.

"Then taste me lower," Cam panted, raising his ass as much as possible with Liam still sitting on him. "I know how much you like eating me. Please, Lee."

Liam did love rimming Cam's perfect little hole. The way he would writhe and whimper was almost enough to send Liam over the edge on its own.

"Dammit," he groaned.

He rutted against Cam for a moment, but the simple words and friction made him crave more. Liam continued to trace the intricate pattern down Cam's back, licking and sucking the flesh as he descended. When he reached Cam's cheeks, he grasped each and massaged, exposing Cam's tight passage. Each time he pulled them apart, Cam pushed back into the motion, the whimpers and moans enough to tempt Liam to skip the appetizer.

Instead, though, he pulled Cam's hips up so Cam was on his knees with his chest on the soft, black sheets of the bed. He loved how Cam's creamy skin looked against the dark colors. Liam licked his way down Cameron's cleft, not stopping as he passed over his entrance. He grazed Cam's taint with his teeth, loving the gasp that escaped. He then licked back up, making several passes but never stopping at the fluttering hole he so desired.

When he finally zeroed in on his target, he alternated nibbling and sucking on the tender flesh there, stabbing into Cam with his tongue.

"Liam, I'm begging you, please... I need.... Dammit, fuck me!" Cameron's voice was high and needy, as it only got when Liam rimmed him. Liam loved that tone.

He reached out and took the bottle of slick, popped the top, and poured a small amount on his fingers before dropping his mouth down to gently suck one of Cam's balls into his mouth.

"Oh God!" Cam panted, shaking hard.

He touched Cam's hole, enthralled with the sounds and the shiver that tore through Cam as he first pet, then slowly pushed his middle finger all the way to the knuckle inside Cam's willing body. Liam switched to the other ball, laving and sucking on it as he pumped his finger in and out of the hottest, tightest body he had ever felt.

Eventually Liam added a second and then third finger, twisting and scissoring as he went. As Cam fucked himself, Liam sat back on his heels, watching as his fingers disappeared over and over again. He was careful not to hit Cam's happy button, though, wanting to savor how his body tightened around his cock, not his fingers.

"If you don't get in me soon, Liam, I'm not going to make it."

"That's okay, baby. I'll pound you through your first and keep filling and stroking you until you're hard and shooting again."

Cam shuddered at his words, his hands scrabbling on the sheets as he slammed back harder, the sounds coming from him no longer coherent. When Liam couldn't take it anymore, he withdrew his fingers and poured more slick into his palm.

Cam twisted his head so he could glower, his silver eyes blown wide. "What the—?" He stopped and stared as Liam made a production of stroking the lube up and down his cock, caressing and squeezing the shaft.

"Head down, ass high, Cam," Liam barked, loving how fast Cam hurried to do as ordered.

When Cam was in place, Liam lined the tip of his rod up to the tight, pulsing hole and gave short, teasing jabs. Cam only tolerated it for a minute or two before he slammed backward, impaling himself on Liam's hard cock in one violent push.

Desperate not to lose it already, Liam held on tight to Cam's hips, holding him in place until his need backed off a bit. The pulsing of Cam's muscles around him made it harder to accomplish, but he wouldn't change a thing about the man under him. Once Liam was certain he wouldn't come, he began slow, full slides, reveling in the exquisite heat wrapped around him.

Cam reached back with one hand, clutching Liam's hip, tugging at him. Liam knew what Cam wanted, but refused to change his pace. Since he still held Cam hard, Cam was completely at his mercy—a fact Liam thoroughly enjoyed.

"What's the matter, Cam?" he asked, thrusting harder and faster for a moment before slowing down again. "What do you need, baby?"

"Dammit, Lee! Fuck me through the goddamn bed!" he roared, tightening around Liam until Liam saw stars.

Liam released Cam's hips, took two handfuls of cheek instead, and pulled them apart. He watched for a moment as his cock slid in, but then pulled back and slammed in hard. Over and over again, he drilled into Cam's willing body, shifting until Cam keened with every thrust. Happy with his angle, he sped up again, his thrusts brutal as he took everything Cam offered and more.

Cam screamed, his body tightening painfully around Liam, but Liam kept pounding through Cam's release, not ready to end the pleasure for either of them. He slowed when Cam's body sagged and his channel unclenched, but did not stop.

He reached around Cam and scooped up some of his spend to use as lube. He wrapped his large hand around Cam's half-hard shaft and stroked in time with his gentler thrusts, squeezing and tugging the way he knew Cam liked best.

The jolt under him from Cameron made him chuckle, as did the begging that started back up again. "God, you're trying to kill me, aren't you?"

"Nope," he argued, adding a twist to the head of Cam's cock as he stroked and thrust. "But I can never get enough of you, so shut up and let me love you," he demanded.

"Liam…."

He pulled out and flipped Cam over, needing to see Cam. Looking into Cam's stormy gray eyes wasn't a want; it was an all-encompassing compulsion.

"What are you—?"

"Keep your eyes open," he barked. As soon as Cam opened them again and met his gaze, he slammed back inside, thrusting so hard he shifted Cam up the bed in increments. "I need to see you come for me, baby. Please, come." His voice bottomed out on the last word.

Electricity crackled deep in his gut and spine, his balls pulled up tight, but he couldn't go over the edge until his lover did. When he wrapped his fingers around Cam's angry red member again and pulled, Cam arched back and his mouth dropped open, but no sound came out. His dick spewed shot after shot of viscous white fluid over Liam's hand and abs.

The sight alone sent Liam hurtling over the razor's edge he'd been hovering on, his body throbbing in time to his heartbeat as he emptied into Cam's body. With the last pulse of his dick, his arms gave out and he slumped down onto Cam's chest, spent.

After a moment Liam shifted and gently withdrew before he collapsed on his side. When Cam didn't move, he chuckled, pulled him over, and wrapped his body around Cameron's still-trembling form.

"Liam?" he whispered.

"Hmm?" Liam nuzzled his lips against Cam's nape.

"Thank you."

Confused, he shifted so he could look into Cameron's eyes. "For what, baby?"

"For being so good to me and always knowing what I need." Cam leaned in, brushing his lips against Liam's so softly, they barely touched.

"I—"

Beep…. Beep…. Beep….

"No! Not yet!"

Beep…. Beep…. Beep….

"Dammit," Liam Grady growled as he opened his eyes to the early morning sun peeking through his curtains. He turned his head away and tried to ignore the evil little noisemaker on his nightstand. Even though he knew it was useless, he reached out and smoothed his hand over the cold sheets.

Another damn dream.

Dreams were the only times he felt happy or fulfilled anymore, not that it did him any good, seeing as his perfect man didn't exist outside his imagination.

Rolling onto his back, Liam roughly rubbed his hands over his face, trying to shake the lingering memory of Cam's touch. Frustrated with life and his lack of a real relationship, he reached out and pounded his fist down on the demonic alarm clock. Satisfied when it went silent, he flipped the sheets off himself. He was annoyed, but not surprised, to see the mess he'd made. It was worse than puberty.

He hopped out of bed and stripped himself and his bed before he headed into the bathroom to grab a quick shower before making it down to the store. The Feathered Quill was a small bookstore he owned near downtown and his pride and joy. However, it would not open itself.

An hour later, he walked the aisles of his shop, breathing in the unique scent of paper and ink that permeated it. The aisles were neat and wide, with a few comfortable chairs scattered about for those who preferred to sit to browse. The carpeting on the floor muted the sounds of countless kinds of footwear, but he also had mirrors in various places so he could see around the store without having to crowd his visitors.

Once satisfied with how welcoming it seemed, Liam headed into the back. He switched on the small CD player he'd set up, the speakers in strategic places throughout the store, and was content when the first notes of Beethoven's "Für Elise" wafted through the store. He grabbed the first case of new books he needed to put out and carried them out to the floor.

The bells Di gave him when he first opened The Feathered Quill still hung on the front door, and when they jangled, he paused as he put out a new set of erotic romances. Moments later, his best friend since they were both in diapers poked her head around the corner. He remained squatting and watched her as she looked around before finally noticing him. A smile lit up her entire face as she glided over to where he worked.

"Hey, Liam. What do ya got there?" Dianne asked, glancing from him to the tasteful sign designating the area for erotic LGBT romances.

He arched one brow at her but held up one of the books to let her see the cover. "This here's a book," he drawled. "Inside it are words, hon. And it's," he added with a gasp, eyes wide, "got boys doing naughty things to each other in it."

She giggled and swatted him on the shoulder before snatching it from his hand. "Brat. I know what it is. I meant who's it by?" She examined the cover and grinned. "It's the newest Grey novel! Sweet!"

"Yes, Di, you can get it today, but I already have your copy behind the desk, so hand it over and back away from the smexy boys in love." He held his hand out, waiting for her to return the book in question.

"Is it signed?" she asked, batting her eyes at him as she finally returned the book in question.

"Duh! I had to order it special, just for you."

Dianne was all of five feet, maybe. She had blonde hair and bright blue eyes that were made even bigger by the wire-rims she wore, and a smile so big he wasn't sure how it fit on her little heart-shaped face. She threw her arms around his neck and hugged him tight. "Thank you, sweetie. You're the best."

A small chuckle slipped out as he watched her, glad he could bring her a little joy. His customers and his best friend seemed to be the only bright spots in his life anymore. Once upon a time, he'd considered his dream lover, Cam, to be one of those, but that was back when it was an occasional dream and he was lonely. Now, torn between wanting to live in his dreams and never wanting to dream again, he didn't know what to do.

"Oh dear." Dianne peered at him over the edge of her wire-rimmed glasses. "What's the matter?"

"Nothing, Di," he said, waving off her solicitous question. He knew if he wasn't careful, she'd be on one of her save-the-nephew kicks. "Now, are you going to stand there all day or help me here?"

"Hmm…. But watching you work is hot," she countered, leering down at him.

For the first time in months, he laughed loud and long, unable to get the image out of his head. "God, I love you, girl," he declared, set the books in his hand down, and stood, scooping her up as he did, and spinning her around.

"So good to hear you laugh again. Now, are you going to tell Auntie Di all about what's bothering you?"

He set her back down and sighed. "Nothing really. I'm just not sleeping well."

Her eyes narrowed as she scowled at him. "Still with the dreams? We need to find you a real boy. One that's cute and sweet and hot as hell between the sheets," she explained, waggling her thin, perfect eyebrows at him as she smirked.

"No more blind dates, Dianne," he grumbled. He bent to finish putting the books away. He thought back to her last three attempts at finding him "Mr. Right" and cringed. They had been the worst dates of his life. Controlling, whiny, and arrogant were not his thing in friends, much less in a partner. "Please."

"Fine," she snapped. "I just want you happy, Liam. That's all."

"I know, and I appreciate it, but—" He stopped speaking when he heard the bells jingle again. "Hold that thought," he whispered before heading to the front of his store to welcome his customers.

The next few hours were a constant barrage of people coming in to browse or to pick up special orders. When things finally settled, he found himself alone in the store, Dianne having left for work a little earlier. He restocked and cleaned a bit. One of the only things he didn't enjoy about his store was the complete hit-or-miss of when shoppers would come.

He was sitting at the counter doodling idly when someone pushed open the door and entered, smiling. A short, thin man headed straight for him as he called out his greeting.

"Hey, I'm here to pick up a couple of art books for Andy at the Indigo Dragon. They in?"

"Yep. Give me just a second." Liam had turned to look through the holds on the shelves behind him, when he heard a gasp. He pulled the book bundle and spun to find out what had caught the man's attention.

Instead of examining a book or one of the little kitschy, impulse items on the counter, the man—*John? Jean? No, Jason, that's it*—held the page Liam had been drawing on, his head tilted slightly. Jason's eyes flicked from the page up to meet Liam's. "You designed this?"

Liam set the books down and took the paper to see what had caught Jason's interest. When he looked at it, he realized he had drawn

Cameron's back, butt, and tattoo. He swallowed hard, not liking someone admiring his Cam—*No, Cam isn't even real, so it's stupid to get jealous!*

"Just something I saw once. Looked cool," he mumbled.

"Dude, you should totally bring this in. Andy or Bass would love to get their hands on this." He traced his finger down the wings reverently. "Bet it would be sweet on the biceps too," Jason added as they both stared at the sketch.

"I'll think about it. Thanks," he added, retrieving the sketch before ringing the items up and bagging them.

Honestly, he had thought many times over the last few months about having a small version of Cameron's tattoo put on his body. He had chickened out every time he had considered the whole needles-and-pain thing, though. However, now that someone else had spoken his secret wish aloud, the idea seemed to haunt his thoughts as he set about helping new customers as they entered behind the retreating man.

CHAPTER 2

CAMERON DANU turned up the radio in his old, but lovingly cared for, black and red Volkswagen Beetle. He'd had it converted so it had all the modern amenities, but he loved that it still had that old-school feel. One of his favorite bands blasted through the speakers as he seat-danced, energizing him enough to finish the last leg of his move to Asheville.

He'd worked at the Fiery Pen Tattoo Parlor until a little over a month ago. Sadly, it had closed because of his boss José's second heart attack. He hadn't been sure what to do next until José had called him with a new job and a new place to live. The uncertainty had been awful, and Cam hated moving away from his friends and the few family members who still spoke to him, but José had convinced him it would be a good move. He'd even arranged for a friend of his to scout out possible apartments for Cam in the area. So, a month later, Cam made the last trip between Blue Ridge, Georgia, and Asheville, North Carolina, bringing his beloved Bug and a few odds and ends given to him at his going-away party to his new loft. It wasn't as though Asheville and Blue Ridge were even that far apart, though it seemed they were, but he would no longer be able to pop by his sister's or visit the woods he'd grown up in. Nor had he ever been to Asheville, for all it wasn't that far away.

He had fallen in love with the little place the moment he'd seen it. It wasn't big, but it was close to where he would be working. The bus system intimidated the hell out of him, so he would have liked the location on principle alone, but thankfully, the apartment and area were perfect. The converted warehouse was cozy and clean, and meant he wouldn't need to drive to work or deal with the bus or the strange people huddled together on it.

Cam had high hopes that with the new job and residence would come a new chance at love. He was tired of the only man who consistently wanted him being someone he'd conjured up when he was still a teen. The fact his dreams had been filled with nothing but his imaginary lover, Liam, for half a year now, had convinced him something drastic needed to change in his life. Either that, or he really was as insane and deranged as his parents insisted before throwing him out.

The GPS chirped, shaking him out of his maudlin thoughts, and instructed him through the maze that was Asheville's roadways. It was one of the few things he wasn't sold on about Asheville, having grown up in such a small community, but he figured it was a good trade-off considering where he now lived and worked. He smiled when he pulled into his parking space at the side of his new home.

He turned the engine off but didn't immediately get out and head up. First, he took the time to say a tiny prayer to the universe that things would improve from here forward. When his cell rang, he jumped, clutching his chest as his heart attempted to exit through his rib cage. He fumbled with it twice but managed to get it to his ear before the person on the other end gave up on him.

"Hello."

"Cameron? It's Bass."

His new boss? *This cannot be good.* "Yeah, this is Cam."

"Cool. Are you back in town yet? I was hoping you could start a little early." Bass's voice dropped and hardened a little as he continued. "I've got a thing to do this this weekend, so I need to get you into the studio early for your orientation and paperwork and all. Can you come in tomorrow?"

Cam laughed, amused at the timing. "Yeah, just got in, so it's no biggie. I'll be there."

"Great," Bass replied, the grin evident in his tone. "Take some time to get settled and rested, and I'll see you around noon tomorrow."

He clicked the cell off and pocketed it before finally opening the door and climbing out of his car. Cameron looked up at the brick wall of his new home and smiled, glad for the change in plans. Waiting around until next week to start work hadn't been the greatest prospect, but now he didn't have to worry. He grabbed the bags from the backseat and headed up, whistling as he went. Cam was certain Bass needing him in early was a good sign and hoped he would love the new shop and the other tattoo artists as much as he had those back home.

He looked around as he stepped through his front door a few minutes later. The open feel was what had sold him on the apartment in the first place, even more so than the location. The apartment had high ceilings with the beams and some of the pipes visible. To his left was the kitchen and dinette area, and to his right was a large open room. He'd bought and set up a silk divider screen to separate the space into a living room and a bedroom. On the wall near the divider was the bathroom door, which was his destination as soon as he finished unloading the car. It didn't have a bathtub, but it had a shower that would hold at least four grown men, he was sure of it, and the pounding, hot water was calling his name after the long drive.

Three more trips and he had everything out of the car, including the food wrappers from his drive up. He dropped his shaving kit on the bed and sat down, exhausted. It was still early, but before he thought better of it, he'd stretched out on the bed and, still dressed, fallen asleep.

An insistent ringing woke Cam sometime later. When he raised his head, he realized it was his cell screaming from his pocket. His thoughts were foggy as he answered, but he smiled when he heard the voice on the other end.

"Cammy?"

"Hey, little sis. How are things with you?"

"Not that little," Sarah grumbled. They were less than a year apart, but he always teased her about being little. The fact they were the same height, five-eight, never counted in his book, though she tried repeatedly to use that to further her position. "Anyway, I wanted to make sure you got in safe. You were supposed to call me."

"Sorry," he mumbled, feeling like an ass for worrying her. "The drive was fine. I just fell asleep when I got in. No big."

"Unless you're the one waiting on a call or text, then it is a big, Cam."

"I know. Miss you already."

"Me too, but staying 'cause of Dan and me would have been silly. Now I'll let you get back to sleep or to your unpacking. I just wanted to check on you. Asheville's such a big place."

"It's not that huge. It's not like I moved to New York or LA."

"Well, it's bigger than here at least."

He could hear the worry in her voice but was thankful she wasn't mad. "True."

She and Dan were the only members of his family who still spoke to him, a fact he was thankful for every day. Without his sister and her husband, he didn't know what he would have done when his parents rejected him after he came out. Not that he'd expected anything different from them, but his sister was still his rock.

"Cam, you're off in your head again, aren't ya?"

He chuckled. "Yeah, just thinking. Don't mind me. Tell you what, I'll call when I get done at work tomorrow and let you know how things are then? That way I'll actually have news. I mean, I did see you this morning and all."

"Snark much?" she teased. "And I still do not count six a.m. as morning, but fine, call me tomorrow. Love you, Cammy."

Six wasn't that early, but he knew she hated to be woken before about noon. Still, he knew she worried and felt bad for not calling. "Love you too, Sarah."

He sat up and placed his cell on the nightstand. Then he scooped up his kit and shuffled to the bathroom to shower and change. It was his first full night in his new life, and he wasn't going to sit at home alone. He'd do his basic food shopping, and then he was going out. Cam stripped out of his clothes, then stepped into the hot shower, intent on getting shaved, clean, and dressed.

Cam wiped the steam off the mirror in front of him. He frowned at his reflection, unsure about his plan for the evening. Considering Blue Ridge had no gay scene, he'd always had to go to clubs out of town but never alone. Would anyone be interested in him? Would anyone interest him? The latter question was the real issue. His dreams had never interfered with his dating life before, but since Liam had become his nightly visitor, no man had truly piqued his interest or desire.

Pushing the thoughts away, he focused on his reflection. His smoky, silver eyes, high cheekbones, angular jaw, and curly, blond mop of hair usually got him attention, but tonight he decided to try a little harder than normal. He grabbed the eyeliner and mascara off the counter and set about doing his eyes the way his sister had taught him. Once done with them, he used some sculpting wax to tame his curls and add an angled layer toward the front, framing his face.

Satisfied with his appearance, he headed to the bedroom area to dig through his closet and bags, searching for just the right look. Twenty minutes later, he slipped his wallet into his tight, low-rise black jeans, added his collection of leather bangles to his right wrist, and smoothed his hands down the dark blue, silk button-down he wore. He stomped into a pair of chunky ankle boots and stood, happy with his appearance, though still nervous about his destination and goal.

He paused at the door and took a deep breath. "Getting back in the game is the goal tonight, not finding Mr. Right. You can do this!"

Feeling slightly foolish for talking to himself, he headed out the door and made sure to lock it before he took the elevator down to the main floor and walked out into the evening air. Cam looked around, pleased to see so many people out—many of whom seemed to be same-sex couples. *Yep, this will be a good move*, he thought as he turned and headed down the street, his destination not too far away.

A drink, some flirting, a little dancing... maybe more.

CAM ROLLED over and curled around his body pillow. He knew it wasn't the body he wanted, but the aching in his heart due to his dreams left him needing something to hold on to a little while longer. The previous night swam through his fuzzy mind, teasing and taunting him with what he'd seen. Or rather, who his obviously drink-addled brain had conjured up for him after a few beers.

He'd been at the bar, getting another drink before heading back out to the dance floor when he'd seen him. Cam knew it was his imagination but had stood there frozen nonetheless. Out writhing with the mass of sleek and gyrating bodies was Liam. *His* Liam!

After a moment's hesitation, he'd tightened his hold on the bottle in his hand and headed out into the mass of bodies, hoping to find the man he'd dreamed of for the last decade, or at least a good look-alike. Right then he would take the guy home if he even slightly resembled Liam.

Half an hour later, he'd sat on a stool on the far edge of the bar, nursing a Jack and Coke, disappointed beyond reason. He'd known chasing after a ghost was pointless, but he'd been so certain he'd seen Liam. Now, hours later, his head hurt, his mouth felt as if it had cotton stuck in it, and he'd spent another night dreaming, wrapped in the arms of a make-believe lover.

At least the dream had been different this time. Instead of sex and panting, he'd spent his sleeping hours curled up on a couch with Liam, cuddling and kissing next to a large fireplace as it crackled with warmth.

Cam burrowed into the pile of pillows at the head of his bed as he considered the change and smiled. He loved kissing and cuddling so much, his last boyfriend had picked on him relentlessly, calling him a chick with a dick. He hated the teasing as much as the idea that guys only cuddled if girls made them. He wasn't a girl, but he loved such things! *Too bad the only guy that wants to cuddle with me is someone I made up.* He sighed and untangled himself from his sheets before heading into the bathroom to relieve himself, clean up, and pop a couple of Aleve before heading into work.

An hour later, coffee cup from the cute little coffeehouse near where he now worked in hand, Cam stood outside the Indigo Dragon, noting how it looked like most tattoo parlors he'd seen. He knew they weren't like many others, though, not with how clean and skilled everyone who worked there was. Bass did not tolerate messy areas or dark lighting. Besides, Cam would never work for a place that didn't meet his artistic standards.

Entering the front area, he noted the standard fare of generic art on one wall. His lip curled involuntarily at the thought of ever putting art such as that on his own body. He tried never to put bland, overused designs like those on his customers, either, but sometimes they insisted. He shifted his backpack on his shoulder higher, thinking of his sample book within it. It held both his sketches and photos of various works he'd done before in Georgia, hoping the customers here would like his style as much as Bass and the other guys had.

"Hey, man. Glad you could make it!" Bass said as he strode across the black-and-white checkered floor. He clapped Cam on the shoulder, a wide smile on his furry face.

Cam faced Bass, slightly intimidated by how huge the man was, the same as he had been the last time they'd met. Bass, short for Sebastian, was six-three, with wide shoulders and biceps as big as Cam's thighs. He had a full beard, trimmed short and neat, giving the bear of a man a little smoothness to his rough. Of course, the fact Bass kept his head shaved added a little to the smooth too, but Cam wasn't about to mention that.

"Any time. You saved me from rearranging the, like, two pieces of furniture I have all weekend," Cam explained with a chuckle. He had more furniture than that, but he wasn't going to explain all that right then.

"Good man. Now," Bass continued, draping his arm across Cam's shoulder and steering him toward a door Cam knew led to the room he'd be using for his own from now on. "Did you bring your things? Your designs and all too?"

"Of course. I have the rest of my gear in the car still. Figured I'd bring it in once I have things how I want 'em in here."

"Cool. José said you had your own setup and tools, but I wasn't sure how much was really yours. He also said you were a bit particular about your area."

Cam tensed, knowing that his OCD about his tools and area could grate on people's nerves at times. He didn't want his new boss pissed at him already.

"Hey, none of that," Bass rumbled, shaking Cam's shoulders roughly. "As long as you respect my space, I'll do the same for you. Besides, I want this place so clean the health inspector doesn't even bother to stop by and inspires jealousy in the hospital OR."

A chuckle slipped out at the rambling. He was glad his boss was more like him than he'd thought. "Great!"

Bass sat on one of the stools in Cam's area. "Now, I've got a few more papers I need you to complete, but that shouldn't take you more than a couple of minutes. I'll help you bring in your equipment after that."

Cam listened with one ear but started moving things around, preparing the area. "That'd be great. Oh, here." He paused to pull his binder out of the backpack. He smoothed a hand down the cover before handing it over.

"This the complete one?" Bass took it carefully in his huge hands before he set it in his lap and opened the cover.

"Yeah. In the back are a few pieces I'm working on for personal use, but otherwise it's all stuff I've done on others in there." Cam continued rearranging the basic shop items for a few more minutes as Bass looked through the book.

When he was finally satisfied with the furniture placement and how the stands and other equipment were situated, he turned but froze at the look on his boss's face. "What's wrong?"

Bass turned so Cam could see the image that had caught his attention. It was the start of the tat he'd designed for his right deltoid and down onto the biceps a little.

"It's so intricate and colorful," Bass said, his deep voice soft. "Who're you planning to have help you do it? You can't do that level of detail yourself. Not at the angles you'll need."

"Yeah, I know." That was the million-dollar question, really. "I had planned to have José do it, but since his heart attack… his hands aren't steady thanks to the meds." Now, he wasn't sure.

"Come on," Bass said. He closed the binder and set it down before he stood up and stalked toward the door. "Once you're settled and comfortable here, we'll help you get your next tat done."

Cam beamed as he followed Bass out the door, happy to have found a place he thought could be a true home for him.

CHAPTER 3

"LIAM?" DI'S voice intruded on his internal rantings as he paced the length of his living room. His apartment wasn't overly large, but he liked it. Usually. Right then, everything annoyed him, including the place he would normally view as his refuge.

"What?" he snapped but then stopped. He took a deep breath then let it out slowly before speaking again. "Sorry, Dianne. This isn't your problem or fault."

"No, it's not, but since you haven't even told me what the issue is, I can't do a thing for you."

He didn't want to tell her, even though she was probably the only person in his life who wouldn't call a shrink the moment the words were out of his mouth. His shoulders drooped as he sighed. "I went out Thursday night." He started pacing again, though it was now more of a way to avoid meeting her gaze than a need to fidget. "And I'm really thinking something's wrong with me, Di."

"You need to explain to me how what happened two days ago has you this agitated still," she countered, staring at him intently. "And what do you mean 'wrong'? You think you're sick or something?" She gulped as she twisted the silver ring on her index finger around and around.

"In the head, maybe," he mumbled. "No, not like that." He waved her concern away. "It's… I don't know what it is, but I think I'm losing my mind."

On his next pass, Dianne grasped his wrist and pulled him to a stop before she manhandled him until he sat on the couch beside her. "Liam, sweetie, I need you to start making sense. What happened that has you so upset?"

"I saw him. I mean… I see him every night, but this time I swear I *really* saw him." He ran his hands through his disheveled hair, not caring how bad it would look afterward. "I was at the club dancing, you know, and well, my dance partner and I stepped off the floor for a more, um, private moment."

She cleared her throat, stopping him midramble. "So you got laid?" Dianne giggled and a light flush spread up her cheeks.

"Just a blowjob, Di. Seriously"—he fidgeted, uncomfortable discussing tricks with her, especially considering how rare such actions were for him—"that's not the important part!" Nor was the fact he hadn't been able to actually go through with it—much to his partner's irritation. For whatever stupid reason, his heart wouldn't let him. He'd felt as though he was cheating on Cam, even though Cameron wasn't real. Well, he didn't think Cam was real…. Maybe…. "The point is, when I was on my way back to the bar afterward, I saw him." Liam shivered, nauseated over the thought of his next words. "Cam was sitting at the far end of the bar drinking, though I'm not certain what. But—"

"Wait, your dream guy is real?" she squealed. Dianne threw her arms around him as she bounced on the cushion beside him. "That's wonderful!"

"Okay, see, now you sound as nuts as I do! He can't be real, Di. That isn't possible. I've dreamed of Cam since I was seventeen. People don't just materialize into reality simply because you want them so desperately, waking up breaks your heart."

"Normally, I would agree, hon," she soothed. The pitying look in her eyes made him wish he'd kept that last bit to himself. "But maybe he's someone you saw once when you were younger and now he's back in the area?"

Liam shook his head before she'd finished speaking. "No, not possible. He has grown and aged in the dreams just like I have. And, well, other than the sadness in his eyes the other night, he looked like he always does in the dreams."

"Hmm…. Have the dreams changed since then and why didn't you go over to him?"

"I, um, I froze when I saw him. Or what I thought was him. By the time I got my feet working again and managed the distance between us, he was gone."

"And the dreams," Di pushed. "Are they the same?"

"No. I came home after he disappeared. Staying at the club wasn't something I could even fathom right then," he added, thinking of how hollow he'd felt, and still felt, for that matter. "I curled up on the couch and fell asleep thinking about Cam." Liam picked at a cuticle as he thought about the dreams the last two nights and how he had not wanted to wake either morning. "The tone of the dreams changed completely after that. Cuddling, kissing, and spending time together as if we were an ordinary couple. That's how they've been since I saw, or thought I saw, him. I wake up and feel like I've just been dumped all over again." He looked down at his best friend and aunt, desperate for help, hope, anything, really. "Something's got to give, Di." He didn't bother hiding how afraid and demented he felt by that point.

He wasn't even sure why the change in the tone of the dreams had happened. Why had they changed to cuddling and couch time instead of fun and sexy time? He had a theory, but it sounded too crazy to share with Di, even crazier than the rest. How did you tell your aunt you were living an entire dream life? One where he had a life like he'd always wanted? Yeah… that didn't sound nuthouse worthy at all, nope!

Dianne was quiet as she tapped one of her perfectly manicured nails on the arm of the couch, staring at him so hard, he fought the impulse to squirm. "What if there's a possibility this Cameron of yours is real and—" Liam started to protest, but she put her small hand over his mouth. "Shush, you. Now listen to me. I've talked to a couple of the guys in my circle, and Nosha suggested he might be able to help you with your dream issues."

"Di, I love you, you know that, but what does your Wicca group have to do with my guy issues?" *Exasperated* wasn't a strong enough word for how he felt. Religion wasn't something he focused on or valued, per se. He wasn't against it, but Di's faith in ancient deities hadn't ever been his thing. Besides, how did religion and hallucinations mix?

"Will you just meet with him?" She cupped his scruffy cheek, her voice soft but determined. "Please? It's not often that he even takes on students like this. He turned away the last man that tried to get him to teach. Don't throw away this chance, especially if it means finding out if your Cam is real—which he is."

He thought about it for a moment, ignoring the last part of her rant, and then sighed. "Can't hurt, I guess." He shrugged. "Don't know what good it'll do, though, so don't get your hopes up, okay?"

Di beamed up at him. "Deal. Now let me make you some tea, and we can visit about things other than your boyfriend."

"Dianne."

She tsk-tsked at him as she stood and headed for the kitchen. Liam sat staring at where she'd disappeared, bemused at how his mental breakdown had somehow turned into circle and teatime.

LIAM SAT in the driver's seat of his Chevrolet Equinox, staring at the building in front of him. It was nothing more than a small house, not intimidating in the least, yet something about this meeting had his nerves on edge. He knew why. He was meeting Di's friend to discuss his dream problems.

In the last week or so, things had only gotten more confusing. He dreamed of Cameron every night, but he spent more and more time each night kissing and cuddling with Cam than engaging in the more carnal activities that had always been the norm between them. He didn't mind the change, exactly, but it made the longing for someone his warped mind had created stronger. Every morning was worse. The empty bed and the quiet of the apartment all combined to hurt him more than any breakup he'd ever gone through.

The last few nights were even more unusual than before. His fingers twitched as he recalled the way Cam's body was changing right before his eyes. He and Cam had been walking, hand in hand, through the park. The sun was bright but not hot. Squirrels played in the treetops, occasionally irritating the birds nearby. A light breeze ruffled their hair as they moved together.

"Do you want to see what I've been working on?" Cam had asked suddenly, his eyes bright. He stopped walking and pulled Liam over to a bench along the path.

Liam chuckled, amused at how excited Cam seemed. "Sure, beautiful. What'd you do?"

"See, I've been working on the designs for a while now, but we just started the actual work," Cam explained as he unzipped his thin, smoky-gray, leather jacket. "I really hope you like it," he added so softly Liam barely caught the words.

He threaded his fingers through Cam's thick mop of curly, blond hair and leaned in, lightly brushing his lips across Cam's soft, full bottom lip. "I'm certain I'll love it," Liam murmured, his lips barely grazing Cam's as he spoke.

Cam leaned in, their mouths lingering against each other for a moment. When he pulled away, Cam slid his coat down his arm to reveal an intricate tattoo on his right deltoid. Liam stared, taking in the various details, before reaching out carefully to run the tip of his index finger along the design now adorning his lover's arm.

"It's beautiful," Liam whispered. There on Cam's upper arm and shoulder was a vibrantly inked dreamcatcher, but it was unlike any he'd seen before. The web part was a complicated Celtic knot that he'd somehow made to appear as having depth instead of being flat against his pale skin. The webbing was a careful weaving of gold and silver strands. The traditional feathers were there as well, each a shockingly bright color. On the right side was a pair of feathered quills, bound to the rim of the dreamcatcher, one silver and the other a deep blue that reminded him of his own eyes. "And the detail.... Amazing."

"Thanks, Lee." Cam sighed as Liam continued tracing the pattern, a shiver running through him as he continued to allow Liam to touch and trace the patterns inked into his flesh. "You inspired this one."

"Me?" Liam couldn't imagine how this could be because of him, but the idea Cameron would mark his body for him made Liam's heart hurt and his groin tighten.

"Mmm.... You. I can't explain it, but your heart inspired all the art that will be a part of this sleeve, but I wanted to start with the top piece. Well, the tree will actually reach up and around this one a bit, but that's not the point."

"Tree?" Liam was getting more and more confused. How did dreamcatchers and trees come from him? "I don't get it. It's gorgeous, truly, but I don't follow the logic."

Cam chuckled. "Babe, there's always Celtic things around you, or didn't you notice? And the dream part made sense when I drew it," he continued, his pale brows furrowing as he paused. "Huh, I can't remember why right now." He shrugged. "Anyway, yes, it's all you in one way or another."

"I love it and I'm sure it will be even better once done. But seriously, Cam, you don't need to ink yourself for me."

"I want to...."

Liam bent forward and traced the edge of the catcher with the tip of his tongue. Cam's breath hitched and shifted into a moan. He loved how Cam's skin and taste always teased his senses.

Liam smiled against Cam's shoulder, pleased at how easily he could derail Cam's ability to think. He shifted Cam onto his lap, kissing and nipping up his arm, across his shoulder and collarbone before sucking a bit of flesh between his lips and teeth to worry. Cam may have marked himself, but it only made Liam want to mark him with his mouth and hands all the more.

Knock. Knock. Knock.

The banging against his window startled Liam out of his musing. He jumped, hitting his head on the ceiling of the car. After he turned, Liam glowered at Dianne as he rubbed the now-sore spot. He popped his door open and grumbled, "Di, please."

She rolled her eyes at him and smirked. "Oh please, if I left it up to you, you'd sit here half the night and then drive home without ever meeting Nosha. Now, out of the car and come along, Liam."

He groaned at how perky she was being, refusing to acknowledge that she might have been right about what he'd do without her there. He still wasn't sold on the idea of dragging others into his dream delusions.

"You know, I can hear your internal monologue going. Now smile and be good," she added, sliding her small hand around his arm. "Nosha is a sweetie. You'll like him if you give him a chance."

In a way, that was part of his worry. What if whatever this guy said did make sense? Would that mean Cam was real or that he really had lost his mind? And if Cam was real, how would he go about finding him?

He closed the car door, clicked the alarm, then walked up the drive with his aunt. Before they reached the front door, it swung open. A tall, thin man about their age stood in the doorway, a broad smile stretched across his angular but handsome face. Liam took a moment to take in his features as the man stared at Di. Thick brows, brown-black hair, and dark hazel eyes behind gold-rimmed glasses, plus the swarthy skin that graced the man gave him a slightly geeky Romeo appearance.

"Hi, Dianne," Nosha said, his voice lighter than Liam expected.

"Hey, Noshie. This is Liam."

It took a moment for Nosha to pull his eyes away from Di, Liam noted. "Hello, Liam."

"Hi." He still wasn't sure what he was doing there. Di and Nosha could just figure out the next step of what to do now on their own. If they could pull themselves away from the other long enough.

Nosha blinked a couple of times but then smiled. "Sorry. Please, come in."

They entered the small, tidy home without any more words. As he walked into a comfortably appointed living room, Liam noticed a small altar against one wall. It resembled the one Di kept in her great room. Little statues, a bowl or two, herbs, a lighter, and a small knife he knew was called an athame, all sat on the small wood stand. Behind it, hanging on the wall, was an ornate painting of a horned, green man and a voluptuous, green-skinned and green-haired woman. Both were nude, but it seemed tasteful and elegant to him, not smutty or naughty in any way.

Their host gestured for them to sit on the plush couch while he chose the wingback chair across from them.

"Did you want anything to drink while we talk?" Nosha looked between the two of them, brows raised.

"No, thank you," they both replied, then burst out laughing at the timing. "Sorry. It's really not that funny," Dianne said, but then ruined the straight face she'd managed when she giggled again.

"Right...." Nosha chuckled and shook his head as he watched them.

"Sorry," Liam said as he worked to control himself better. Once they both were calm, he gestured to their host to begin.

"Never seen Dianne giggle so much before. I approve."

"Noshie, I laugh all the time. Don't you remember?"

He shrugged but didn't respond. Instead, Nosha faced Liam again and spoke. "Di says you might have a dream walker visiting you, or possibly that you might be the one visiting."

"A dream what?"

"A dream walker. A dream walker is someone who works with and within dreams to do a great many things. They can create dream spaces, heal, meet with others in places they create, or even work with other worlds and realms."

Liam stared at Nosha, trying to figure out if he'd heard him right. After puzzling out the words for a moment, he asked, "You mean you two think either Cam, if he's even real, or I, travel through dreams to meet and spend time together? That we've done so since we were teens?"

Nosha beamed at him and nodded. "That's it exactly! See, he gets it," Nosha said, regarding Dianne again. "And you said he'd be difficult."

"Just wait, Noshie. That's not belief you're hearing."

"Harrumph." He crossed his arms over his chest, a slight frown marring his features.

"She's right. I don't mean to be rude, but that has to be the most absurd thing I have heard in a long while. People don't travel through dreams," he stated, trying to sound firm, though the idea made him curious at the same time. The thought that Cam was really real was too good to be true, in his opinion. But if he was....

"I can see you wondering if I might be right, even as you try to discount me. Give me a chance to show you that things might not be as you've been led to believe. That the world is a more magical and wondrous place than you've been taught."

Liam sat there, thinking hard about what Di and Nosha said. Could dream travel be real? Maybe he actually had seen Cam at the club? He regarded Dianne and then Nosha before opening his mouth to speak. No sound came out. He cleared his throat and tried again. "I'm not certain I buy all this, but if there's even a chance you're right, I need to try."

Dianne bounced beside him, throwing her arms around him, the motion oddly reminiscent of when he'd agreed to meet with Nosha in the first place. Nosha clapped his hands together loudly. Dianne and Nosha wore huge smiles as they gazed at Liam, which managed to make him more nervous, not less, as he assumed the gesture was meant to do.

"Great!" Nosha said. He leaned forward and rested his elbows on his thighs. "Now, there are many ways to enter the dream realm, Liam. Meditation, shamanic journeying, and lucid dreaming are all possibilities. Though, for some people, it's just something they can *do*." Nosha looked him up and down, head tilted as he did so. "That's what I think we're looking at in this case."

"That I'm a what?" he asked even as he was positive he didn't want to hear the answer.

"A true and natural dream walker."

CHAPTER 4

THE BUZZING of the tattoo gun in Cam's hand was one of the most soothing sounds he'd ever heard. He relished designing the artwork almost as much as he loved doing the actual tats. He knew a lot of people thought the sound scary, or unnerving at the very least, but not him. No, for him, being behind the pen was where he ruled.

Cam took a moment to wipe the skin before him again before he lifted the gun back to Jay's shoulder and continued the intricate design there. As he worked on the curls of the feathers for the dragon, he heard the chimes for the front door. Thankfully, he also heard boots clomp down the short hall toward the front, so he ignored the sound and continued working. He was almost done with the session and didn't want anything to interrupt him right then.

"How's it looking," Jay asked, holding still even as he spoke.

"Good, man. Just a little more and we'll be done for today."

"Sweet!" Jay yelled, wiggling in the chair slightly.

Cam pulled the gun away as he laughed. "Dude, don't do that! You make me mess this up and I'll beat ya like I own ya."

"Ooh, scary," Jay teased.

At five-eight and with a slender body, Cam knew no one would ever be afraid of him, but joking around with his customers was half the fun of his occupation.

"Sorry, but I gotta pee and the vibration isn't helping me here."

He shook his head as he calmed. "Tell you what," Cameron offered. "Why don't you take a potty break and then I'll finish this last bit?"

"Uh-huh. Finish this piece up and then I'll go. Please?"

With a shrug, Cam bent back to his work, smiling at how the feathered serpent was coming out.

"Wait, did you really just say *potty*?" Jay asked incredulously.

"Well, you *were* doing the pee-pee dance after all," Cam countered before focusing again on the delicate feathering.

"Still! I'm not five, man."

"No shit, you don't say. Fine, you can go piss or jack off, or whatever, just be a good boy for me right now and stay still. 'Kay?"

Twenty minutes later, he covered the fresh tattoo and sent Jay on his way before cleaning up his area. He was so focused on his task he didn't hear anyone approach until there was a knock on the door to his room. Cam jumped and spun around, a squeak slipping through his lips.

Bass stood in the doorway, a rumbling laugh accompanying the smirk on his rugged, fuzzy face.

Cam put his fists on his narrow hips and glowered back. "What?"

"Sorry, Cam," Bass said, hands up in surrender, his face mostly serious. "I've got a guy out here that wants to discuss a wing tat, and it looks so much like what's on your back, I thought you should come out. Maybe see if you can tailor it for him."

Cam stared at Bass a moment before he started moving toward the front. "Like mine? But I designed mine and have never allowed it to be photographed or anything. It's not even in my portfolio," he muttered as he followed behind Bass.

"I know, you told me before, but I swear, that's what it looks like. And well, you seem to have a knack for that kind of work."

Cam smiled at the praise, knowing what it took to impress someone as talented at Bass. "All right. Show me this guy and his—" His voice stopped working the same time he glanced up. Caught in the Technicolor blue eyes he'd only ever seen in his dreams, Cam could barely manage to breathe, much less think. However, even with his mind spinning out of control, he would know those eyes, and that face, anywhere!

Standing at the counter, staring back at him, mouth open, was Liam. Cam's gaze swept down and back up his body, taking in his height, the tan skin, and tidy brown hair, before settling again on the eyes he'd loved since he was a teen.

"Cam?" Liam's deep voice croaked out. He took a half step toward Cam but then froze again.

He nodded and then shook his head, even as he doubted his sanity. "Lee…. Liam?"

"You two know each other?" Bass asked, looking back and forth between them.

Cam stepped forward and raised his hand but stopped short of touching Liam. He couldn't make his hand move any closer. He was vaguely aware of Bass beside him and that his hand shook, but his entire focus revolved around the apparition before him.

"Cammy?" Bass tried again. "Say something, man. You're starting to freak everyone out here."

Liam swallowed so hard his Adam's apple bobbed, drawing Cam's eyes.

"Cameron? You…. You're real?" Liam choked out before stepping forward. He rubbed his rough cheek against Cam's outstretched hand.

The moment he felt Liam's skin, he lost his tentative hold on reality. The sensuous feel of it pulled a soft moan from him—well, he thought the sound came from himself, it might have been from Liam. Before he realized what he was doing, he'd spun on his heel and taken off. He fled into his studio room, then slammed the door and leaned against it with all his weight. In his dreams a door would not be enough to stop Liam—not the way he could toss Cam around during sex—but it was all his addled brain could think up. Not that he'd ever run from Liam in his dreams. He'd run *to* Liam. Never *from*.

He couldn't remember his flight there, but he prayed the hallucination would go away quickly. He would call his insurance, find a good shrink in the area, and get help, he decided as his legs gave out and he slid down the door. He prayed this never got back to his parents. They already thought him crazy and damaged as it was. They'd even tried sending him to one of those "pray the gay away" camps when he was a teen. Then his dream visits from Liam had been all that kept him sane. But now…. How could Liam be real, no matter what he'd thought he'd seen the other night?

Moments later, there was a knock on the door, so hard it vibrated through him as the flimsy bit of wood shook on its hinges. "Cameron?" Bass's voice came through the door, but no one turned the knob. "What is going on?"

"Is he gone?" Cam choked out.

"No, Cam, I'm still here," Liam called out, his voice soft, soothing. "Please open the door."

"You're not real!"

"Uh, Cam, he looks real to me. You're really starting to scare me now. How 'bout you open the door and talk about this like a grown-assed man. Okay?"

Cam sat on the floor, arguing with himself, trying to convince himself that if Bass could see Liam, he wasn't really crazy. Maybe. Besides, there was no way his parents could ever send him away again, even if he were crazy.

After a few minutes of debating and worrying, Cam slowly stood and dusted himself off. He couldn't believe he'd freaked out and ran. Dream come to life or no, he wasn't a coward!

He took a deep breath before turning to open the door. Cam could hear Liam and Bass whispering through it, their voices too muffled for him to make out the words. As he turned the doorknob and slowly pulled the door open, he squared his shoulders, hoping to seem a little calmer, if nothing else.

No one was in front of the door when he blinked open his eyes. Confused, he peeked around the corner, looking for both Bass and Liam. He could still hear them, after all.

The two men stood together near the front counter again, but no one else was there. They both stopped speaking as soon as he stepped into the hallway.

"Cam?" Bass said the same time Liam asked, "Cameron?"

"I… I'm sorry about that. I'm not usually that much of a spaz."

"I know," Liam replied and gave him a small smile. "Can we, maybe, sit and talk a little?" He gestured to the far wall where a row of chairs sat empty. "I think we need to."

Looking around the room first, he met Bass's clear, green eyes. "I, um, I don't have another appointment until later this evening."

"Go on, take your break and maybe later you can explain all this to me?"

He nodded, not that he had any idea how to explain away his stupid freak-out. He had no intention of ever discussing the horrors of where his parents had sent him in their futile quest to "cure" him of his gayness. "I'll be at the coffeehouse around the corner." Cam then faced Liam again and did his best to smile. "Coffee?"

"Sure, my treat." Liam opened the front door and gestured, waiting for Cam to exit before he stepped outside.

Cam looked around, blinking in the bright light of the day. He tensed when a large, warm hand settled against his lower back.

"Relax. It's just coffee, beautiful."

Trying to ignore the pet name, Cam turned and walked down the sidewalk, stepping to the side enough that Liam's hand slipped away. He could still feel the heat as if that simple touch had branded him. He needed a clear head if he was going to survive this, and Liam touching him wasn't helping him calm down any—not with how much he wanted to sink into Liam's strength and presence as he did in their dreams. Well, that and he really didn't think dropping to his knees for Liam would get him any answers about what the hell was going on.

LIAM WALKED beside Cam, noting every nuance of the man he'd been with most of his life, even if they'd never met while awake before. He was entranced with how Cam moved. He thought of the way Cam had spoken using his hands to emphasize and punctuate his voice when they were inside the tattoo shop, and even the little sidestep to separate them didn't surprise or bother Liam any. Liam had expected it, truthfully, but he'd needed to feel Cam, to know he wasn't imagining all this, either— that fleeting touch in the tattoo shop hadn't been nearly enough.

Working with Nosha the last couple of weeks had been interesting, and he'd started to believe Cam *might* be real. However, seeing and touching Cam was very different from trying to willfully take control of his dreams or debating Cameron's possible existence. And touching him? Liam suppressed a shiver as he opened the door for Cam to enter the little coffee shop.

"Thanks," Cam murmured. "You always do things like this in the dreams too," he added so softly Liam almost missed it.

Liam smiled, hoping Cam could adjust to this new knowledge and glad he'd noticed how Liam acted both in their dreams and now.

Thankfully, it wasn't busy right then, so they got their coffees and were seated at the farthest table from the other patrons in a few minutes. Liam waited, watching Cam as he fidgeted with his cup, steadfastly refusing to meet Liam's eyes.

Liam cleared his throat and asked, "Will you look at me, please?"

Cam raised his head slowly before finally meeting his gaze. "I don't understand how you're here. You're supposed to only exist in my head. Well, in my dreams, anyway."

Liam chuckled, thinking of how he'd made the same argument with Di and Nosha not that long ago about his seeing Cam at the club.

"I'm still not entirely certain how all this works, but I'm quite real. As are you, it seems."

The silver eyes before him flashed a moment before Cam snorted softly, then smiled, almost. "Why don't you seem more, I don't know, upset? I mean, this should be just as much of a shock for you as it is for me. Or do you go around invading people's dreams and doing all those things with others you do with me all the time?"

He blinked hard as he thought about what to say and which questions to even answer. "I saw you at the club, but by the time I got my legs to work, you were gone. Since then I've been studying about dreams enough that I mostly believed you existed… somewhere. Though, honestly, I didn't expect to find you when I set out to ask about getting a tattoo."

"Why a tat? Why now, I mean?"

"It'll sound corny," Liam mumbled, looking away from Cam. *Because I wanted some part of you to be with me… to be real… for me.*

"Come on, tell me."

Liam shook his head, grasping for something to change the subject. Instead of answering, he flashed a smile at Cam. "Do you really have a new tattoo on your shoulder and arm?"

"Huh?" Cam looked at him as if he had grown a second head, before blinking hard and nodding slowly. "Bass did part of the work on it, considering where it is, but yeah. The…."

"The dream catcher with the feathered quills?"

"How'd you know that?"

"You showed me in our dream. It was beautiful, not that your explanation made sense to me then, but…" he explained with a shrug.

"So, what does this mean? I mean, I've never had a figment of my imagination walk up and say hello before."

Liam watched Cam take a few sips of his coffee as he debated the reality before him and the logic he thought was right until a few weeks ago. Honestly, he was a bit freaked out too, but after how shaken Cam had been, he knew he had to keep it together, for Cam's sake if not his own. "I don't know, other than it seems we've been seeking each other out for more than a decade."

"Seeking?"

He nodded. "Yeah. Nosha—that's my aunt's 'friend' who's been working with me on dream walking and dream control—says our spirits

have been… I don't really understand it all yet, but we've been searching for one another."

"I don't get it," Cameron stated, voice flat. Liam couldn't tell if Cam didn't believe him, or if he was really that confused—not that Liam could blame Cameron, considering how confusing much of it was to him still, and he was the dream walker and weaver in training.

"Me either. Not really, but look, the dreams changed for you recently too, right?"

"Yeah. You were dancing the night I thought I saw you, but disappeared when I tried to find you among all the dancing masses."

The sudden heat crawling up his cheeks and down his throat was unwelcome, as was the memory of his one and only attempt at sexual release that hadn't stemmed from Cam in well over half a year. The fact he'd failed only added to his embarrassment, though in a way he was kind of glad for having not gone through with it. He shifted, suddenly uncomfortable with his actions that night. "That night, when I fell asleep, the dreams changed and have been more like, I don't know, dates or couple time, than how they were before."

Cam started nodding before he'd gotten past the word *dates*. "Yeah, they did. But I still don't get how and"—Cam's gaze went hard, pinning him in his seat—"I don't like the idea that someone's invading my dreams without my permission."

"It wasn't deliberate. At least, not at first. I—"

"Look… it needs to stop," Cam said. "I can't keep doing this. Just…." He stood up so fast he knocked the chair over and fled—it was the only way Liam could think to describe the way Cameron hurried away from him.

"Wait! Cam!" Liam yelled as he hopped up and sprinted after the man he knew was a part of him. They had shared things, done things together, that he had never considered with anyone else. Things he didn't *want* with anyone else. He caught up with Cam just outside the door. "Please, wait."

Cam stood with his back to him, trembling, not saying a word, but not moving away, either.

"I wasn't trying to hurt you, Cam. It wasn't even something I knew I was doing before a few weeks ago. But come on." Liam took a deep breath before offering Cam something he knew would hurt to do, if he

even could. "I'll try to stay out of your dreams, if you really want, but please, let me see you again. In the waking world. Please."

"I'm not convinced I'm not in a padded cell somewhere, imagining all this as it is, because this is nuts. You know that, right? 'Souls searching through dreams' is crazy."

"I thought so too at first, but I'm right here. You can see me, feel me. I'm real and so is this connection between us."

"I can't do this, Lee. Not right now."

"I've always loved it when you called me that. No other man has ever called me that," Liam said, keeping his voice soft.

Cam turned his head but didn't look at him, either. "Please, don't visit my dreams again. Please don't try to visit me in real life, either. I— This isn't— I can't…. Just…." Cam shook his head. "I'm sorry." He walked away, leaving Liam standing on the sidewalk.

He had no idea how long he stood there, staring after Cam. Liam had lost sight of Cam long ago, but he couldn't make himself move. His phone rang a few times, but he ignored it, not caring who it was. It wouldn't be Cam, so why bother? Eventually, he moved again, finding his way home, not that he knew how he got there or even cared he'd made it safely. The only thing he could focus on was Cameron's parting words and how hollow he suddenly felt inside.

CHAPTER 5

TWO DAYS later, Liam stood in a kitchen he knew, but he was uncertain how he had ended up there. He looked around and found Cam bent over, rummaging in the fridge, his pert little butt in nothing but a pair of tight boxer briefs. Liam groaned as he moved closer to Cam and slid his hands over the smooth cotton, feeling the tight muscles beneath flex as Cam jumped and spun around.

"Dammit, Lee, don't sneak up on me like that," Cam groused, though the pout was ruined when the edges of his lips turned up in a small smile.

"Sorry, beautiful, but how could I resist such a tempting and delicious offering?"

"Uh-uh. Stroking the ego won't help you this time."

Liam smirked and slid one hand down to lightly rub up and down Cam's length. Cam's eyes closed as a low moan slipped out. His hips pushed forward, his body begging for touch. "Your ego wasn't what I had in mind, baby."

"Oh, God, Liam. Please," Cam begged. He threaded one hand into Liam's hair and tugged him down until their lips met in a hard clashing of teeth, tongue, and yum.

Liam slipped one hand inside Cam's briefs, then wrapped his fingers around the hard shaft that had been hiding within. He pulled and stroked the hot, hard flesh as he continued to kiss Cam as if he hadn't touched Cam in ages. He wanted Cam so bad he couldn't think straight.

He captured the moans Cam let out as they continued to devour each other, relishing each one as if it were his first and last ever. Liam clutched at Cam's hip, desperate for his lover's touch. He ripped his mouth away, panting for breath, never letting up on his slow pumping of Cam's cock.

"So perfect," he panted, relishing the little mewling sounds Cam made every time Liam skated his fingers over Cam's cockhead, how Cam's eyes were blown wide in desire.

"I need you in me, Lee. I don't wanna wait...."

Liam grabbed Cam's briefs and tore them off his tight little body, desperate to be back inside *his* Cam. After slamming Cam against the wall, Liam kicked Cam's feet apart before he dropped to his knees and swallowed Cam whole.

Cam screamed, but Liam didn't care. He was going to take everything Cam offered and then some! Setting a fast pace, he bobbed up and down on Cam's straining cock, making it wet and slippery. Using some of the excess wetness, he slipped his fingers behind Cam's balls, rubbing them along Cam's taint until he reached Cam's tight hole. Teasing and tapping Cam's needy entrance, Liam shivered as precome squirted on his tongue, the taste making him even harder than before.

Shaking above him, Cam pushed back against Liam's fingers, begging with both words and action for exactly what Liam wanted to give. Wetting his fingers more, he slipped first one, then two inside the most perfect heat ever.

Cam could only whisper Liam's name as he splayed his fingers across Liam's shoulders, digging his nails in as he rocked back and forth between Liam's mouth and the invading digits. "Lee.... Dammit, gonna come if you don't...."

Liam quickly added a third finger. He popped off Cam's dick long enough to grin up at him. "That's the idea, babe."

"No. Inside first," Cam gasped out. "Need you filling me."

Wordlessly, Liam withdrew his fingers and stood, pinning Cam against the wall again. He pressed his body against Cam's as he devoured his lover's tender, kiss-swollen lips. As they ground against each other, Liam's thin hold on his control snapped and need ripped through him like never before.

"Mine!" Liam growled. He dragged his hands down Cam's back, relishing how he arched into the touch, before cupping his ass hard. He squeezed and thrust harder, desperate but determined to give Cam what he asked for.

He grabbed the back of Cam's thighs and pulled, lifting Cam off his feet. Cam wrapped his arms and legs around Liam as he shifted Cam where he wanted him. Liam rubbed his hard dick against Cam's opening as he dipped his head to lick and suck on one pert nipple.

Cam screamed and trembled in his arms, but Liam didn't let up. Instead, he maneuvered around enough to torture the other nipple as he shifted his hips until he felt the tip of his cock against Cam's fluttering hole.

"Please, baby," Cam begged, vibrating in his arms.

Liam used his weight and strength to angle Cam how he wanted him. As soon as he was certain Cam was in the right place, he thrust up, and in one powerful, deep push he filled his lover.

Cam's fingers dug into Liam's back and neck, and he panted, "Please…. More…. Oh God, more…."

"I love it when you beg," Liam growled against Cam's lips as he thrust harder, faster, determined to take Cam where Cam's body begged to go. He continued to slam into Cam as he balanced Cam against the wall, holding him there with the weight of his body and sheer determination. He pulled Cam up as his back bowed, giving Liam a better angle to drive into him, pummeling his body and happy spot hard.

Cam tensed, scrabbling his hands against the slick wall as he keened out his release. Rope after rope painted both their abdomens as Liam fucked him through his orgasm. Even once Cam sagged against him, Liam didn't stop. He merely slowed down to enjoy the friction and how Cam's body clenched around his.

He didn't want to come, but to stay like that forever, wallowing in his lover. To stay wrapped in Cam's heat and passion was his desire.

"Lee? No one but you makes me like this, I swear," Cam panted against his shoulder as he curled around him, holding on as Liam continued the slow slide in and out. "Can't be without this, without you."

Something niggled at the back of Liam's memory, but he couldn't catch it, too wrapped up in the way Cam shifted and pulsed around him.

"Don't stay away again," Cam begged as he undulated against Liam's abdomen. His cock hard again, Cam's dick slid smoothly in the viscous fluid between them. "I need…."

"Need you too, beautiful," he whispered against Cam's lips before he dove back in, tangling his tongue with Cam's, needing to be inside Cam in every way possible. Liam picked up his pace, thrusting hard again inside his lover, pulling his cheeks apart to let him in deeper.

Cam sucked hard on Liam's tongue, rocking against him. Liam's balls drew up tight and as the first tingles shot up his spine, he increased his speed even as his need for the beautiful man in his arms grew.

"Fill me, Lee. Please, come for me. I need to feel you dripping from me for the rest of the night."

Shuddering, Liam's thrusts faltered and the world whited out as he emptied inside Cam's willing body.

Moments, or possibly hours later, he focused his eyes again to find Cam curled up in his lap as he sat on the bed. Cam's fingers toyed with Liam's chest curls, and his breath ghosted over one nipple.

Liam looked around confused. How the hell did they get from the kitchen to the bedroom?

"Missed you," Cam murmured into his chest.

Missed me? Place shifted? What the…?

With a sudden and painful flash, he realized this was all a dream. He'd just had sex with Cam in a shared dream! He started to tremble as the understanding of what he'd just done impaled his heart. The painful truth that he had just touched Cam after he'd forbidden him to ever visit his dreams again, caused his stomach to roll even within the shared dream space.

Next thing he knew, he was sitting upright, tears streaming down his face as he gasped and curled in on himself on the couch. He had tried so hard to stay awake, to not go to Cameron. As if Cam hadn't rejected him already, now Liam was certain Cam would hate him.

When the tears ceased to flow and the shuddering stopped somewhat, Liam managed to get his hands to work enough to text Dianne. All he typed was "I failed" before hitting Send and dropping the phone on the floor beside him.

He racked his brain as he fought to stay awake again, for any ideas on how to block himself from doing what he'd just done to Cam again. He couldn't bear the thought of how angry Cameron would be when he woke. The only thing in his favor was Liam didn't think Cam knew where his bookstore was, so maybe he wouldn't have to face him and his anger quite yet. Wouldn't have to see the pain and violation in the eyes he loved.

Before he thought better of it, he got up and headed into the kitchen. Rummaging around in the cupboards, he found an unopened bottle of whiskey and set out with the intention of getting so drunk he would pass out. He thought he remembered Nosha saying alcohol would mess up his ability to travel in dreams. He hoped like hell the man was right.

"DAMMIT, LIAM," Dianne snapped, snatching the bottle out of his hand for the second time that night.

When he'd passed out two nights before, he hadn't dreamed of Cam, so he had decided that being drunk was better than hurting Cam.

Besides, he didn't care about much right then. Cam didn't want him, he couldn't stomach the thought of being with anyone else, and sleeping was dangerous, as it seemed he couldn't behave himself. "Give it back, Di."

"No. This has to stop! This isn't like you, sweetheart. What happened?"

The thought of telling her what he'd done nearly brought all the alcohol he'd already consumed that night back up. He shook his head but stopped when the room started to sway. "Nothing," he mumbled as he tried to take the bottle back.

"Liam Bradén Grady," both blurry Diannes snapped at him. "You listen to me, you little shit. I don't care what you did, or what you think you did, this isn't the answer! You'll never meet a nice boy and settle down if you drive yourself into an early grave or become an alcoholic or both."

"Nice boy?" He sneered at her, angry that he had to explain *why* drinking was better than the alternative. "Yeah, I found one of those. He not only doesn't want me, but also ordered me to never visit him in his dreams again! This'll keep me from dreaming, from dream walking, dammit," he roared, before collapsing back onto the couch, drained and hurting.

"Oh, hon. You mean you found your Cameron?"

He nodded but didn't look at her. He couldn't bring himself to do that yet.

"That's a good thing, isn't it?" Dianne asked. She pushed his hair out of his eyes, then tilted his head back with firm but gentle movements.

Closing his eyes, Liam felt a tear escape. He had hoped he was all out of them, but no, the traitors were visiting him again. "No. Not when he doesn't want anything to do with me. Cam doesn't even want me visiting him in his dreams anymore. I—" he choked off, unable to tell her he'd accidentally taken advantage of Cam after his demand to stay away.

"Oh, Liam. I'm so sorry. That's what you tried to tell me the other night, isn't it?"

"Yeah," he breathed out. "I found Cam, and he's just as beautiful and bouncy and perfect as he is in our dreams, but he…. It doesn't matter. I have to stay out of his dreams. I won't hurt him like that again, Di. This is the only way I know to stop myself from seeking him out. Please," he begged, reaching out to where she'd set the bottle of bourbon on the coffee table. "Please don't get in my way."

Dianne looked at him hard but didn't move to stop him. He'd already had enough that there was no burn when he took another mouthful and swallowed.

"We'll find you another way, hon. I'll talk to Nosha and see if he can help, okay?"

Taking another pull of the liquor, he nodded, resting his head on the back of the couch. He didn't know what the other man could do for him, but for now, this worked, and that was all that mattered.

Liam was used to being alone. He'd only had a few relationships, and the—attempted—anonymous sex he's sought the night at the club was even rarer for him. He simply wasn't built for tricks or short-term flings. He wanted a partner. To love and be loved. Many of his friends had teased him over the years about his old-fashioned ideas of sex and love, but that's just the way he was. Deep inside, he knew he was built for just one man. The problem was, he was afraid that man was Cam.

He didn't remember falling asleep, but eventually, the world was dark and quiet, and for the third night in a row, he didn't dream of his lover, just as he had promised.

THE NEXT week was a series of days working at the bookstore and nights drinking himself into a stupor. Liam dodged every call or text from Dianne. He even went so far as to park his car in the guest parking area instead of his usual spot to make it harder for her to find him. Not that it worked all the time. Or that she couldn't get in when he wasn't home.

When Liam got home earlier that night, he'd been dismayed to find not only all the liquor in his apartment gone, but supper on the table and Dianne in his kitchen. It was so 1950s sitcom, it sort of scared him for a moment.

Liam set down the fresh stock of whiskey and vodka—placing the bags with his stash under the sink so she wouldn't easily find it—before he stomped into the dining area, glowering down at Dianne. "What the hell are you doing here, Di?"

"Making sure you eat once in a while," she replied calmly. Her huge, blue eyes peeked out from behind her delicate gold wire-rimmed spectacles as she stared up at him. "You've lost weight, sweetie, and you didn't have much spare to begin with. You're not going to the gym, you're not answering your cell, and you've ducked out both times I've tried to get you to meet with Nosha."

He rubbed his hands roughly over his face, noting again how coarse his stubble was as it scritched loudly against his skin. Dropping his arms to his sides, Liam turned away from her. "Your wannabe boyfriend can't help me undo what I've already done," he mumbled, not meeting her eyes as he fidgeted.

"Sit down, Liam."

Lost in his own pain, he didn't move right away.

"Now," she added, pushing and tugging until he was hovering next to his usual spot at the table.

"I don't need a sitter, Di," Liam snapped, wishing she would go home and leave him alone. He wanted a drink, not the food in front of him. He hadn't had an appetite since the day Cam had walked away.

"Liam? What are you thinking about?" Di asked, wrapping her arms around his shoulders. "Come on, talk to me. You can't keep this up, hon. Not and come out on the other side sane and still breathing."

"All I care about right now is not hurting Cam anymore." Shaking his head, trying to banish the pain he'd been drowning in, he glowered down at his plate. "If I eat, will you leave me alone?"

Dianne let out a huge, put-upon sigh, but nodded. "Fine. But this cannot continue, and you know it. You need to let us help you."

The high-pitched, thready laugh that escaped him wasn't attractive or sane-sounding, but right then, Liam didn't care. *Help?* "Help? I did things your way and look what I got. You convinced me Cam was real and that the dreams were real only to have him turn away from me. Yeah, that helped *so* much." He stabbed at the chicken and rice on his plate, uninterested in eating it but hoping doing so would hurry her the hell up.

"That's not fair, Liam. You had a chance to adjust to the idea of Cameron being real. He didn't. Did you even think of that? Maybe if you give it time—"

"No," Liam bellowed, slamming his fork back down. "No time. No trying. No hoping for a sunset of dreams and fuzzy hearts. I won't violate his dreams again!" He stood, turned, and stormed into the kitchen, grabbed the vodka he'd stashed earlier, and headed into his bedroom.

Liam slammed the door before locking it, knowing he'd wind up with Di following him in there as well if he didn't. He twisted the cap off and then downed a fourth of the bottle before coming up for air again. He just wanted to protect Cam from him and to stop hurting so much. Was that really too much to ask?

He stripped down to his boxers and flopped on the bed, ignoring Dianne's demands for him to open the door and talk. Liam flipped on the radio, turning it up in a vain effort to drown out her incessant pleading. He proceeded to drain the large bottle, welcoming the numbing elixir even as his body shook and his heart bled all over his thoughts.

CHAPTER 6

CAM SAT at his drafting table, sketching out a new tattoo for a customer. In the short time he had been working in Asheville, there was already a demand for his scheduled time and a list of designs and ideas he needed to make into reality for his clientele. He loved his work, and even more, he loved seeing the finished piece and the grins that always accompanied his pieces.

The music was loud in the shop, but he didn't mind. Lately, quiet was getting harder for him to deal with. Too much quiet and his thoughts turned to Liam, which would only serve to make him feel even lonelier than he already was. He missed Liam more than he'd have thought possible, especially since he'd never really spent any awake time with the man. How someone could affect him so much was beyond him, but to keep his thoughts from going there, he bounced to the beat and worked on the sketch in front of him. It was of a Burton-styled Mad Hatter and grown-up Alice, coiled together. He'd never have thought of it himself, but Sonny had been adamant they would be perfect together. Now that he was drawing it out, he had to kind of agree with him.

A soft knock on his studio door cut off his musings about other possible Alice tattoos. When he set down his pencil and turned, the pixie of a woman in his doorway greeted him with a tentative smile. "Are you Cameron?" she asked, her blue eyes bright in her tiny, heart-shaped face.

"That's me. What can I do for you?"

"My name's Dianne, and I need to talk to you about Liam Grady."

He froze at the name, unsure why this woman wanted to discuss Liam. "What about him?" Cam asked, his voice hesitant even to his own ears.

"Look, can I come in and sit down?" The determination and annoyance flashing in Dianne's eyes unnerved Cameron even as it intrigued him. "Or do you really want everyone to hear your business?"

Heat rushed up Cam's cheeks and down his neck, but he tried to ignore it. "Sorry, ma'am. Come in, please."

"Better," she replied before closing the door behind her and perching on the edge of his work stool. "Now, I hope I'm right and you're the Cam

Liam's been dream-sharing with for years." As soon as he nodded, she flashed him a wide, bright smile and continued, "Good! I'm so happy to finally meet you. I just hope you can help me."

"I don't know what I can do for you unless you want a tattoo. I mean, that's what I do here," Cam explained, gesturing to his half-finished design and tools. "Or what this has to do with Lee."

"Oh, I like how you say his name. Maybe this will work," she added. "Look, I know you don't know me, but I'm Liam's aunt, and I need your help before it's too late and we lose him forever."

The lost, faraway look in her eyes worried him. *Lose him?* "What do you mean lose him?" *What's wrong with Liam, and is that why the dreams stopped?*

"I don't know what happened exactly, but he said you didn't want to see him and all, but that he visited your dreams again once. On accident, I'll have you know," she stated forcefully, startling him. "But now he's so afraid of hurting you again, he's drinking himself to death to block his ability to dream."

He didn't know what to think or say but opened his mouth anyway. No sound came out, though. He ended up snapping it shut, feeling foolish. *Drinking to stop the dreams?* "What do you mean hurting me?" he finally managed to ask. He couldn't think of any reason Liam would think that way.

"I'm a little fuzzy on the details, but he thinks he'll hurt you if he dream walks again. Or rather, he believes he already has hurt you somehow, but I can't get the story out of him. Last time I tried, he locked himself in his room with the radio on so loud I'm certain he couldn't hear me on the other side of the door." Dianne shifted on the stool, her huge eyes looking up at him, wet and imploring. "I need your help before it's too late and he loses himself completely to the pain, guilt, and alcohol."

Cam struggled to make sense out of what she was saying, but he didn't want Liam hurting. The thought of him drinking himself stupid to try to protect Cam made a twisted kind of sense, though he didn't approve of the idea at all. "I only met him the one time, and while I did tell him not to visit me again, I don't understand the drinking thing. Of course, I don't understand how this dream-thingy of his works, either. I mean, seriously, how do you travel without your body?" Cam raised his right brow as he continued to stare at her. He still didn't understand it even though he couldn't completely deny it was possible—he'd spent too many years dreaming of Liam to not believe at least a little.

"Did you mean it?" she asked, leaning forward and patting his hand as it sat on his knee. "Do you really not want to know him?"

Confused at how she jumped around topics, he nodded, but then shook his head. "I did when I said it, but no, not really. I mean, I was so shocked to find out Lee was real I couldn't, I mean… I panicked," he mumbled, looking down at his scuffed Converse high-tops as he wiggled his toes inside them. "He came back once, but that's all since the day we met here. If it weren't for Bass, my boss, knowing Liam, I would honestly think I'd hallucinated the whole meeting."

"Oh Goddess, you two are a pair! He thinks you hate him, and you look sad over him not visiting again." The woman stood and gave him a hug, that he was a tiny bit ashamed to realize he needed right then. "Will you help me, then?" she asked, smoothing his fuzzy, blond mop off his forehead and out of his eyes.

"I don't want him hurt, Dianne. I just… I panicked and ran," Cam added, looking away again.

"It's been almost a month since he started drinking every night." Dianne sighed and sat back again. "Look, even if you don't want to date Liam, could you maybe, I don't know, talk to him? Try to get him to stop the drinking. I mean"—she peered up at him, her eyes wide and beseeching—"at least talk to him and tell him you don't hate him, please?"

Cam nodded and tried to smile but knew he failed by the sad look on the woman's face. "I'll try, but where? He won't come here again if he's really taking things that far. Besides, I don't know where he is other than in the city somewhere, and while Asheville's not *huge*, it's not exactly tiny, either."

A bright, bubbly laugh escaped from Dianne. "He's right; you are too sweet and cute to be real." She sobered after a moment but continued to smile. "He works not far from here, but his bookstore isn't the best place for heart-to-hearts. Um…." She drummed her silver-and-purple nails on her leg. "I'm planning on breaking in and making him dinner again tonight. Would you like to come over for dinner?"

He looked at her, trying to figure out if she was serious or if this was some kind of messed-up coercion tactic to get him over for a dinner date. She seemed so sincere and honest, though, Cam didn't think she was playing him. He hoped not, at least. Truth be told, he had been fighting with himself about asking Bass where Liam worked and going over to talk to him before this visit, so he figured it was a coincidence, not a trick. He just hoped he was right. "All right, but I work tonight, so it has to be either really late or I need the time so I can make sure to block it out on the schedule."

"Wonderful," Dianne chirped, jumped up, and threw her arms around his neck. "You have no idea how happy you just made me."

He gently patted her back, wondering if she was always this touchy-feely. It wasn't that he minded hugs, but they didn't even know each other yet. Cam chuckled and smiled. "Okay. Let's go look at what I have set for tonight, and then we can plan this intervention of yours."

CAM LOOKED down at himself, nervous like he had never been before. He looked at the seemingly nonthreatening door but couldn't get his hand to raise. Talking to Dianne earlier, this seemed a simple enough mission: help her calm Liam down and see if maybe they could be friends or something. Now, however, he stood frozen on Liam's doorstep, unsure if this was the best or worst idea ever.

This is stupid! I want the man, so why is talking to him so hard? It's not like I don't know him, haven't had the best sex of my life with him, don't know that he likes to cuddle—and won't make fun of me for it—and will even talk to me like a human the next day. This should be simple, so why isn't it? Cameron knew why, in part at least. He'd been in love with Dream Liam since he was fifteen. He was terrified the real Liam wouldn't be as loving, sweet, hot, sexy, or perfect for him as the dream version was. Still, he knew he needed to get past this and to stop letting his fear rule the situation. That's how this got all messed up in the first place.

"Go home, Di!" Liam's voice rumbled through the door, startling Cam out of his paralysis. "I don't need a sitter."

He couldn't hear her reply but figured he needed to man up before he ruined Dianne's plans. Closing his eyes, Cam took a deep breath and released it after a moment. He took the single step forward needed to reach the door and rang the bell.

Moments later, the door flew open as Liam bellowed, "What do you—?" His words died in his throat as he stared down at Cam.

Cameron gave him a small smile. "Hi, Lee."

Liam stood there, gawking, his mouth opening and closing, but no sound escaped.

"Can I come in?" Cam asked, knowing how unreal this probably seemed to Liam. Hell, it seemed that way to him too, but he couldn't let what had happened that day at the coffee shop destroy Lee.

The man blinked hard and nodded. "Uh, s—sure. Please," he added, moving quickly out of the way. He led Cam into a nice little living room with a comfortable-looking couch, plush chairs, an enormous flat-screen TV, and a few scattered accent tables and lamps. Cam noticed two of the walls and part of the third were covered in very full bookshelves. He smiled to himself, knowing Liam ran a bookstore. The setup made sense and seemed so "him."

"Thank you."

"Who's at the door, Liam?" Dianne's voice called out from another room.

Liam didn't answer; he merely continued to look at Cam, his bloodshot eyes never setting on any one spot for long. Cam did the same, noticing how Liam didn't look as he had before. His eyes looked so tired, dark, and puffy. Liam had always been clean-shaven in the dreams, but now he had stubble, but like he hadn't bothered to shave, not that sexy, close-shaven-beard look so many men pull off so well. Cam also noted how Liam's hands shook and how he kept swallowing hard. He looked like hell, but at the same time, Cam wanted nothing more than to throw himself into Liam's arms and live there.

"Oh, hello," Dianne said from beside him. "Liam, say hello to your company."

"Hello, Cameron." He sounded more like he was just responding to her demand than actually engaging his brain, but Cam didn't care.

"Hi, Lee. Nice place." Cam groaned internally. *Nice place? Really?*

"Thanks. Um, wha—what are you doing here?" Liam asked, looking away from him for the first time and directly at Dianne.

"I invited him over for dinner. Had you not started yelling, you might have noticed there are three settings on the table, not two." Dianne stood, all five-two of her, with her arms folded across her chest, glowering up at Liam. "Now, offer to take his coat and bring him to the dining room. Dinner's ready."

Liam's body jerked as he turned back to face Cam, but for the first time, Cam saw a small smile cross his face. "Right. May I take your coat and, um, would you like to stay for dinner? I know she asked you already, or you wouldn't be here, but…. Have dinner with us, please?"

"I'd love to." Cam slipped his jacket off and handed it over quickly.

He watched as Lee took off for a moment and then came back sans coat. Liam held out his still-trembling hand, gesturing Cam toward the other doorway. When he stepped through, he found a dark cherrywood oval table with high-back chairs in the center of the room. One wall housed a china hutch, and there was a beautiful buffet table along the back wall. The room wasn't large, but it felt welcoming nonetheless. Looking at the table again, he noted there *were* three settings laid out. He wondered what they were having to need so many forks and spoons but tried to ignore the nervous flutter in his stomach at the thought of messing this up.

"You two sit, and I'll serve the food and drinks," Dianne added, staring pointedly at Liam. Cam fought not to laugh at the cowed look on Lee's face.

Liam stepped over to the chair next to the head of the table and pulled it out. "Join me?" he asked, looking from Cam to the chair again.

"Thanks." Cam let Liam seat him and smiled as Liam took the chair at the head of the table. He'd been expecting the man to be rip-roaring drunk and belligerent, not quiet and accommodating. Maybe things weren't as bad as Dianne seemed to think?

He opened his mouth to ask about what was going on, but Dianne bustled in with bowls of some kind of creamy, red soup, interrupting him. Moments later, she returned with bread, butter, and drinks for them before sitting across from Cam.

Cam observed the man he both wanted and feared. Enjoying the soup and the meal that followed, he noted how exhausted Liam seemed. Neither of them spoke much, and as dinner wore on, he noticed how Lee avoided direct eye contact. Was he doing that because he was nervous or because he still thought Cam didn't want anything to do with him?

When Dianne brought out bowls of ice cream, Cam couldn't stand it any longer. "Are you going to talk to me or just covertly stare at me all night?"

"I, um, sorry?"

"I don't want you to be sorry unless it's for not taking proper care of yourself."

Liam slumped even further into his seat. He picked at the cold desert but didn't actually eat any. But then, Cam had noticed Liam hadn't eaten much of his dinner, either, more moving the food around than anything. "Why are you here?" Liam finally blurted out.

"Your sweet aunt here—" He turned toward the woman in question. "Though you're way too cute and young to be his aunt," Cam added, smirking at Dianne. "—convinced me to come over and talk to you. But almost every word out of you has been prompted since I arrived. Before then, all I heard was you yelling."

Dianne stood and collected her bowl and spoon before heading to the kitchen. A few moments later, Cam noticed her in the doorway, her coat on already. "I'm heading out, Liam, Cam. Liam, talk to him, please, and Cam, be gentle with him, okay?"

Cam nodded and flashed her a smile before she kissed the top of Liam's head and disappeared out the front door. When he heard the door click closed, Cam turned back to Liam. "Well?"

"You said you didn't want anything to do with me. Why are you here?" Liam's voice was so soft Cam barely heard him.

"My imagination had just come to life before my eyes, Liam. I didn't know how to deal with that, and you acted as if it was just a given that we were a couple or something. It freaked me the hell out. But that's no reason to drink and hurt yourself like this," he continued, becoming more upset the longer he sat there. The more he noticed how thin and drawn Liam was, the more he understood Dianne's reasons for hunting him down. He'd have done the same if their roles were reversed.

"I had water and apple juice with dinner. I hardly think that's inappropriate," Liam countered.

Cam looked at Liam hard, knowing what Dianne had already revealed about Liam's recent drinking issues. What he'd observed before he stepped inside also told him juice wasn't Liam's usual evening beverage of choice. "I'm not arguing with you, Lee. I don't know why you are drinking yourself into a stupor every night, but that sweet little thing that just left seems to have convinced herself it's over me. That's bullshit and we both know it. You have no reason to drink over me, and you know it." Cam folded his arms across his chest, trying to make his look hard, if not intimidating. "So you can sit there and lie to me, or you can talk to me about all this drinking nonsense and maybe we can figure out how you can function without the booze."

He watched as Liam seemed to crumble in on himself and stared down at the table. After a minute or two of nothing, Cam sighed and stood. "Come on. You're going to get a shower and some sleep, with*out* any liquid assistance."

Liam shook his head even as Cam pulled him up out of the chair. "I—"

"No, and that's final, Lee. You don't want to tell me what this is about, fine. I can be patient, but you've lost weight, you're scruffy, and you look like you slept in your clothes. I may have only met you awake once, but even I know that's not like you. Now, shower," Cam continued, nudging Liam toward the hall he hoped led to the bath and bedroom.

CHAPTER 7

CAMERON LOOKED around the room, unable to believe he was in Liam's home. Just as bizarre to him was the idea that he was sitting on a chair in the guy's bedroom awaiting the man in question's return—once he showered and shaved. While Cam *had* decided to find Lee and try talking things out with him, the entire situation was a bit surreal. Who starts a relationship and keeps it up for years in a dream? Worse, he couldn't figure out why Liam was drinking the way Dianne described. And while he hadn't witnessed the drunkenness, Liam's odd attitude changes and the shakes made him believe her. The obvious loss of weight and the weariness only added to his concerns for Liam.

The water from the shower stopping cut off his musings and drew his focus back to the present. Cam fought not to pace as he waited, getting more concerned and itchier under his skin as the minutes ticked by. When the bathroom door finally opened, Liam leaned in the doorway, dressed only in a pair of silver sleep pants. However, Cam also noted he still had the beard scruff on his face, and while his hair was damp and he looked clean, his eyes were still bloodshot and hollow.

"Uh-uh, Liam. I said shave too," Cam chastised gently. He'd stood, intending to shoo Lee back inside to finish up when he noticed Liam's hands were trembling again, or still more likely.

"I, um…." Liam held up one unsteady hand in explanation but wouldn't meet Cam's gaze.

He took in how tired and beaten down Liam seemed and made a decision to do something he had never done before for anyone but himself. "All right, then I'll do it for you and then tuck you in before I head back to work."

Brows scrunched, Liam stared at Cam blankly. "Do what?"

"Shave you, of course. Now, where's your stuff?"

Liam's eyes widened comically, and he swallowed so hard his Adam's apple bobbed before he spoke. "I…. Do you know how to use a straight razor?"

Cam froze a moment but then shrugged. "Not done it in a while, but my papa taught me when I was a kid to"—his voice dropped an octave—"shave like a real man." Cam's voice went back to normal as he continued. "But I can do it if you'll trust me with a razor."

Liam nodded, his gazed darting from Cam to the floor and back before he dutifully shuffled back into the bathroom. Liam stood in front of the sink and mirror. "This is it," he mumbled, gesturing to where his razor lay folded next to his shaving soap, mug, and brush.

Looking around, Cam frowned. Liam was a half a foot or so taller than Cam was, so he wasn't confident he could reach up safely from behind, and he knew he couldn't face Liam and do it. He couldn't tie a tie on someone else, either, but he didn't figure Liam needed that kind of help right then.

In the corner, behind the door, Cam noticed a small step stool. He snagged it and set it behind where Liam stood slouched against the counter. Cam briefly wondered why he had the stool but figured he could ask later. After wetting the brush, he began to work up a lather. He knew Liam had just been in the shower but hoped the entire ritual would help soothe Lee's obviously frazzled nerves.

Cam worked carefully, softening and lifting the coarse stubble covering Liam's strong, but too-thin jaw and cheeks. After a few minutes, Liam sighed and leaned back against Cam's chest. Cameron shifted so he could support Liam's weight before he asked Liam to hand over the straight-edged razor.

"Lee?" Cam whispered into his ear and nuzzled Liam's temple a moment. "I need you to stay still, okay?"

"Mmm…. Still, okay." Liam's voice was soft, almost dreamy sounding as it washed over Cam. His gut cramped, but he ignored it and forced himself to focus on the task at hand.

Cam moved slowly, pulling Liam's skin taut before scraping the extremely sharp razor along it, careful to be thorough but without injuring the pitiful man in his arms. When Cam shifted to work on Lee's neck, Liam hummed softly and closed his eyes. Cam was extra careful as he swiped the blade along Liam's Adam's apple, not wanting to injure him.

As he was wiping the last of the lather from Liam's face, Cam felt the lightest of touches along his outer thighs. He looked down to see Liam's long fingers brush back and forth against the soft material of his pants. The other hand dug into Cam's thigh as Liam clutched him. Cam gasped softly, irritated with his body as his cock hardened immediately, becoming a steel bar digging into Liam's backside.

Involuntarily, he flicked his gaze down, and thanks to the mirror, he could see how Liam's cock grew harder the longer he stared. He wanted to climb Liam, but now was neither the time nor was he going to be a trick for the man. Cam swayed gently, rocking Liam side to side as he finished cleaning Liam up.

He kissed the side of Liam's head before pulling back. "There, now don't you feel better?"

"Much." Lee hummed, nestling back into Cam more. "Thank you, Cameron."

"You're welcome, Liam. Now let's get you into bed, hmm?"

Liam merely nodded, allowing Cam to direct and guide him to the king-size poster bed in his room. Once settled, Liam looked up with bleary eyes but didn't say anything.

"Look, I'd really like to know what's going on, but for now you need sleep and I need to get back to work. So maybe sometime tomorrow you could give me a call and we can try that coffee thing again? You won't *drink* and I promise not to run again. Deal?"

The blind nod worried Cam, but he figured it was the best he could hope for at the moment.

"Now, please sleep, okay?" He pulled the sheet and comforter over Liam before smoothing his brown locks out of his eyes. "And no getting up after I leave to drink," Cam added, hoping Liam would listen to him.

When Cam began to pull away, Liam's hand shot out, his fingers wrapping around Cam's wrist with a strength he wouldn't have expected, considering how Liam had acted so far. "Why are you doing this? Why help me?"

Cam looked from where Lee held him tight enough he thought there might be marks later—a thought he secretly enjoyed but wasn't going to share just yet—back to Liam's Technicolor blue eyes. "Look, I don't get what's happening between us or with you. I know I bailed on you when we met the first time, but I can't let you self-destruct like this." Cam rubbed the back of his neck, searching for the right words but not finding them. "When I see you next, I'd really like the tall, sexy, strong man back instead of the self-abusive one. 'Kay? We can talk all this out once you're fully awake and thoroughly sober. I'll leave my business card here for you," he added, pulling out one of his cards and setting it on the nightstand. "Call me."

Liam finally let go and sank back down into the thick pillow-top bed. Cam settled the blanket around him again before he quietly stepped out of the room. He took a minute to clean up their glasses and ice cream dishes before turning out the light and locking up behind himself.

Walking back to his car, he nearly turned around more than once but continued, knowing Liam needed sleep and he had work to do still. The justifications didn't help much, but he knew they both needed to be awake and ready to talk. Cam just hoped Liam would be back to himself soon and that he would call.

CAM SAT in the plush chair he usually used for clients with his shirt off as Bass worked on the newest addition to his shoulder and arm. After that first disastrous meeting with Liam, he'd almost stopped work on his sleeve. That had lasted all of one day before he'd been right back at work tweaking the design and even adding more to his sketch than he'd originally planned. Now, as he looked down to where Bass worked on the bits of leaf and branch that curled up to almost meet his collarbone, he was thankful he had continued. The design was in many ways Liam, but at the same time, he loved each bit and knew he would be happy when it was completed.

"You going to tell me where you disappeared to last night after the book guy's little firebrand came by?" Bass didn't look up, but Cam also knew it was more a demand than a real question by the tone alone.

He snorted, thinking of how she'd run all over Liam the night before. "Good way to describe her. She wanted me to go over and meet with Liam. You know, the *book guy*?"

"Fine, so I know his name. I also know you've been weird since he came by a month ago, so you ready to talk yet?"

"You're just asking me now because you know I can't get away, aren't you?"

"Damn skippy, I am. Now, spill."

Cam fought not to laugh at the snarky bear of a man beside him. "Don't know what to tell you, Bass. I mean, I told you about the whole freaky dream thing already." Bass nodded but didn't pause in his work. "Well, it seems something's wrong with Lee, but I don't know what. I, um, told him to call me and left him my card, but he hasn't yet."

"It's only the next day, Cam. You can't get bent out of shape that fast. He has a shop to run too, you know."

"I know." Cam sighed. "I…. It was weird seeing him like he was last night. The dreams stopped right after I told him to not do it again, but if I hadn't seen him that day here, I'm not sure I would have realized it was him last night. He looked that bad."

"You gonna—?"

Cam's cell ringing cut Bass off, which he was silently pleased over. Bass was a great boss, and they'd become friends in the short time he'd worked there, but Bass was too nosy when it came to Liam and the freaky dream thing.

Bass moved away, letting Cam get to the noisy thing before it switched over to voice mail. He didn't recognize the number but answered anyway. "This is Cameron."

"Hi, Cam."

It took a moment, but then his brain kicked in and he realized it was Liam on the phone. "Lee? You called!"

"You said to call. Is this a bad time?" Liam sounded more awake and focused but just as sad as he had the night before.

"No, well, Bass is working on my arm, but I have a minute."

"You still want to meet up for coffee? I close tonight at eight."

He fought the urge to laugh at how shy Liam sounded. The man was many things, but shy just didn't fit the Lee he knew. "Let me check."

Cam gestured to his desk behind Bass, whispering, "Schedule, please."

Bass smirked but handed it over. Cam checked it quickly before replying, "I can meet you after eight tonight, then, if you like."

"I'll be there at eight thirty."

"Great! I can't wait to see you again." Was that his voice? Yeah? He really had said that.

"Thanks for that, Cam. I don't want to interrupt your artwork getting done on your arm. Do you think you'll let me see it sometime soon? I know what I saw in the dream looked great, but I'd really love to see it in person, with my waking eyes."

Cam refused to look at Bass as he knew he'd pretty much melted at Liam's words. *Does he know how sweet he is or how special words like those are to someone like me?* "If you're a good boy, I just might, depending on how it feels. It's going to be a little sore tonight, though."

"I understand. Something to look forward to." Cam heard bells jingle in the background before Liam sighed and said, "I have to go. Business calls and all. I'll see you later, Cam. Bye."

"Bye, Lee."

After he hung up, Cam felt better than he had in over a month. He settled back in the chair, smiling so hard his cheeks hurt. He was startled out of his thoughts about later when Bass swatted his tender arm.

"What the hell?"

"You going to let me finish our session here, or you want it left like this?" Bass grinned. When Cam pouted at him, Bass laughed so loud, Jason and Del poked their heads in to see what was going on. "Moon on your own time, Cammy."

"I was not," Cam sputtered, knowing he had been doing just that. He couldn't help it. Even with as freaked out as the situation made him, there was something special about Liam. Cam longed to get to know Liam, and not just how he was in the dreams. "Fine," he forced out as he chuckled along with Bass. "Maybe I was. A little. But, yeah, could you finish up, please? I've got an appointment soon."

Bass set back to work but then pulled away again and frowned. "You're going to be sore. Why didn't you tell me? We could have waited to work on yours."

"It's a design appointment, Bass. I won't do the inking until next week. Relax, would ya? Besides, I work sore all the time. Now," he added, pointing to the unfinished tree, "back to work, please. I'd like to be done before they show up."

Grumbling, Bass got back to work. Cam watched him carefully as he brought Cam's design to life. They chatted some, but most of the day Cam spent either working on designs for his customers or on obsessing about his coffee date for that evening.

More than once, Cam found himself lost in memories of past dreams, times he wished had been real. But then he still wasn't sure if those dreams should be considered real or not. He had no one to ask about such things, and while they felt so real at the time, when he awoke, they always faded some. He never completely forgot them the way he did the non-Liam dreams, though.

"Hey, Cam!" Jason barked from his doorway. "Bass said for you to get out of here so you're not late. Where ya going?" he added softly.

Cam looked up, blinking hard as he tried to focus his eyes on the short, even to him, thin man staring at him. Jason was nice but tended to blend in with the environment. He was about five-five, with mousy-brown hair and eyes to match. But what made him so frustrating was that he seemed to want to blend. He was always soft-spoken, dressed in neutral colors, and stayed out of the way. Except for today, of course.

"To get coffee, but"—Cam looked at his watch—"that's not for more than an hour still."

Jason's eyes widened as he continued to stare. "Oh, it's a date thing. Shouldn't you go home and get cleaned up, then? You're—" He paused and gestured up and down at Cam. "Well, spotted."

He tilted his head as he stared at Jason. *Spotted?* "Huh?"

"Look at your hands, Cam. Your face is kind of the same," Jason added, a light pink touching his cheeks. "Unless your guy goes in for the whole absentminded-artist thing, of course."

Cam looked down at his hands, and sure enough, there was ink and graphite on his fingers and the side of one hand. He could only imagine how his face looked right then. He grinned and nodded. "Yeah, I guess Bass might be right about me. All right, tell him I'll head out in a few and be back later. Oh, and thanks, Jason. I want to look hot, not like a hot mess."

Jason headed away, but Cam could hear the soft chuckles as he hurried to clean things up and put his designs away and then headed out and down the street to his apartment. He got a few odd looks from people on his way, but he was in too good a mood to care. He was going to meet up with Liam, and this time he was prepared and determined to learn more about the man who he'd known yet not known since he was a teen.

CHAPTER 8

CAMERON STROLLED down the sidewalk, then turned the corner and paused to stare at the innocuous coffee shop situated there. He'd been there many times since he moved, but this time was different. This time he was willingly meeting with Liam, and he hoped he'd get some real answers about what was going on with their dreams and with the drinking thing. The way Liam looked the night before still haunted Cam.

He looked down at the dark, low-rise dress pants he wore and smoothed his hands over the silver silk button-down. He tugged his leather jacket closed again before opening the door and stepping inside the café.

Liam sat at a small table in the back corner, his eyes fixed on Cam as he walked over. Cam nearly tripped twice trying to cover the short distance, his heart beating so loud he was certain those he passed could hear. When he finally reached Liam, he gave a small smile as he glanced at Liam's face and body.

Liam was dressed much nicer than he had been the last time Cam had seen him. A teal sweater, tight enough to show off his defined chest and long enough to cover the backs of his hands graced Liam's upper body. From the angle at which he stood, Cam could see Liam wore black dress jeans and a pair of Docs on his feet. Liam was clean-shaven again or possibly still, and while he was still too thin, he seemed better rested and more steady than he had.

"Hello, Liam." Cam sat across from him, draping his jacket over the back of the chair. When Liam smiled, Cam smiled in return, thrilled Liam seemed pleased to see him again. "One of those for me?" he asked, noting the coffee cup in front of where he now sat.

"It's what Shay said you preferred," Liam explained, gesturing over to where the perky, blond-and-purple-haired barista worked.

Cam picked up the cup, enjoying the delicious blend of spice and sweet as he took a sip of his chai latte. "Mmm, perfect. Thanks."

Liam nodded, but neither of them spoke again for a minute. Cam wasn't sure what to say, so he focused on his drink, hoping Liam would come up with something before he had to.

"Thank you for last night." Liam flushed bright red and stared down at the tabletop suddenly. "I mean… uh… thank you for everything you did. I did as you asked."

Pleased more than he figured he ought to be, Cam set his cup down, reached across the table, and cupped Liam's chin lightly. He gave a gentle nudge, and Liam finally raised his head again. "I'm glad. You really had me worried last night."

"Sorry."

"I don't want *sorrys*, Lee. I want to know what's going on, both with the dreams and with the drinking."

His shoulders slumped. After a moment, Liam nodded. "Fine." He picked up his drink, then took a moment to stare at it before taking a sip. He cleared his throat. "Dianne's friend Nosha is a dream walker and dream weaver. He's been one most of his life, or so he says. Anyway, it seems I have as well but didn't know it until recently. After the night I saw you at the club, I talked to Di, and she introduced me to Nosha. Since then, he's been trying to teach me how to control it." Lee swallowed hard, his eyes wet, but no tears escaped as he continued. "My control wasn't as good as it needed to be, though, and I swear I tried to not visit you after you said not to again."

The pain and guilt that flickered across Liam's handsome face confused Cam even more than his words. He reached over and covered Liam's empty hand with his own. "I don't understand, Lee. The dreams did stop, and what's that got to do with the drinking?"

"That's how I stopped them after the one slipup."

Cam thought about it, but it still didn't make sense to him. And what "slipup"? "Look, I don't get all this," he said, gesturing around him vaguely. "But drinking like your aunt said you were won't fix things. That guy I met last night, him?" Cam squeezed Lee's hand lightly. "Yeah, that's not the guy I've known since forever. Hell, he's not the kind of man I'd want to meet. Drunks aren't my thing."

"I didn't know what else to do. I couldn't take the chance of hurting you—" Liam closed his eyes tight.

The slight tremble in the hand he still held surprised Cam, as did the words. "You've never hurt me in any of the dreams, so why do you think you would do so now?"

Liam pulled his hand away from Cam. Cameron wanted to chase after it, but he let Lee have his space, for now. "How can you say that after what I did to you?"

"Lee, look at me, please." It seemed to take forever, but Liam did finally meet his gaze. The pain there forced a gasp from Cam. "Oh, hon. What on earth do you think you did to me? I know I ranted at you, but the only time the dreams hurt was the morning after, when I woke up alone."

"I visited you again after you told me not to, and did… things I shouldn't have with you. Not after what you said."

Cameron sat in stunned silence as he tried to make sense of Liam's words but couldn't. He racked his brain for anything Liam had ever done in their dreams that he could feel such pain and guilt over but drew a blank. Finally, he set his cup down, reached over, and took Liam's white-knuckled grasp from his mostly empty coffee cup. He tugged Liam up to standing. "Come on, Lee. We're going to get out of here and walk some. Not everybody needs to be able to hear us, and I think you could use the air."

Liam nodded slowly as he let Cam direct him outside. Cam stopped long enough to slide his jacket back on and waited while Liam did the same. After they'd walked in silence for a bit, Cam bumped Liam's shoulder but hissed when the earlier tattoo work made itself known again.

"What? You're hurt?" Liam asked, pulling Cam to a stop. He tugged on Cam's jacket, trying to expose the injured arm. "You're wearing too many damn clothes," Liam grumbled.

Cam giggled, swatting at Liam's attempt to check him for injury. "Never been told that before."

Liam froze, eyes wide. "Oh God, I didn't mean it like that."

Giving his best pout, Cam batted his lashes up at Liam. "Too bad."

The groan was very telling, as was the nervous chuckle. "You're hurt and picking on me at the same time. It must not be too bad, then."

"There's no wound, Lee. Seriously. Bass just worked on my sleeve more today, and the skin is still a little tender. That's all."

"You're still working on it? I thought…. Never mind what I thought."

"No, don't do that. What did you want to say?"

Cam resettled the jacket on his shoulders as he waited for Liam to answer. When he did, he shocked Cam again. "I thought you'd change your mind about it since you didn't want anything to do with me, with the dreams, with us."

He sighed, unsure how to make Liam understand his earlier reaction. "Look, I did think about changing it, for like a day, but it was the shock talking. Kind of like my yelling at you. Same thing, really. After I had calmed down, I realized that was a stupid thing to do, and so I continued working on the tat. I, um"—Cam shifted from foot to foot— "I've missed your dreams. I mean, I've missed spending time with you like we did in the dreams, but I was scared to try to find you. Sarah, my sister, said I should when we talked about it, but I mean, dreams aren't supposed to be real, man."

"You… missed the dreams? But you said no and I still… I don't understand," Liam groaned and tugged on his short hair. "How could you miss me if you hate me?"

"I don't hate you! I just didn't know how to handle you being real." The thought of Liam going to such lengths to stay away hurt, even though he knew it's what he'd demanded the first time they'd met. "I mean, if you don't want to share dreams with me, fine, but there has to be a better way than drinking, Liam."

Liam looked even more confused than before. "I only did that for you. Because I couldn't trust myself not to visit or take advantage of you again."

"See, you said it again. While I may not be the one traveling, or what-the-hell-ever it is you do to visit me, I don't remember you ever doing anything in the dreams I didn't want, ask for, participate in, or demand of you. When, exactly, did you 'take advantage' of me?"

"He doesn't remember?" Liam muttered, Cam assumed to himself, before looking up again. "After we met. Do you remember a shared dream right after that?"

Heat crept up Cam's cheeks. Thankful for the dark, he hoped Liam wouldn't notice. "Once, but they stopped after that. You were, uh, very athletic as I recall."

"And that doesn't bother you? You said…."

He could have kicked himself when the light finally went on in his head. "Wait, the dream in the kitchen. That's what freaked you out? I remember a lot of things I said in that dream, but *no* and *stop* were *not* part of the list."

"You'd already said no before, though. So that means I shouldn't have visited you in the first place, much less done… things like that… with you."

Cam tilted his head back and stared at the inky night sky dotted with stars and the occasional shadowy cloud. Contemplating what he'd just learned, Cam reached over and took Liam's hand again. After a moment, he threaded his fingers through Lee's loosely. "Come on, I want to do something with you before I have to send you home for the night."

"Oh-kay," Liam said, his voice soft, slow.

He walked them around to one of the fancier restaurants in the area. They had an outdoor garden, and while the flowers were dormant because of the winter cold, it was the fountain Cameron was after. He pulled Liam along with him, stopping at the side. Once there, Cam dug in his pocket and pulled out a couple of coins before handing one to Liam. He turned and faced the mostly still water. The wind kicking up caused a few ripples, but even so, it was quiet and calm where they were.

"Close your eyes, make a wish, then toss the coin in. You can't tell me what your wish is, and you can't ask what mine is, either."

"Coin toss? That's your response to what all I said?" Liam asked incredulously.

"Yep," he replied with a smirk. "Now, make a wish and toss. Since it's our first real date, I think it's a perfect thing to begin with."

Cam closed his eyes and focused on the coin and his wish. He knew Liam thought him nuts, but even though he'd freaked and run, Cam had a feeling that being with Liam was where he belonged. He held an odd hope for their future. Making his wish, he tossed the coin and watched as it made a small splash in the water. Cameron turned and watched as Liam chewed on his bottom lip, eyes scrunched closed.

When Liam finally tossed in his coin, Cam swore it took an eternity to finally make its splash as it hit and sank beneath the water. Not saying a thing, Liam sidestepped closer and slipped his arm around Cam's shoulder. "Thank you," he croaked.

The warmth coming off Liam and the light musky scent combined and went straight to Cam's head—both of them. With a contented sigh, he snuggled against Liam's side a little more and wrapped his arm around Liam's waist.

After a few moments, Cam pulled back but didn't release his hold on Liam. He turned his face up to see Liam looking down on him. His deep marine-blue gaze fixed on Cam's and held him pinned there.

Cam watched in slow motion as Liam slowly bent down, his pink lips inching closer. He held his breath as he waited for Liam to take the final step, but instead he rubbed his nose along Cam's and smiled. "First date?"

Huh? "Yeah. Date. I want to get to know you, so date." Did the man not want to date him? The way he'd spoken before, Cam had thought Liam would have encouraged the declaration, but now he wasn't so sure.

Liam's face lit up, a wide smile spreading across his handsome features. "Yeah, I'd like that too."

"Good. Now—"Cam looked down at his watch and winced. "—I need to get back to work soon, so why don't you walk me back to the shop, then go home and get some rest." Liam nodded and sighed as Cam continued gently touching him, caressing Liam's cheek and slipping his fingers into Lee's short hair. "Your eyes," he continued, reaching up to trace right beneath Liam's right eye, "are still bruised-looking, Lee. I'd really like you healthy, okay?"

"Yeah, but, um," Liam mumbled, shifting his weight from foot to foot.

"And if you happen to visit me in my dreams, it's okay. I promise." He really hoped Liam was done with the self-abusive guilt thing.

"Thank you." Liam wrapped his arms around Cam and pulled him close. Cam loved having Liam act more like he remembered from the dreams. Maybe, once they got to know each other more, they could do other activities that were more carnal too.

As they headed down the sidewalk again, Cam slid his arm around Liam's waist, enjoying sharing warmth and being close enough that every breath pulled in more of Liam's intoxicating scent. He couldn't put his finger on what Lee wore, but it had a slightly spicy, warm, and musky aroma that made separating at the front of the Indigo Dragon harder than he expected. But, after a brief, chaste kiss, he left Liam at the door and hurried directly back to his work area. He was determined to finish the design he needed for his first client the next morning before he went home for the night. Well, and to not obsess about the man he'd just spent the best pseudodate with ever.

LIAM STOOD outside the tattoo shop, debating what to do next. On the one hand, Cam had given him permission to dream walk again and had asked him not to drink anymore. But on the other, he didn't actually have control over his dream travel without the booze. Mind made up, he turned and headed home.

He pulled out his cell and scrolled through his contact list, debating which one to call first. After a moment of thought, he smirked and pushed the Call button.

"Hello?"

"Nosha? It's Liam."

"Liam? What can I do for you? It's a little late at night for a social call."

"I know, and I'm sorry for that, but I wanted to find out if you would still be willing to teach me?" Liam wasn't sure Nosha would say yes, not after his actions over the last few weeks, but he had to try. He knew Nosha didn't take on dream weaver students often, so Liam's walking out on the training had been a slap in the face, and he would have to work hard to make it up and prove himself now. Besides, Cameron deserved better than what Liam was now.

"Maybe. Stop by tomorrow after you close and we'll discuss it. And you better be sober and clean," Nosha added with a grumble.

"I will be."

"Just don't make me regret this, Liam. And call Di. She's been going crazy over you. She's a good person and doesn't deserve all this."

Liam knew how much they liked each other, even if neither Dianne nor Nosha seemed ready to admit it. "I'll call her as soon as I get home. And Nosha, thank you."

With more hope than he'd felt in ages, Liam walked back home, determined to learn all he could about dreams. He was ecstatic Cameron wanted to try dating but knew he needed to get a handle on his strange ability if he had any hope of being worthy of such a man.

If he had to beg Nosha, he would do it. He wasn't about to mess up with Cameron again. Not ever again if he had a choice.

CHAPTER 9

ONCE AGAIN, Liam sat outside Nosha's home, but unlike last time, he wasn't skeptical or dreading the meeting. Well, he was, but only the part where he had to apologize and hope Nosha would forgive him. Dianne and he had talked half the previous night away before he'd crashed still holding his cell. He'd woken up barely in time to grab coffee before he hurried out so he could open the bookstore before his first customer knocked. He never opened late; his regulars would worry, something that still dumbfounded him at times.

Taking a deep breath, Liam hopped out of his Equinox and hurried up the walk to Nosha's door. As he raised his hand to knock, it opened, revealing Nosha in baggy jeans and an oversized blue T-shirt. Nosha's attire was in direct contrast to his own choices of dress slacks and a fitted, gray turtleneck—well, mostly fitted. It had fit better a month ago. "Hi, Nosha."

Nosha looked him over a moment before he opened the door more and waved Liam inside. "Come on in," Nosha said before leaving him in the entryway and walking into the living room. "Take a seat and explain to me why you ditched out on the work you were doing here and why you want back in now. Training isn't a game, and my time is worth far more than you seem to believe."

Liam nodded as he considered how to explain his mistaken beliefs and fears that made him act as he had. After a moment of thought, running through how he'd planned and practiced his explanation, he gave as concise a rundown of everything, minus the fun, naughty bits, as he could manage.

"Wait, so let me get this straight—no pun intended—you had sex while in a dream with your would-be boyfriend and freaked out?" Nosha asked, eyes wide and the corners of his thin lips turned down.

"Well, um, yes, but you're missing the point. I thought I'd hurt him! How would you feel if you thought you had hurt Dianne? Especially that way," Liam snapped, folding his arms across his chest. He knew *now* that Cameron didn't hate him or feel used, but at the time that's exactly what he'd thought, and he did *not* appreciate Nosha not taking that point seriously.

"I wouldn't do that!"

"Neither would I!" He then added softly, "Not if I could help it. But it's what I believed. I'm still not convinced seeing Cam's a good idea," Liam explained, even as the thought of not seeing Cam carved away at his heart. "He said I could visit his dreams and that he wants to try dating, but...."

"But what, Liam? There's obviously something between you or you wouldn't have sought him out for so long."

"What if I really hurt him next time?"

"And that brings us back to why you're sitting on my couch at nine at night, right?" Nosha nodded, not waiting for Liam to answer. "All right, but we do this completely my way this time. You will be prompt, ready, and you will do all the little exercises I suggested last time. And I don't care who you pray to, call on, whatever, but I want to start working on your control while you're in a protective circle, if—" Nosha stared at him hard a moment before continuing. "—you're really serious about not just learning control but exploring your potential. Don't answer me yet," he countered when Liam opened his mouth to reply. "I want you to take your time and really think about it. This isn't a game, and faith isn't a toy. You have to decide what you truly want and how. I will teach you, but it will also be my way."

"I understand that, Nosha. I will practice, learn, and respect your ways even though I've never been religious myself. I'm not against your faith," he quickly clarified. "I've just never really had much faith in faith. Of course, I don't really know much about Wicca. Unfortunately, I never paid Dianne much mind when she started talking religion and such."

"I know. Di told me how you were raised, but if you want to work with guides, Deity, and the spiritual planes, you need to respect them and theirs." Nosha shifted forward, resting his elbows on his bony knees. "But, if you're willing to learn, I'm willing to train you. Now, let's work out our schedule and discuss where you want to go with it."

Liam thanked any deity willing to hear him that Nosha hadn't lumped him into the same category as the last guy who'd petitioned for Nosha's training—and been turned away. He spent the next two hours entranced with all the ins and outs of what Nosha wanted him to do, and this time, he was determined to work hard and develop his abilities. If

Cameron was really willing to give him a chance, he could do no less for the man—or for himself.

By the time he got home, Liam was so exhausted he did little more than kick off his shoes and sprawl across his bed. He didn't remember his head hitting the pillow.

CAM OPENED the front door to his loft, whistling as he walked in. "Honey, I'm home," he called out as he tended to do when there were strangers in the hall or he was feeling particularly lonely and didn't want to admit to living alone.

"Great! Did you have a good night at work?" Liam stood in his living room, wearing lounge pants and nothing else. At least, nothing he could see, but one never knew with Lee.

He quickly closed the door and stalked over to where Lee stood, smiling as he took in his lover's sleep-tousled hair and wide grin. "Mmm.... Okay, but it's even better now, hon." Cam hummed as he wrapped his arms around Liam.

"That's what I like to hear, Cameron." Liam's hands slipped around his waist, shifting down to cup Cam's butt, thumbs caressing the skin of his lower back lightly as he went.

Cam moaned and pushed back into the hands, needing Liam's touch. Leaning in, Cam kissed a wet trail down Liam's neck to his collarbone, continuing down until he reached one of Lee's pert nipples. Liam moaned when Cam curled the tip of his tongue around the tiny nub, teasing and licking it before sucking it into his mouth to worry the sensitive bit of flesh with lips and teeth.

Liam rocked against him, giving Cameron the delicious friction he craved. As a reward, Cam switched to lave the other nipple, tormenting the first with his fingers as he did, reveling in the sounds pouring out of Liam. When he whimpered, Cameron added teasing nips to the chest beneath his lips.

A strangled groan slipped out of Liam before he grasped Cam's shoulders and forced an arm's length between them. Cam looked up, confused and a little hurt. "What's wrong?"

Liam licked his lips, drawing Cam's gaze there before he calmed enough to speak. "Cam, baby, we need to slow down a bit. I want to spend time with you, not just jump you."

Bemused, Cam tried to muddle through his lust-fogged mind enough to understand, but the logic evaded him. Finally, he met Liam's eyes again before asking in a voice much smaller than he intended, "You don't want me?" He winced at how pathetic and needy he sounded, but he couldn't think of a time Liam, his Lee, had ever pushed him away.

"Oh, love, of course I do. But I want to do more than just maul you," he explained, pulling Cam back against his chest.

"Okay, Lee." Still confused, Cam wrapped his arms around Liam, trying to ignore the sting he'd felt. "Did you have something in mind?"

"Many things, but…." Lee tugged Cam to the couch. Liam sat first, then pulled Cam down so he straddled Lee's thighs.

"This isn't the way to keep my mind off sex with you, ya know." Cam wriggled, thrilled to feel Liam's hard member when he rocked forward.

Liam chuckled, and the deep rumble slid down his spine, coiling tightly around Cam's groin. "Cam, be good."

"Don't wanna be good," he purred, rocking against Liam's impressive bulge. "Want to be under you."

The strangled sound that tore out of Liam only served to make Cam want him more. Cam bent again to claim one of Liam's pert nipples, sucking and teasing it until Liam writhed and whimpered beneath him. Determined to have Lee, Cam slid down Liam's body, licking and nibbling as he went. When his knees hit the soft carpet, he bent and pressed his nose against Liam's groin, taking in the dark, musky scent there.

"Lee?" Cam asked, staring up at his lover through his lashes. "Can we talk after I show you how much I want you?"

Not waiting for an answer, he tugged down the waistband of the silky sleep pants until just the crown of Liam's member poked out. Cam flicked his tongue out, lapping at the soft skin, swirling around and around before stabbing into the slit and then gently sucking the tip into his mouth.

The panting and groans he ripped out of Liam made Cam so hard it bordered on pain. He continued to devour and torment his lover, ignoring his own need. Finally, annoyed with the material in his way, Cam shoved the pants down until both Lee's cock and balls were exposed.

"Cam," Lee moaned. "I wan-wanted to— Argh!" He roared and thrust up hard when Cam swallowed him to the root in one smooth motion. Humming, Cam used his tongue, lips, and teeth carefully to torment and excite as he set a quick pace, bobbing up and down. The feel, the taste, the power to reduce a man to a mindless puddle, it all excited and satisfied something within him. Cam loved giving head, but especially to Liam.

"Baby," Liam tried again, but Cam wasn't having it. He wanted Lee insane with his need for him. Period. He teased and petted Liam's sac before rubbing lightly behind his balls.

"Dammit, Cam," Liam roared and lunged forward, pressing Cam back into the plush carpet. Liam's lips crashed down on his, tongue pressing in and staking claim to every point he touched.

Cam groaned, startled, but even more in need when Liam's large hands pressed between them and ripped his top open. Before he could process fully what had just happened, Lee pinched and tugged his nipples. He arched under Liam and screamed, frantic to feel more skin, more touch, just more. And to come. Definitely to come!

"Come on, baby. Give it to me," Liam demanded, nipping and licking up Cam's jaw and down his neck. He never stopped frotting against Cam, giving him the most delicious sensations. At the command, Cam lost his hold on what little control he'd still managed and keened as he shot again and again inside his jeans. Somewhere in there, he heard Lee roar out his own release.

Eventually Cam calmed as Liam peppered his face and chest with little kisses. "Wow."

"Wow indeed, my Cam. Mauling you really wasn't my intention, though. I wanted you to know that…." Liam looked around, a curious expression on his beatific face. It changed in a blink to annoyance. "Dammit. I wanted…. Never mind what I wanted. Look, call me in the morning, okay?"

Confused, Cam nodded but then shook his head. "Just stay, Lee."

"I can't, baby. Now be good, get some rest, and call me when you wake up."

"I—"

Cam rolled over, blinking his eyes open and looked around. He was in bed, alone. He reached out and patted the sheets, but nope, they were cold and there were no signs anyone had been there. Cam was too tired to puzzle it out right then and decided he'd rather just go back to his dreams. He tugged the pillow beside him to his chest, curled around it, and drifted off again, hoping to find Liam when he got there. The thought that he was supposed to do something for Liam flitted through his mind as he floated between sleep and wake, but he couldn't keep hold of it long enough to find it.

"Later," he mumbled to no one as sleep again claimed him.

UNABLE TO be still, Liam paced Nosha's small living room, frustrated. He'd tried the last three nights to contact Cam while he slept. Well, technically, he had visited Cameron. What he'd failed to do was to actually have a conversation of any importance, or get Cam to call him, for that matter.

"Liam, stop. My poor floors can't take your incessant pounding."

Jerking to a halt, Liam glanced to where Nosha sat, calm and collected in the same comfy chair he always used, staring at Liam. "Sorry, but I don't know what I'm doing wrong. I'm going to Cam when I choose, just like we planned. I'm taking control of the dream." He ran his fingers through his short-cropped hair again, knowing he probably had the whole mad-scientist look going on right then. "Well, as much as anyone can with how, er, determined he is to distract me. Heck, I've even taken control of things like place and clothing, deliberately, once. But get him to remember something as simple as 'call me'? Nope, can't do that one."

"As fun as it is to watch you like this, it would be better if you calmed down a bit. Things aren't as bad as you seem to think."

"He's not called me since our... I don't even know if that was a date or not. For coffee, but not the point, though—"

"What is your point?" Nosha asked midrant. "The guy said he wanted to date you, right? He said you could visit his dreams again. From the color you turn when that's mentioned, I'm assuming he's happy in his dreams for you to be there."

"Yes, but, oh God, I sound like a sixteen-year-old whining 'Why hasn't he called!'" Liam groaned and pulled his hair as he did before dropping his hands to his sides. "Okay, I'm an adult. I can deal with this in a mature fashion."

Nosha's rumbling laugh didn't overly help his confidence or mood. "It's really not that funny, man. This is my life here."

"I know it is. I'm just glad to see you finally get that. But look, I'm not a couples counselor. What I am is a priest and a dream walker that promised to guide and teach you. You really need to calm so you can focus."

"Yeah, I know. Sorry for flaking out again."

"It's all right." Nosha shrugged and smiled. "Now, why don't you go change into the stuff you brought in your bag there and I'll set things up for the circle and meditation."

"Huh?"

"I want you to work though one of the meditations I mentioned once we cast the circle."

"Right, sorry." Liam nodded, then grabbed his bag from where he'd left it by the front door and went to change in the guest bathroom. A pair of sweats and a loose T-shirt didn't seem like much for doing ritual stuff, but meditating while uncomfortable didn't really work, and he knew it. He was still struggling a bit with the whole religious aspect of his training, but not like he'd expected.

Unlike Di, he wasn't raised with religion of any kind. Oh, he knew the basics of Christianity, but that was about it. He knew enough to not put his foot in it at school, but he never really thought about it or paid much attention. He knew even less about Wicca and paganism, even though his grandparents and aunt were multigenerational followers. Liam liked the little circle-casting work they had done so far. He enjoyed the way it made him feel energized yet peaceful. The part that surprised him, though, was how he felt connected to something bigger than himself during those times.

Liam folded his clothes and placed them back in his duffel, looked at himself one more time in the mirror, then squared his shoulders and turned to the door. In that moment, he decided he would really try hard to embrace not only the dream work, but the concept of guides and Deity in his life. As he stepped into the living room again, he felt lighter and more hopeful than he had in years.

CHAPTER 10

LIAM BEGAN by placing quartz points at the four corners around him as Nosha handed him each one. He then settled on the floor in the center of the room, cross-legged with Nosha directly across from him. Once satisfied with their placement and his comfort, Liam nodded to Nosha. They then blessed and consecrated the area for training and work.

Afterward, Nosha leaned over and pushed Play on an old CD player. Soon they were surrounded by low drumming and wordless chants. "I'm going to guide you this time. It's a little different than what we've been doing, but I feel this is what you need right now. You need to meet your guides, more specifically."

"Understood," Liam murmured, already working to put himself in the mindset needed for meditation and lucid dreaming. He knew a little of what Nosha intended, but truth be told, he was more than a little excited to move his training forward—not something he would have ever thought to feel, but now he wished he'd started learning earlier.

As Nosha led him through the intro meditation, Liam found himself sinking deeper and deeper into himself, until he no longer sat in Nosha's living room and the sounds changed around him. When Liam opened his eyes and looked around, he noticed he sat on the edge of the same fountain Cam had taken him to the second time they met for coffee. This time, however, it was light out and Cam wasn't there. Curious, Liam looked around, taking in the bright sun, the gentle breeze, and the sounds of water splashing in the fountain he and Cam had tossed coins into the other night.

When Liam looked again, there was a young man sitting on the edge of the fountain watching him as he trailed his fingers through the clear water beside him. "Finally decided to see the truth within, have you, lad?" the young man asked.

Liam was struck by the youth and power of his visitor. The man was tall, well over six feet, with strawberry-blond hair, eyes like green flames, and a smile that made him think of wicked, naughty things. "I, um…. Who are you?"

"Always a good question to start with, but not one that's easily answered. For now, think of me as simply your guide."

"My guide? I thought Nosha was to be my guide." Liam had never had anyone visit in his dreams like this. He was the one in control, well, since he'd learned to take control, that is. The only person to fight him on that was Cam, but a sexy and wanting Cameron was not really something to struggle against anyway.

"Eh, he's your mortal teacher, but he's not one of your spirit guides or your patrons. He is a lovely human, though," the man said with a wink. "But right now, I'd like to help you find your way again. Really, you've been very naughty, and not in any of the fun ways," his guide continued with a small smirk. "You were given a gift, yet you've hidden from and squandered it." As the guide spoke, his lips turned down in a pout, but instead of it being cute, it hurt Liam's heart to witness.

"I'm sorry. I didn't mean to. I didn't even know about the dream thing until recently, and really, I need something to call you other than 'you.'"

The laugh that rang out from the beautiful young man sounded like a great many bells tinkling at once. Light and playful, yet ethereal and mesmerizing at the same time. "Angus, then, since you so insist. That's what humans tend to call me. But that is neither here nor there, lad, for you were meant to be a walker and a healer, but you've lost your way somehow."

Liam listened, enchanted by the way he spoke and the beautiful accent—the man, Angus, sounded a lot like his grandda, or what he would have sounded like had he been young, Liam thought.

Angus gestured to the fountain, and a moment later, a single coin floated up, broke the surface of the water, then slowly spun in midair, finally coming to rest suspended in front of Liam. "This is the token your beloved one tossed into the waters the other night. That night he made a wish and a choice. One for you and one for him."

Frozen, Liam wanted to reach out and touch the coin, gather it and keep it. Another part of him wanted the coin put right back where Cam had tossed it, concerned that whatever his wish had been would somehow be tainted otherwise. With a great deal of effort, he cleared his throat of the large object that had suddenly taken up residence there. "Please, put it back. That's Cam's wish and should stay where it belongs. Where he placed it."

"Ay, that it is, but do you know what he wished for? What his hope was that night?"

"No, I don't, and I don't want you to tell me, either," Liam added quickly. "Only Cam can tell me that and only if he truly wants me to know." Liam couldn't decide if he was crazy or not to not ask if the being, Angus, knew what the wish was. However, he was certain it was something Cam should tell him, no one else.

A wide smile broke across Angus' enchanting face. "That he should and so he shall, but not until you give him reason to, Liam. First, though, you need to learn all you can about dreams, healing, and your lover, though I would recommend you try spending time with him outside your dreams. As much fun as dreams can be, they should never replace the waking world. Nor should you continue to hide from yourself.

"Learn, grow, and love, for those are the greatest things in life, whether it be one of a few hours or of an eternity. Without love, the world is a dark and painful place. And yet, all are capable of love, if they are willing to seek it, fight for it, nurture it."

"You sound like my grams, back when I was little."

Angus's eyes seemed to lose focus for a moment, a soft smile touching his perfect lips. "Yes, Aislin was a beautiful woman, both inside and out." His eyes snapped back to Liam's. "But until you let go of your fears and embrace the life and gifts you have, you will never be happy. You will never hold the most precious gift anyone can possess."

"And that would be?" Though Liam had a good idea what the answer should be, he feared voicing it right then.

"Why, the heart of the one you love, of course. Now, please listen carefully. When you return to the waking world, you must embrace all of who you are, and I do mean all. You must also be willing to fight for yourself and your relationship. And finally, you need to open yourself to the wonders around you."

"I'll try, but—"

"No, there is no try and there are no buts. You must do as I say, or you will cost more than your own joy and love. No man is a singular entity, Liam. We all touch and influence the world around us, be you mortal, spirit, or being."

Liam nodded, not wishing to anger his guide.

"But what fears are you talking about, Angus? I'm learning to dream walk and dream weave, just like I'm supposed to. I'm embracing my gift, as you and Nosha call it. I'm dating Cam now, which the dream walking is really responsible for, so I suppose I should consider it a gift, right?"

"For much of that you'll have to look within. But some I can help you with. You have allowed the biases of your parents to taint your view of your gifts, otherwise you wouldn't only now be learning and training with the mortal, Nosha. You also need to stop worrying about why the young one Cameron ran, and if he'll get bored or if he'll leave." Angus snorted and gave Liam a strange look that made Liam feel as if he should apologize for thinking such, even though it had happened to him more than once. "Or if he's too cute, as if that makes your coupling less promising somehow." Like Cam couldn't do better than boring ol' Liam. "Souls only seek their other half. Now return to your life, son, but don't discuss what all I've said to you. This time was for you. But before you go, do you wish the coin to keep, or would you rather it be returned to the well?"

"The fountain, please."

"Blessings of the heart, my little one," Angus replied as the world faded around him, shifting and reforming until he was awake back in Nosha's home.

"Where did you go?" Nosha asked, tone sharp as his gaze penetrated Liam's thoughts.

"Where you sent me, I would presume. You said I needed to meet my guides, and I did. Well, one of them, at least."

"Huh, well, not quite how I'd intended it to go, but spirits often do things in their own way."

"It was... interesting, to say the least, but he said not to discuss it with anyone." Liam could see the curiosity burning in Nosha's eyes but was certain that keeping the conversation to himself was the right thing, even if he didn't know why yet. Instead, they spent the next hour or so working on lucid dreaming techniques and control.

"All right, you can pack up and head home. You've been working hard and it's late. Don't push yourself too hard and get some rest."

Gathering his things, Liam agreed and left, intending to head straight home and fall into bed.

AFTER CLOSING the Feathered Quill late the next night, Liam stopped by the florist before driving over to the Indigo Dragon. He'd stayed open for Nate, a friend and loyal customer who had a penchant for kinky romance. He hated crowds and had been out of town for work.

Considering Liam's own romantic hopes, he couldn't help but stay to let Nate get his fix of sex and love. Unfortunately, it was drizzling out by the time he left, but he wasn't about to let a little wet get in his way. Not now that he'd mustered the courage to go after Cameron again—while awake.

Thankful when he found a parking spot close to the front of the tattoo shop, Liam pulled into the spot, then carefully picked up the flowers he'd set on the passenger seat before he stepped out and dodged the drops of pseudorain. Liam just couldn't call it rain with how sporadic it was, but either way, he didn't want to show up looking like a drowned rat.

Moments later, Liam ducked inside the shop, blinking at how bright it always was inside. He looked around, but the only person he spotted was the blue-haired girl he'd met once before. Sadly, he couldn't remember her name for the life of him.

"Hey, who are those for?" she asked, a huge smile on her face.

"I'm looking for Cam, Cameron Danu?"

"He's working on a really sweet tat right now, but if you want to wait, I'll go tell him you're here." She smiled at him again and pointed to the empty chairs across from her. "Are you Liam, by the way?"

Liam nodded, hoping her knowing his name meant Cam would be happy to see him. Well, happy to see him in the waking world. Cam was always happy in their dreams. Kicking himself for not thinking to call first, he replied, "Yeah, I don't want to interrupt him, though."

The girl giggled and waved his comment away as she hurried down the hall to Cam's door. Liam watched as she knocked, then stuck her head inside, but he couldn't hear what was said. Deciding the chair would be best, he settled down to wait. He just hoped it wasn't a long tattoo job, or that he'd at least arrived at the end, not the beginning of the work.

Twenty minutes later, a huge man—he had to be close to seven feet tall and all muscle—entered the waiting room, stalking more than walking across it to stop and chat with the blue-haired woman. Before Liam could try to figure out where the new ink would be on the man, Cameron stepped out and headed straight for Liam. "Hi."

Liam swallowed hard as he took in all of Cam. He was dressed in distressed, black jeans with holes in the knees, a tight, silver mesh T-shirt, and a pair of old-school Converse high tops. Cam's silver eyes were set off by the smoky-gray liner around them, and all his tattoos were visible thanks to the mesh.

"Hey, Cam. Um, these are for you." Liam held out the flowers, feeling a bit awkward with the other two people looking at him. Or, he assumed they were looking as he only had eyes for Cam.

"That's... wow, I've never gotten flowers brought to me at work before."

"I thought maybe, if you had time, we could try spending a little time together. Um, awake I mean?" He felt as if he were sixteen again, an even more awkward sixteen than he'd actually been.

"I love them, thank you. As for time, I actually have a break now between ink sessions. Would you like to go for a walk or for coffee?"

Liam couldn't help it. He knew he was grinning like a loon, but he didn't care. Cam seemed honestly happy that Liam was there and was willing to go out, so what if the others thought him crazy? "I'd like that."

The perky woman bounded over, leaving the newly tattooed man at the counter. Her smile was almost as wide as Liam thought his probably was. "Cammy, why don't you let me take your flowers so you can go? I'll find something to put them in and make sure they have water."

"Thanks, Heather." Cameron gave her the flowers after touching one of the petals gently and smiling again. "I'll be back in time for my next appointment."

"I know. You're never late, hon. Now go have a nice time with your guy." Heather bounded back to the counter where the huge man still stood, a dopey grin on his face as he stared at Liam and Cam.

Before Liam could think up anything to say, Cam slid his hand down Liam's arm to twine their fingers together. "Come on, I owe you a coffee."

"Don't you want a jacket? Or an umbrella?"

Cam's sigh was loud and pointed. "If I must," he grumbled but then winked. Not letting go of Liam, Cam pulled him back to Cam's room. He let go only long enough to toss on his jacket, taking Liam's hand again as soon as it was settled to his liking. "Okay, now we can go. And really, that's not rain out there. I'll be fine."

Liam wanted to protest as it was not only wet, but chilly still, though Cam had already tugged him most of the way to the front door before he thought to say anything. He mentally shrugged it off, figuring Cameron would know his body and limits better than Liam would.

"So, coffee?"

"Yeah, for now." Cam slowed so they walked together instead of Liam being towed around. "I figure we can start with coffee and maybe move to real food and such later?"

The coffee shop was only down the street and around the corner, so before Liam knew it, they were inside and had their drinks—triple-espresso-shot french vanilla latte with a shot of macadamia nut syrup for Cam and, at Cam's suggestion, a chai latte for Liam.

Once they were sitting at one of the small tables in the back corner, Liam looked at Cam, meeting and holding his hypnotizing silver gaze. "Thank you. How have you been?"

Cam tipped his head to the side as he replied, "Thanks? What for?"

Liam just gestured to the drinks and the shop around them.

"Uh, Lee, you've visited me almost every night since I said you could again, so I'm not sure why coffee is a big thing, but it's great to actually *see you*, see you."

The chuckle slipped out as Liam nodded. "It's good to see you in person too. I like the dreams"—Liam's face heated to the point that he knew not only was he blushing, but even his ears were probably pink—"but I want to actually spend time with you while awake."

"Yeah, me too. I kept hoping you'd come by."

"When we were together in the dreams, I told you to call me when you woke up." The fact Cam never did bugged Liam, but he knew not everyone retained much from their dreams, unlike how he couldn't forget his. "Of course, you tended to distract me every time," he added with a wink and a smirk. "Not that I minded."

"Uh-huh. I don't remember you saying no," Cam countered as he fought not to laugh—and mostly failed.

"Brat." Liam swatted at Cam but made sure not to connect hard. "You know what I mean."

"Yeah, I do. Sometimes after I woke up, I kept feeling like I was forgetting something, but I could never figure out what. Maybe that was it?" Cam shrugged and took a sip of his latte. "But the point I was making is that I want to date you in the real world, like I said the other night at the fountain."

The dream vision of Angus and the fountain flashed through Liam's mind again as he watched Cam talk. He loved how animated Cam always was, and in that moment, it was hard for Liam to keep his mind on dating instead of sex. But Angus was right, and Liam knew it. If he wanted a real relationship with Cam, it had to be in the waking world.

The idea that Cam knew something was off pleased Liam more than he thought it probably ought. "That's wonderful! Maybe with a bit more practice, I'll be able to actually get messages to you in a dream. That would make things easier." And more fun, but he wasn't going to say that out loud.

"That would be cool, but, um." Cam paused as he nibbled his bottom lip. Liam wanted to lean in and free it from Cam's teeth, maybe nibble and suck on it a bit himself, but as their waking relationship wasn't like that—yet—he refrained. "I like the dream visits, don't get me wrong, but I want a real partner, not just dreams. I've had that since I was a teen," he continued with a pointed stare. "What I need is reality and a waking-time relationship."

"That's what I want too, Cam. I promise. I honestly don't mean for every dream to wind up with us in bed, but you pouncing me makes it kinda hard to remember what I was trying to do." That was the hard part, how every time he tried to dream walk to Cam, the sexy man did everything he could to derail the dream and land them in bed, against the wall, on the floor, the counter….

"Well, then, stop showing up all sexy and all." Cam's smirk was both endearing and annoying. "Besides, you're the one in control of the dream, right?"

"In theory."

"But?"

"You jump on me, wrap those long legs around my waist, grind against me while kissing the life out of me. I think that kind of makes you the one taking over."

Cam squeaked as his face flamed. "Don't say that so loud," he snapped.

"No one's paying us a bit of attention. Well, until you raised your voice there." Liam wanted to laugh almost as much as he wanted to tug Cam over and into his lap. "But that *is* how most of my visits lately have gone."

"So not the point." Cam straightened up, his voice low. "But I promise to behave if you want to ask me out on a real date."

"Not sure if that's an incentive or not, but—" Liam took a deep breath and again met Cam's gaze. "—Cameron, would you like to go out on a real date with me?"

CHAPTER 11

CAM SUCKED in a breath as his sister snickered over the line. "What the hell is that supposed to mean, Sarah?"

"It means, Cameron," and God but he hated the way she drawled his name, "that you shouldn't demand that your boyfriend take you out on a date if you didn't want him to... wait for it... take you out on a date." He didn't appreciate that way she drew out the last word or how she then proceeded to spell the word *date*, slowly, in case he'd missed it the first time.

"I *do* want him to take me out. I'm just nervous about where we're going and what I need to wear and... and... I've not been on a real date in forever. Plus, you know my track record with men." Crappy and crappier. Of course, he'd been involved with Liam—sorta—for half his life, but he couldn't tell her that. Even though she knew about his having dreamed of Liam and all, he still wasn't ready to have some long conversation about dream walkers with her. Hell, he still had trouble grasping it, and Liam *was* his boyfriend... kinda. He hoped. "I mean, he's smart and sweet and a little on the conservative-appearance side of things. Then there's me." Cam looked down at the partly completed tattoo sleeve on his arm, his ripped jeans that sat so low on his hips he'd been accused of defying the law of gravity to keep them up—more than once—to his purple-painted toenails poking out from under the edge of the tattered pant cuff. His fingernails matched his toes as did the new eyeliner he'd just put on before his phone had rung.

Her giggle was not encouraging. "So he'll have to class you up a little, Cammy. No biggie."

Oh, he is a biggie, all right. Not that he was about to tell her that! "You're a funny bumpkin, ya are. I just meant we're a little odd for each other. I don't think it's a bad thing, really, just that I don't want to embarrass him or something."

"Then just ask where you're going so you know what to wear for your date. It's not that hard. Girls do it all the time. Just make sure not to lose your style trying to impress him. No turning yourself inside out for this guy, Cam. If *he's* really good enough for *you*, then he likes you the way you are, not the way he thinks he can make you change into."

That was his little sis. Always his champion. "Liam doesn't want to change me like that, sissy. Promise. I just want him to understand I'm taking him seriously too."

"Good. Now, when can Dan and I come up to visit you? We'd love to see you and hang out."

"Any time you want. There are some great malls and things around here. I might can even sneak you into my favorite coffeehouse, though you'll have to promise not to mention that coffee chain you're infected by, or you might not be allowed inside."

Her slightly high-pitched growl had him laughing so hard he nearly dropped his cell. God but he loved his sister!

"I do *not* drink bad coffee! You need to stop that nonsense right now, Cam."

"Nope. Until you give up that unholy addiction to that… stuff, the best I can do is try regular interventions and to sneak you into my fave coffeehouse when you come up to visit. You'll love it, I promise."

"You're evil, ya know."

"I do, and you love me just as I am."

The sigh that came through the phone was so loud it could have been heard even without it, he was certain. "I do. God help me, but I do. Let me talk to Dan and I'll text you when we can come visit. By then, hopefully, you'll have secured your boy enough that we can meet him. I want to make sure he's good enough for my big brother."

"Sarah…."

"Nope, you do not get to 'Sarah' me. When I started dating Dan, you did the same, so deal. It's my right as your sister to make sure he's good enough for you. Now go finish getting ready for work. Try asking your boyfriend where he's taking you so you know what to wear for your date, and relax. You know this guy already likes you. I mean, he's been stalking your dreams, so he must think you're awfully damn cute."

"That's damn sexy, thank you very much!"

"Yeah, yeah, yeah. Sisters do not think their brothers are sexy. It's just… eww! No!"

He had to give her that point. She was cute, but only Dan was allowed to think his sister was sexy. But Liam, now Liam was supposed to think Cameron was sexy as far as Cameron was concerned. He drew in a deep breath and let it out slowly, making sure she could hear him. "Fine. Burst my little bubble. Actually, right now I need to finish getting dressed and out the door or my boss is going to get pissed. I don't have a client scheduled first thing, but still. He likes us there on time. Plus, I have some design work to finish."

"Okay, get to work. Just don't forget to call your guy and ask about dress code or where you're going, one or the other. 'Kay?"

"Yes, sissy. I will. Love you." Cameron made a big, loud kiss sound before he hung up, her giggle ringing in his ears.

"Now if life were only as easy as she makes it seem." Cameron shook his head as he went to find his favorite pair of beat-up Chucks so he could get his shoes on and get out the door and to the Indigo Dragon on time.

By the time Cameron had stopped and gotten himself a hot macadamia nut, double mocha latte and settled at his drafting table in his tattoo room, he was mostly mentally set to work. Cameron set his latest design sketch on his table and sighed happily. He loved how eclectic his clients were and how free they were in letting him play with and tweak design ideas. The current one was of a Canada lynx coiled around a sensuous male form that wore nothing but a low-rise pair of harem-style pants and a wicked, fanged smile. It had seemed like a somewhat strange combination, as Cameron thought that vampires and felines weren't supposed to get along in the stories—at least in the ones he'd read—but what did he know? It was a great commission, and the art was turning out beautifully. He couldn't wait to show his client and begin work.

"Hey, Cammy," Bass's voice boomed into Cameron's concentration, bringing the rest of the world back into focus.

Cam looked up, blinking a few times as he looked around before he finally found where Bass stood. "Yeah, boss?"

"Got a new guy for you. You got time now?" Bass asked as he gestured at the artwork Cameron had just been finishing the final details on.

"Yep. Why don't I go out and introduce myself while you look at my design here? When I'm done with the initial meeting—he wants something custom, not just wall art, right?" Cameron paused, hoping Bass wasn't sticking him with dull primary tat art from the stock on every tattoo parlor wall in the country. Bass knew how much he hated that.

"Yeah, he wants something special. Since it's something with wings and feathers, I thought you'd be the best choice, plus you're next on rotation."

Bass's voice was clear, but he was also apparently already distracted by the art on Cam's desk, much to Cam's delight. He loved watching people, but especially those in his field, get sucked into his designs.

"Cool, then I'll be back."

Bass waved him away after agreeing.

Cam smirked to himself as he wiped off his hands—he never could figure out how he wound up with so much graphite on his fingers—then walked to the front of the tattoo shop. He was eager to see his new canvas and work out the design he'd need to impart upon it.

BY THE time Liam arrived to pick Cam up, Liam was so nervous he wasn't entirely sure he would be able to eat dinner. Dianne insisted his being like this was stupid. He'd been with Cam off and on since they were teens. They'd talked on the phone almost daily since they'd decided to try to actually date. There was no doubt that they liked each other or that they were compatible, really. Yet the sense that if he didn't do everything right, he'd lose the best thing he'd ever find hung over his head nevertheless. It was a feeling he hated more and more as time progressed.

If he didn't want Cameron so much, didn't want a real and lasting future with the sweet, outrageous man, he'd say screw it and walk away. Instead, Liam took a deep breath and looked down at himself. He checked to make sure his black slacks were neat and his blue silk button-down shirt was straight before he raised his hand and knocked on the door to Cam's loft.

When the door opened, Liam's breath whooshed out of him. Cam stood there in silver pinstriped dress slacks, a shimmery, indigo button-down top, and a matching vest with a thin set of chains in the same shimmery purple color going from one set of pockets on the vest to the pocket on the other side. His ears had a mass of silver and purple studs and hoops alternating in color and type. Cameron's silver eyes were lined in purple, and his nails were a shiny purple tipped in silver.

Liam wasn't sure, but he didn't think he'd ever seen a hotter person. "You look… I'm not sure I have the right word, Cam. Just wow!"

Cam smiled, his pale cheeks tinting pink. "Thanks, Lee. You look great too. Um, is this okay for where we're going?" Cameron held his arms out and proceeded to turn in place, showing off not only the set of silver rings on his right hand, but his delicious butt as well.

It took Liam swallowing the lump in his throat twice, but he eventually managed to force out, "You look perfect, hon. Possibly too good for them, in fact."

"We still going the same place you mentioned earlier?"

"Yes." Lee nodded and smiled softly. "To Limones on Eagle Street. It's a cross between Californian and Mexican cooking. It's good food that's a little different but pretty interesting."

Cam locked up, and as they walked out together, he wrapped his right arm around Liam's left. The touch sent a thrill up Liam's spine and helped calm his nerves a little. The show of affection was enough to let Liam's heart rate settle a notch.

When they reached the outside, Cameron looked up from under his long eyelashes and gave a soft smile. "Um, I know you asked me on the date, but would you mind if I drove? I'd love to take you out in my little baby. Sarah thinks it's silly, but...." Cam stopped speaking and shrugged, the pink in his cheeks even darker than before.

"I'd love that. You mean your VW Bug, right?"

"Yeah." Cam sighed and smiled, the bounce back in his step. "It totally looks old school, but it's not."

Liam chuckled as Cameron pulled him along, and before he knew it, he was seated in the passenger seat of Cam's Bug and they were on their way to Limones.

When they arrived, Liam insisted Cam stay in the car until he got out and went around to open the door for Cameron. "Such a sweet and old-fashioned thing to do, Lee. Thank you."

"It might be old fashioned, I suppose, but it's also about respect and courtesy."

"I wasn't complaining, Liam. I promise. I've never had anyone do that for me. Ever. I think it's nice." Cam stretched up and kissed Liam's cheek quickly. "Now, take me inside and feed me, please. I've been looking forward to this since you told me where we're going. I've heard this place is fantastic."

"I've never had a dish I didn't like." Liam just hoped that held true now that he was taking Cameron there for their first, of hopefully many, dates.

He'd thought ahead and made reservations, something he was thankful for when he saw how busy they were. It didn't take long for them to be seated, though.

"Kora will be your server tonight," the host who'd introduced himself as Juan said as he gestured to a petite woman with a bright smile and a set of menus in hand. "Let her know if you need anything tonight."

After he had stepped away, she introduced herself. "Hi, I'm Kora, as Juan said." She placed their menus for them and smiled again. "Do you know what you would like to drink or do you need a few minutes?"

"I'd like the Palata de Naranja," Liam said. Since he wasn't driving, he didn't have to worry, and since Cam had made him stop drinking so heavily, he'd only had one beer. This wouldn't be construed as him drinking too much. He hoped. "If you don't mind," he added, looking at Cameron.

"That's fine with me." Cam waved one long-fingered hand as if shooing away Liam's worry, which the motion did. "Since I'm driving, I'll only allow myself one drink and only this early on, so let me have the Basil Refrescante. After that, I'll just have sweet iced tea."

"No problem, I just need to see some IDs, sirs."

Cam sighed but pulled out his wallet and showed Kora his driver's license. She turned and waited for Liam to do the same.

"Thank you. I'll put those in and come back to take your appetizer and entrée order."

"Thank you," they said together, then laughed.

"So," Cameron asked. "What are you thinking now?"

"You mean as far as what I want for dinner or...?"

"Dinner, hon. I think it's too soon to ask you your intentions toward me, isn't it?" Cam asked, one sculpted eyebrow raised.

Liam busied himself with the menu, humming and oohing over the different options as if he had no idea what he wanted to eat. Not only did he know what he wanted to eat, he knew what he wanted as far as Cam went too. The thing was, he was terrified to ask for it. What if Cam didn't want long-term with him? What if he was too business and homebody for Cam? What if he was too weird with the whole dream walker slash dream weaver thing?

"Hon? Liam? Lee!" Cam's voice broke into Liam's circling thoughts and panic.

"Huh?"

"Liam, the nice server is back and would like our order now."

"Oh, right." Liam knew he was blushing, the heat on his face and ears made that more than obvious, but he tried to ignore it as he ordered. "I'll have the roasted mushroom nachos to start, please."

"That comes with chile pasilla salsa, crema, pico de gallo, and pickled jalapeños."

"That's all fine. And for dinner I want the Seared Sea Scallops."

"With stone-ground grits, wild mushrooms, mango salsa, and micro greens?"

"Yes. It's all sounds excellent. Thank you."

"Wonderful. And for you, sir?" she asked Cam.

"Mmm, I think I'll have the grilled scallops to start. They sound so yum."

"They are," Kora said and winked. "Those come with carrot-fennel salad, watermelon, and jicama-pineapple pico. Is that all okay?"

"Perfect. And for my dinner I think I'll have the Grilled Tuna."

"It comes with beluga lentils, yellow wax beans, poblano-spinach sauce, and mango chutney."

"Can I get regular snap beans instead of the wax ones?"

"Of course. Anything else?"

"No. Thanks."

Kora left with their orders, and they lapsed into quiet again, but this time it wasn't so tense. After a few moments, Cameron nudged his foot. "You don't need to worry so much, Lee. I was only teasing about intentions earlier. This is a first date, but it's not like we don't at least know each other a little already, right? So instead of stressing, why don't we just enjoy our dinner and each other's company some? Honestly, I just want to get to know more about you, the guy, not the guy you can make yourself seem to be when you have time to plan."

Liam nodded and smiled. "Yeah, I want to know you the same way. I mean, I know I've managed to freak you out, disappoint you, and worry you already. But really, I'm not like that. I run a bookstore. I love the written word, love finding rare books for customers, and like to spend time with my small collection of friends and family. Well, and now I spend what seems like an awful lot of time training with Nosha, my aunt's priest, and ought-to-be boyfriend."

"I'd like to meet this Nosha person. And yeah, when your aunt—she still doesn't seem old enough to be your aunt, by the way—mentioned that guy she wanted you to train with, she got that same happy sigh to her voice that my sister got to hers when she talked about the guy that's now her husband."

Liam smiled and relaxed back into his seat more as they continued talking. Chatting he could do when they didn't fixate on the future. The more they talked, the more he calmed, and by the time their food arrived, he was able to eat, though they did decide to share their appetizers and entrées.

CHAPTER 12

"THAT WAS so good." Cameron sat back and sighed as he reached for his almost-empty glass of sweet iced tea. Everything had been cooked perfectly as far as he was concerned. He was almost tempted to stretch out and lounge back against the chair, but the restaurant was just a little too upscale for that. Plus, even though in a way he'd been dating Liam for years, he still wanted not to do anything that might embarrass himself, or Liam. Liam, once he'd relaxed, had been funny, intelligent, and cute. Cam had also appreciated that Liam had only had a single beer with dinner, on top of the drink with their appetizers, then switched to Pepsi. Cam never wanted to see Liam descend back into that scary drunk he'd found when Dianne had intervened not that long ago. "Thank you for bringing me here."

"You're more than welcome, Cam. And worth it." Liam gave Cam that same soft, shy smile he had most of the time since he'd picked Cameron up for their date. Cam was torn between thinking it was endearing and wondering why Liam was so worried Cam wouldn't want to continue dating him. "Thank you for wanting to come."

"Did you have anything planned for after dinner?"

"Actually, yes. But that's for after we're done here." Liam's smile was broad and his blue eyes twinkled as he gazed at Cameron after speaking.

Cam couldn't help but return the smile. "So let's get the check and head for the next thing, then. I can't wait to see what you have planned."

Liam looked over to where he hoped the waitress was and held up one hand when she looked his way. When she was close enough to hear, he said, "Check, please."

It didn't take long for Kora to cash them out, with Liam leaving a nice tip as both the food and the service had been excellent.

"I thought we could do something simple," Liam said as he slipped his right arm over Cam's shoulders. Cam did the same around Liam's waist. "We need to stop by one of the shops near Biltmore to pick up the basket I ordered, then we'll be set."

"Sounds good to me. What's in the basket, though?"

"Nosy." Liam managed about three seconds before he laughed at Cameron's deliberately campy pout. "Fine, fine. Dessert, coffee... nothing major. It's the place we're going and the company that's important really."

Cam curled into Liam's side a little more as they made their way back to the car, happier than he could ever remember being on a first date. Usually, he was either trying to find a way to tactfully leave or was too nervous to really enjoy it. This time, however, Cameron didn't feel either emotion. Instead, he wanted the night to go on and on and hoped Liam felt the same.

"Sounds good to me. I'm always up for coffee."

"Yeah, I sort of guessed that." Liam squeezed his shoulders slightly. "You seem to be even more addicted to it that I am."

"Hey, coffee is necessary. It's one of the five main food groups, I'll have you know."

"Really? And those would be?" Liam asked, barely choking back his laughter.

Cam stopped and pulled away so he could face Liam. He made sure his face was as serious as he could manage, and as he spoke, he counted off on his fingers. "One, coffee. Two, seafood. Three, produce— no judging, I like my fruits and veggies. Four, sweets. And five, meat."

"Wow. I'm not sure if I should be impressed by your list or frightened. I'm leaning toward laughing, personally."

"Yeah," Cam said, losing the battle and giggling. "Me too. But seriously, coffee is vital to me. I have a Keurig because waiting for the whole pot to be ready takes too long. I just got it and already can't remember how I got along before!"

"Okay, even I'm not that bad. Wow! But don't worry, I won't deny you your caffeine fix, I promise."

"Good, because that would be a terrible thing. Here we are." Cameron pulled away, though he didn't want to, opened the car, and slid into the driver's seat. Once he and Liam were buckled, he took Liam's hand and twined their fingers for a moment. "Where are we going?"

Cam released Liam's hand as he unfortunately needed his for the gear shift, then backed out of the parking spot. He carefully followed Liam's directions through town and to the quaint set of shops near Biltmore House. Eventually, they made it to their destination. They parked near the French Broad River, and, basket in Liam's arms, they walked down to the grassy area near the Lagoon where across the river they could see what was referred to as the "castle view" of Biltmore House.

It was evening, but the sun was still up, though not very high. Liam spread out a plain blue blanket before setting down the basket. He then sat, tugging Cam down with him. "Come on. Someone needs to help me drink this dark chocolate, macadamia nut mocha and eat the little Nutella brownies I got to go with them."

Cam moaned so decadently, Liam was instantly hard. It was the exact same sound, he was certain of it, that Cam made when they were having sex… at least in their dreams. Liam shifted, trying not to draw attention to his *issue* while relieving some of the pressure from his pants on his now-aching dick. Cameron shouldn't be allowed to make that sound outside of sex! Ever!

With a sudden thump, Cam was sitting beside Liam, his huge silver eyes wide and his hands already lifting the basket away from Liam. "Really?"

Giant thermoses and a large plate of brownies covered with a plastic dome appeared in the basket's place, and in no time, Liam had managed to wrestle his portion of the drink from Cam.

"Oh, God, dis is gud," Cam mumbled around one, or possibly two, of the brownies.

Liam couldn't help but laugh. He picked up one and took a much smaller bite. It wasn't that he didn't like them too, he did, but obviously not to the level Cameron did. After Liam had finished a second brownie, he stretched out, resting on his side so he could see Cam and still sip his mocha and simply enjoy the view—mostly that of his date.

"Enjoying yourself, beautiful?" he asked after Cam finished a couple more.

Cam took a napkin out of the basket, and once he'd wiped his hands and face, replied, "I am. That was delicious, and this is amazing. I've seen the Biltmore House—who around here hasn't?—but it looks like a castle from here. And thank you for thinking of this for me. It's sweet. Most guys would have tried taking me dancing to show me off or home to try to get me into bed. I like that you did something to try to make me happy and to spend time with me."

"Well, that's because I like you for you, beautiful, not for the fact you look like you're barely legal."

"I do not," Cam said with a sniff, but the effect was ruined when he smirked a moment later.

"I bet you still get carded to see rated-R movies," Liam teased.

"Huff! I do not." Cameron's bottom lip pooched out. "But I do always get carded, as you noticed at the restaurant."

"Yeah, but I did too. At least you didn't get indignant about it."

"No point. But I really do like this for an after-dinner outing. I've never been taken on a sort of picnic like this before. It's kinda cool."

"Thanks." Liam collected the empty plates and used napkins, then dumped it all back into the basket before he moved it to the side. He tugged Cam closer. "Do you mind if I get a little closer to you? Or should I go back to my side of the blanket?"

"Oh no, I think my side is definitely the better side to be on. You should stay." Cameron screwed the lid back onto his thermos and set it aside before doing the same to Liam's. He snuggled up close to Liam. "In fact, I think I'm getting a little chilly."

Liam smirked but enjoyed the playful tone Cam took as he wiggled closer and wrapped one arm around Liam's side. "Well, we can't have that, now can we?" But instead of continuing the banter, Liam took a slow breath and let it out carefully. He leaned in and gently pressed his lips to just the edge of Cam's mouth. Not pushing for more, but offering if Cam wanted.

Cam moaned and parted his lips enough to dart his tongue out and flick it against Liam's bottom lip before he shifted enough to pull Liam's bottom lip into his mouth and suck for a fleeting moment. Liam went up in flames, he was certain. All he could think was *Cam, hunger, more.* He pushed forward, taking Cam's mouth in a deep and hungry kiss, much as he had for years in their dreams. Delving between Cam's parted lips with his tongue, tasting and tangling it with Cam's, laying claim to everything it touched. He nipped Cam's lips, sucked on his tongue, and did everything he knew would drive his lover insane, all while making sure they couldn't grind on each other. No way was he going to explain to a cop why they were having sex in public and why that shouldn't be frowned upon.

The whimpers and moans from Cam nearly caused Liam's resolve to crumble, but the thought of jail time helped to keep him and Cameron in check, much to Cam's annoyance if his sounds and attempts to push his groin against Liam were anything to go by. When he finally tore himself away from Cam, his need for oxygen having hit critical levels, Cam whined and clutched at Liam.

"Need...."

"Not here, beautiful." Though, God, but he wanted to!

"But—"

"Public area." No way was he getting arrested for public indecency or public sex or how the hell ever the cops wrote that up! Nu-uh! Nope. Not happening, he reminded himself. He'd made it to thirty-two without having been arrested, he'd like to keep right on adding years to that marker, thanks.

"Dammit!" Cam sat up and ran his hands through his hair shakily. "Why'd you start that, then, Lee?" Cam groused, the hard edge of want still riding him if his growly voice and blown pupils were any marker. Liam wasn't any happier, he was just being a little more logical. A very little.

"Actually, you started that. If you really want to continue, then we need to go back to either your place or mine. But we can't stay here."

"Which is closer?" Cameron asked, his voice husky, but his eyes closed and his hands balled into fists at his sides.

"Mine, I think."

"Good. Come on." Cam hopped up, snatched up the basket, and strode off, his walk a little off. It only took a moment for Liam to realize why— Cam was just as hard as he was. Liam scrambled up, barely remembering to grab the blanket before he followed Cameron to the car.

Neither spoke as Cam wove through the streets of Asheville until they were outside Liam's home. If he'd been asked, Liam could not have said one thing about the trip between the river and his apartment, other than it was too damn long.

As soon as Cam pulled the Bug into a parking spot, mostly aligned with the lines, and stopped, Liam was out of the car and desperate to get his keys out of his pocket. Steering Cam inside and upstairs wasn't the easiest, but he managed, mostly by using his own body to push and pull Cameron along with him.

"Cam," Liam said as he panted against Cam's lips. "I need you to unwind just long enough for me to unlock the door so we can get inside, beautiful. And as much as I want you, I'm not up for sharing even the view." And if Cameron was as loving and giving in the waking world as he was in their dreams, Liam wasn't sure how he'd survive letting Cam leave after this was over. Not that he wanted to let him leave anyway, but he was trying hard not to get ahead of himself.

It only took Liam two tries to get his apartment door open and Cameron inside. He shoved the door closed and just hoped it latched, as all his attention was once again on his lover who seemed to be all hands and lips again.

"Lee, please," Cam begged as he ground his rigid cock against Liam's trapped length.

"Bed."

"Now."

"Floors are too hard, baby. Bed." Liam pulled away, grasped Cameron's seeking hands, and tugged him along, not even bothering with the pretense of showing him around. Cam had been to Liam's already. Hell, he'd been in Liam's bedroom and en suite, so it wasn't as though he didn't know where Liam was dragging him.

They quickly divested each other of their clothes between kisses. This seemed easier in the dreams, where he could just make Cam be naked, but watching as Cameron's beautiful, tightly muscled body was revealed was even better. Liam made a mental note to take the time, later, to map every luscious inch of Cam's creamy, pale skin, but right then, all he wanted was to taste one part of Cam.

With a not-so-gentle push, Liam managed to get Cam on his big bed. *Damn but he looks perfect there!*

Cam squeaked but then grinned wide. "How do you want me?"

Instead of answering, Liam crawled up onto the bed and leaned over Cam. He reached out and trailed one finger through the small pool of precome already dripping from the tip of Cam's dick. Cam groaned and squirmed and panted. "I want to taste you, beautiful. I want to choke myself with this until I come and can't taste anything but you on my tongue for the rest of the night."

The loud whimper from Cam made Liam smile. "Like that idea?"

"Uh-huh, but I wanna taste too, Lee." Cameron patted the bed beside him. "Flip around so I can get at you at the same time?"

Liam happily complied.

He didn't waste time asking anything more. As soon as he was on his side, his head level with Cam's cock, he immediately lapped at the slit, taking in the taste of his love along with the first feel of overheated flesh eager for his touch. Cam tasted even better in real life than he'd ever imagined either in dreams or in his waking fantasies. He groaned and licked until the head was clean before he sucked Cam into his mouth, not stopping until the tip of Cameron's cock hit the back of his mouth.

Focusing on Cam was hard as Cameron did everything Liam loved, driving his need higher and drawing his orgasm closer. Not to be outdone, Liam redoubled his efforts. He added his fingers in, stroking Cam's balls, tugging and teasing just the way he knew Cam liked. Humming and sucking, licking and teasing up the underside vein. Nibbling with his lips around the flared head, flicking his tongue against the little button of flesh on the smooth spot where the ridge thinned. Digging into the slit over and over, fucking it with the tip of his tongue until Cam writhed and cursed.

When Cameron's sounds turned truly desperate, Liam used some of his spit to wet one finger, then used it to tease Cam's tight little hole. Cam thrust back, his sounds louder and the suction around Liam's own cock so tight and perfect, he forgot what he was doing for a moment. But not even Cam's talented mouth could distract him from his goal for long. He pulled back, licking and sucking, until just the head of Cam's dick was in his mouth, and he carefully worked his finger inside Cam's perfect heat.

Liam didn't manage more than a few shallow thrusts of his finger before Cam stiffened and came, pumping copious amounts of thick, salty fluid into Liam's waiting mouth. He swallowed, loving that this was his Cam he was taking inside himself even as he pushed his finger in far enough to brush and nudge against Cam's happy button, drawing out another near shout and a little more come for him to lap up.

He'd been so caught up in what he was doing and tasting that when his own orgasm hit a moment later, it was almost as much a shock as it was bliss. The sensations of joy, lightning, and *ohmyfuckinggod* ripped through him as they always did, though even clearer than they ever had in their dreams. As Liam's world whited out, he was positive Cam claimed even more of his heart and body, and that as good as their dreams had been, he wanted more of the waking Cameron!

CHAPTER 13

"YOU NEED to hire someone to help out at the store, Liam." Dianne stood with her hands on her hips in the middle of the shop as Liam tried to stock the newest paperbacks from his favorite two gay romance publishers. Try as he might, ignoring her had never been the easiest thing—not even when they were little and he could hide behind his mom or run away and get away with it.

Still, he tried by saying nothing as he continued to tidy the store, adding books to shelves, rearranging and reordering so everything drew the eye but remained neat.

"Liam, do *not* ignore me."

Giving up, Liam sighed and rolled his eyes—making sure she saw him. "What is it you need, Di, dear?"

"For you to hire an assistant. Someone to help run the store so you can have a day off or leave early or come in late. You know, so you can have a life and spend more time with your sweetling."

"Sweetling? Really?" *What the hell?* "I don't think I even want to know where you got that one from. And I have Saul, who works part-time for me already. What, he doesn't count now? The date with Cam I *just* went on doesn't count?" It did. Damn did it ever! After they'd cleaned up the night before, they had collapsed into each other's arms and slept. Liam hadn't even dreamed, not that he remembered, at least.

"I can help you find someone," Dianne continued as if he hadn't spoken. "If you'll let me, that is. Chell, one of the younger women in my circle, is in college for some kind of library science degree. She wants to work in a library eventually, but for now, working here would be great for her. She needs the extra income, and it would let her be around books."

"Di, I have someone that works for me already. You've met Saul. Hell, I'm pretty sure you even like him—though not as much as you like Nosha."

"Saul's fine, but he's only here a couple of days a week. If you're going to have any kind of real personal life with Cameron, plus keep up your training with Nosha and have any time for you, you need at least one more worker. What's wrong with hiring Chell? If you don't like Chell, I'm sure I could find you someone else that's interested in books and that's still good with people too."

That was his aunt, always managing people. She did at her work—damn human resources manager!—so why not when she was at his work too?

"Dianne, it's not that I have a problem with Chell. I don't even know her or her qualifications, to have an opinion yet. It's that I don't like a lot of people messing in my business and that I don't see a need. Saul helps out when I need. He even came in for some extra hours so I could take Cam out when I asked him too. Saul works hard when he's here, and I like working my own store. It's not a huge chain or something where I need a bunch of workers, hon."

"You often stay late to catch up on work because you stay so busy during the day. Even with the fact that so many people are going to e-books and such, you have a loyal customer base, and the special-order service means you'll always have business. If you had another worker, you could have more time, less stress, and the store would be better off for it too. Now, when would you like Chell to come for her interview? Would you like me to find you any others, or do you want to see what you think of her first?"

Might as well just give in and interview the woman. Di won't give, and I know it. Ugh! "Fine, Di. I'll talk to your friend, but, and this is a major one, if I don't think she's right for my store, I will not hire her. I will concede that having another worker might help, that maybe having Saul work a little more might also be nice, but I will not be bullied, even by you, into hiring someone not suitable. Agreed?"

"Well of course not! I would never want you to do that. I know you won't hire anyone but who you truly think is the best choice. I only suggested her because I know her and know what her goals are. I believe you will like her and that she would be a good helper for your store. Now that you've agreed to be reasonable, tell me about your date."

"Really?" First the store and now the date with Cam? "Why don't you get your own date and stop trying to live vicariously through me? I bet Nosha would love to take you out."

Dianne's smile fell off her face so fast Liam almost doubted it had ever been there. Her shoulders slumped and she looked away. "I can't do that, and I don't like him that way."

"Bullshit. I've seen the way you look at him. It's the same way he looks at you. So why can't you go out with him? What's wrong with him?" *What am I missing?*

She fidgeted, not raising her gaze, then sighed. "Nothing is wrong with him that I know of, but he's my priest. He's… I don't know. How do you ask your priest out on a date? Plus he's so powerful and so much more trained and all than I am."

Liam paused to think over what she'd said and then how to reply. He didn't want to word anything wrong and make things worse for her. "He's not Roman Catholic, hon. It's not against your beliefs or tenets for him to have a relationship, sex and romance included, so why can't he have love with you? As for powerful… I don't know what to tell you there. But I don't think that matters to him. He seems to like you as you are. Besides, clergy in many faiths have spouses, so why can't a Wiccan priest?"

The thought that she, his indomitable aunt and best friend would feel intimidated by the status of the man she wanted had never occurred to him before. It was almost too bizarre for him to fathom. If it weren't for her admitting to it herself, he'd never have believed it. Now that she had, he didn't know what to make of it other than to encourage her to move past her fears. If she could bully him into Cam's arms, then he could do the same for her. He smiled, making sure to let her see it as he thought about ways to get Dianne and Nosha together.

"No, wipe that grin off your face now," Di snapped, her hands going to her hips as she glared.

"What?" he asked as he cocked his head, making his smile wider and his voice a little higher. "I have no idea what you're talking about now. I thought we were talking about me hiring someone new and my date."

"No, no, no. You will not meddle in my love life!" Dianne's voice cracked as she shook her head.

Liam dropped the smirk and snagged her wrists loosely. "Di, hon, you know I would never do anything to hurt you, so calm down. Please." He tugged her into his arms, curling them around her protectively. "But do you hear yourself? You butt into mine constantly. You just tried to demand info about my date after attempting to run my shop for me. It's kinda the same thing, ya know? I'm trying to make sure you're happy, just like you are me. That's all."

Dianne looked up at him with her big, bright blue eyes behind her gold-framed glasses and blinked hard a few times. "I know you're not really trying to be bad, Liam, but Nosha is…. He's… I don't want to get my hopes up and then have him not think I'm good enough to date or something. There are others in the coven that are prettier, smarter, better at the things you still only refer to as my 'pagan stuff.' I never attract the good ones, so…."

"Yeah, well, maybe you just don't pay attention to the good ones. I know the man has serious eyes for you. When you stop by during our training sessions, he tends to forget I'm there," Liam explained with a chuckle. He never minded as he kept hoping Dianne would take the hint and accept what Nosha was so obviously offering her. How she could be so good with figuring out people when it came to friends, work, his love life, et cetera but never her own was a huge mystery to Liam. One he thought needed to change.

"He does not! He takes your training very seriously, even if you still don't want to embrace the spirituality of what we do. He spends a lot of time trying to help you and you're not even officially a member of his coven."

He couldn't help it, Liam chuckled, then full-out laughed at her indignation.

"Do *not* laugh at me," she hissed as the doorbells chimed and one of Liam's favorite customers came in.

"Play nice," Liam whispered as he set down the last few books and stepped over to where Nate Keegan stood. He was a little over six feet tall, with inky-black hair, buzzed on the sides, long on top that flopped into his eye. Nate's blue, near-violet, eyes, porcelain skin, pouty lips, and slightly androgynous body and face had intrigued and attracted Liam when they'd first met. However, Liam had quickly figured out that Nate was a submissive, and because Liam wasn't a Dom, they would be better off as friends. That had been almost three years ago, and the only regret Liam had was that he was now happy with Cameron, but as far as he knew, Nate was still alone. Nate had trouble finding a Dom who could see past his twisted legs, after all—stupid men.

Liam noted Dianne stepped to the next aisle and nodded toward Nate.

"Hey, Nate. What can I do for you today?"

"Thought I'd come by and visit," Nate replied, his British accent catching Liam's attention as it always did. Liam, like most people he knew, loved accents, especially British, Irish, Scottish, and Australian. Cam didn't have one, but that was about the only *flaw* he'd found in his Cam so far. "That and to see what new came in. You know how much I like to read."

"And even though you love your computers as much as many people do their pets or family, you still prefer paper to e-books."

"That I do." Nate's lips quirked up on one side.

"I have a few new things in, even a few BDSM romance books in the M/M section you might like." Liam smiled when Nate blushed and fidgeted with the purple forearm crutches he used. They were the strangest shape, but Nate swore they were infinitely more comfortable than traditional ones. "Oh, and I need to introduce you to Cameron sometime soon."

"Cameron?" Nate stopped his progress toward the section of the store Liam had pointed out. "Who's that? You're not trying to set me up with some friend of yours, are you?"

"I promised I wouldn't do that, and I won't. I've even managed to stop Di from meddling too much."

"Then who's Cameron?" The worry and edge to Nate's voice didn't change. Liam hated how Nate's exes had battered the man's sense of self so badly. He was a beautiful and sweet man, sexy too, truth be told. But his legs were twisted—some kind of birth defect—and he had arthritis, and that made things difficult for him, sadly. Well, romantically, it did.

"Cameron is my boyfriend. Well, we've had one official date, but I intend to keep him." They'd been together forever, so Liam didn't feel bad about using the term. It fit as far as he was concerned.

"Oh… he's why you haven't been around other than to work lately? Is he why you were so upset there for a while?" Nate's voice went from excited to worried in a heartbeat. He stood taller, his shoulders back, and the usually shy man was suddenly gone. In his place was someone Liam rarely saw—Nate Laurie Keegan, ready to kick ass if needed to protect his friends. "He's not hurting you somehow, is he?"

Liam reached out and put one hand on Nate's shoulder gently. "Nate, hon, calm down. No, Cam didn't hurt me. Yes, we had a rough patch and I was a bit off—"

If that wasn't an understatement, Liam didn't know what was, but he wasn't about to tell Nate about the drinking or the dreams. They were friends, but he doubted most people would believe he'd been dream walking to Cameron since they were teens.

"—but that was more a matter of misunderstandings and miscommunication than anything. He would never hurt me. You're my friend and I want you to meet him, that's all."

"Well, okay, then. You know I like meeting your friends."

"Yeah, now, how about we find you something new to read while Dianne finishes pouting?"

Nate leaned in and stage-whispered, "What's she pouting for?"

"Boy troubles. She's *skerred* to ask her beau out on a date."

Dianne stomped over to them and snapped, "He is *not* my beau."

"But you want him to be," Nate countered softly. "That's why you're so mad at Liam for teasing you about him. Who is he?"

"I…. That's so not the point, Nate."

"Di, poppet, who is this man?"

"He's…. Nosha's my priest."

Nate shrugged one shoulder and hummed softly. "He's still human and you're Wiccan, not Roman Catholic, so I don't see the problem. If you like him and he likes you. Or are you not into the same things?" Nate's voice dropped to a near-whisper. "That could be a problem, but…."

"I wouldn't know as I've never talked about such things with him. He's my *priest*!"

Liam looked at Nate and shrugged when he noted the same confusion in Nate's eyes that he was certain was in his own. "I don't get it, either. How about I show you naughty books with whips, leather, spanking, candles, and more in them while she decides what to do about Nosha and which of her coven sisters she's going to demand I hire?"

"Ohhh…." Nate's eyes lit up as he bounced on his toes and smiled. "That sounds perfect. Wait? You're hiring someone, but she's informing you who?"

Liam chuckled and nodded. "Basically, yeah. You know Di. It's better to just give in and accept that she knows best in these situations. Besides, she's probably right. I am always behind with inventory, stocking, cleaning, etcetera. Plus, I would like to have a little more free time to spend with Cam, and he works late hours."

"Makes sense. I don't have to worry about that, even if I did date, as I work from home, but just make sure it's someone you can trust. And I'd love to meet your boyfriend." Nate paused and looked down at his legs. He wore loose-legged pants, so other than the fact his shoes stuck out at odd angles, you couldn't see how twisted his legs were. "Do you think he'll mind meeting me?"

"Nate?" Liam began as he looked Nate over from head to toe and back. "You actually do the same basic thing as far as the smoky-eye and makeup thing goes, though you look nothing alike. But you're a very handsome man and a friend of mine. Why would he mind you? You think he might be jealous of how hot you are?"

The way Nate's pale skin suddenly mottled with near-fuchsia, bypassing pink and red, had Liam biting the inside of his cheek to keep from laughing. "I am not! And he has no reason to be jealous of me, you twit. I just, I'd like your boyfriend to like me."

"You are and he will. Now, stop being so sensitive about your legs. They are not what makes you, you. Now let's get you some hot men to read about, and then I'll see about when I can get you and Cam in the same room at the same time."

Now that Liam was back to himself, free of his fears and the influence of the alcohol, he was more determined than ever to be a good friend to those he was close to. He didn't have many he truly considered friends, but those he did, he would reconnect with and do his best to help where he could. Dianne and Nate were the two he thought he needed the most, but right then, getting his hands on Cameron was higher on his list of needs than teasing Dianne or nudging Nosha. Even if they did need a good boot to the butt.

CHAPTER 14

CAMERON RAN his fingers over his right wrist, even though there weren't any marks still. The morning after the first time he and Liam had finally been together in the real, waking world, he'd woken with light bruising on not just his lips and hips, but his wrists. He'd found an odd sort of satisfaction in touching and tracing the marks on his wrists off and on throughout the day and was disappointed the skin was now back to the usual smooth, pale cream color it always was. He knew the signs of their lovemaking wouldn't last; they never did, even with how light and easy to mark as he was. This was the first time that fact had disappointed him, though.

The worst part was that even though it had been only a day, he struggled to believe everything had been real. When Liam had touched him, there had been no hesitancy, no fumbling, nothing that was normal when with a new partner for the first time. He'd touched Cam the perfect way each and every time. Things hadn't been perfect exactly, of course. They'd had to actually remove their clothes, and there was the matter of moving and getting comfortable and such, but the familiarity and knowledge in Liam's touch and motions unnerved Cameron—well, they did now he'd had time to think about things. At the time, he'd been a little distracted with Liam and the *ohmygoddoitagain!* that was happening.

The next morning they had made love again. Cameron couldn't call it sex even though they'd only just started seeing each other in the real world. But then work had intruded. Liam had left to tend to his bookstore, and later Cam had gone to work at the Indigo Dragon where he currently was.

They had talked on the phone, and Liam had even stopped by after he'd closed the shop that night with coffee and a snack for Cameron before he went over to Nosha's for one of his late-night work sessions. But it was now the next day and there were no more signs left, and the niggling feeling of unreality was pushing in on Cam. Was their relationship real? Were his feelings for Liam real? Or was this something born out of loneliness and need? And why had sex felt so… comfortable? It had been hot, passionate, perfect, needy, but also… comfortable was the only word his mind could seem to settle on. Was it the years of dream sharing? And would that sense of comfort always be there? Was that even a good thing?

Cam startled so hard he nearly fell off the stool at his drafting table when Bass's voice intruded on his circling and increasingly worried thoughts, along with Bass's huge hand patting Cameron's shoulder roughly. "Cammy? You okay?"

"Huh?"

"Well, I've tried to ask you a question like three times now, but you haven't responded. Hell, you didn't even move."

"Oh, sorry. I was, um, thinking. What'd ya need?"

"Thinking? Not sure if that's a good thing."

"I'm not either, but I'm okay. What's up, man?"

"Well, that Celtic knot sleeve you're doing is here for his last session. I was up front already so thought I'd let you know when you didn't respond to Mandy paging you."

Cam knew he was blushing, but he couldn't do anything about it. The heat on his face only made him want to duck away more, which he figured probably made the color brighter. He hated getting so fixated and zoning out like that, but that was how his brain worked. At least it was only Bass that knew how much of a space case he was. "Sorry. I have everything set up, so give me just a couple of minutes and I'll be right out to get him."

"No worries. He's calm as ever. But, um, if you don't mind me asking… when you came in yesterday you were all smiles, and then today you've slowly gotten more, I don't know, edgy and sullen?" Bass's voice ticked up at the end, making the sentence into a question, though Cam was certain it wasn't really. "You sure you're okay, Cam?"

"Just nervous about a guy, no worries. I'm good."

Bass didn't look as though he believed Cameron but dropped the subject, much to Cam's relief. After another long look, Bass left the room and Cam got to work pulling out the ink he'd need and making sure he had everything perfect before he stepped out to welcome Raven for their last session. The sleeve was coming out great—mocha knot work on Raven's caramel, smooth skin that went from the ball of his shoulder to his wrist.

"Hi, Raven. Ready?"

"Always." Raven flashed a perfect, straight smile at Cameron as he stood up from the waiting room chair and sauntered into Cam's little domain. "I can't wait to let it finish healing up and then show off the full sleeve."

"Just make sure to tell them who did your work and I'll be happy." Cam batted his lashes as he finished, camping his voice a little, pleased when Raven chuckled. The man had a gorgeous, deep voice, and his laugh was enough to turn a man's knees to jelly. Well, it would be if not for Liam. He sighed, then almost sighed again at the thought of the first one. *One great date and I turn into a teen? Ugh!*

"Have no doubt, Cameron. I always try to lift up local talent when I can."

Cam grinned. He loved hearing praise like that. "Sweet. Now, be good and stay still. I don't want to mess anything up, especially now. I've never done a knot work in relief before but am loving it, especially on your skin."

Raven sighed dramatically and slumped his shoulders as Cam dipped into the first round of ink. "Are you hitting on me *again*? You're just not my type, honey."

Fighting not to laugh, Cam replied, "Nope, that's true. Silk is for shirts, crops are for farmers, and wax should stay on the candle."

"I am wounded, sir. Truly wounded. You would think by your words that I was into something kinky." How Raven said all that with wide eyes and a slight frown was beyond Cam. He knew full well what Raven was "into." The man was a freakin' Dom! A rather popular and sought-after one from what he'd heard.

"You know," Cam said after a moment, then lost the fight not to smile. "If I didn't know better, I'd almost believe you were offended by the insinuation of sexual deviancy."

Raven laughed loudly and nodded. "Offended? Hell, I consider that to be one of my best features. Still, I do love how you worded all that. Now, you going to torture me or just stare at my arm?"

"If you'd stop shaking your arm while you giggle I would." Raven calmed quickly and Cam got to work.

After a little while, Raven spoke again. "So, I heard you went out with someone. You found someone since you moved up here or someone follow you up from home?"

"Nosy." Raven shrugged his other shoulder and made a sort of *eh* noise but didn't say anything. "It's complicated, sorta, but Liam took me out to dinner and then for dessert."

"That's good, right? I mean, you're the keeper kind of guy, not the trick sort, so what has you all quiet and sighing? You're always bouncy and chatty, but not today."

Cam thought about it and realized Raven was right. It wasn't just how he'd acted in front of Bass, he really was off today. "Sorry. Guess I'm just overanalyzing things and crap. Don't mind me. I promise it won't affect the awesomeness of your tat!"

"Well, that at least sounds more like the puppy of a man I'm used to you being," Raven said with a chuckle. Cameron jutted his bottom lip out, but Raven ignored him. "Nope, I don't accept pouting out of my boys, so no way will I out of you. Though you do do it well," he added with a headshake. "If your guy is right for you, then talk to him. Don't stress yourself and get an ulcer at...." Raven looked Cam over as Cam tried to ignore him and work. "What are you? All of twenty? Twenty-two at the most?"

"Thirty, but thanks. And we've talked and he stopped by. It's not that, it's...." He took a deep breath and focused on a tight edge for a moment before he continued—more stalling for time as he tried to think about how to explain the issue. "Most of it would make no sense to anyone but me, but I guess the part that would is that being with Liam feels unreal. No, that's not right. Like a dream. No, that's not quite right, either." *How do I explain that it feels like I'm back in a dream, not in the waking world when I'm with Liam? That it's all too perfect?* "It's more like a dream than reality, and when he's not here, it's hard to believe 'us' exists. And yes, I realize that sounds completely nuts and like a teen whining about why he won't call or something but...."

Raven was quiet for a few minutes while Cameron continued to work, worried he'd said too much and Raven now regretted talking to Cam like a friend instead of just as a service provider. When he did finally speak, Cameron nearly jumped. Only his focus and experience with his work saved him—and the tattoo.

"It doesn't sound nuts at all. It actually sounds like some subs I've known. Sometimes they feel insecure about their Dom's affection or attention and need something that will remind them who they belong to. I know you're not a sub, but that doesn't mean you don't have that kind of worry. I mean, the guy obviously makes you very happy, but then you fear he'll leave or lose interest or something." It wasn't a question, Cam knew that by the tone, but he nodded anyway. It was that, but the dream sharing, walking, weaving thing added to the unreality of it, but he couldn't explain that to Raven. Not unless he wanted the man to think he really was crazy. Eccentric was one thing, but totally nuts was another and not high on his list of desires for his life. "You know, that's part of the logic behind having a sub wear a cuff or collar or piece of jewelry when they're not with their Dom, right? It's not just ownership—well, not just for the Dom—but for the security and possession… to let the sub feel and know they are chosen and wanted."

"What's that got to do with me? I'm not a sub and I don't want a collar, thanks."

"Think, Cam. If you're having trouble with how happy he makes you, with things feeling real when he's not around, maybe you could modify that idea and have him mark you in some way that would allow you to still feel the connection. Something tangible you could touch and *know* he wants you. It's not like the idea is exclusive to the kink community." The implied *duh* was louder in the room than Raven's voice or Cam's equipment.

Cameron thought about it as he bent to his work. Wasn't that what he'd been doing with the bruises on his wrist? They were tangible proof of Liam's interest and that it had *actually* happened. "I'll have to think about it, but yeah, that makes sense. No collars, though. I respect your lifestyle and all, but I'm no sub, nor am I a furry."

Raven laughed loudly, moving so much that Cam feared for the tattoo, so he pulled back and waited.

"I don't know, Cam. With that fuzzy mop of hair on your head and all, you'd make a great puppy."

This time, Cam's pout was real, as was his indignation. "I am not a puppy. I'm a grown man. Not a boy, a puppy, an *anything cutesy you want to insert*, thank you so very much."

That just sent Raven into more hysterics, much to Cameron's annoyance. Eventually, Raven calmed and settled down. "Sorry, Cam. Really. I know you hate being teased, but if you could have seen your face. Damn! Seriously, though, just talk to your boyfriend. If you were a sub friend, I'd tell you to talk to your Dom. Communication is the only way relationships work, no matter what kind."

"You sure you're a guy? Men do *not* talk." Cam smirked as he tugged Raven's arm back into position and returned to work.

"Uff. Hey, not so hard."

"Baby."

"Bully."

"This coming from a Dom, I'm not sure if I should be insulted or flattered."

"I do not abuse my boys," Raven's voice no longer held any of the earlier playfulness or joy. "I would never harm anyone in my care or allow anyone to be abused that I could help or protect."

Cam paused his work again and raised his head so his gaze fully met Raven's. "I know that, Raven. I was teasing only. I know the difference. Just 'cause I'm not into your lifestyle doesn't mean I don't understand that BDSM isn't abuse."

"Sorry. It's a touchy subject. I get tired of people assuming one is the other when it's not."

"Yeah, I bet. It's hard enough being gay without the kink prejudice added on, I'm sure. I was listening to your advice, though, and I'll try talking to him. I'm not sure what to say that will make sense to him being we've had kind of a weird start to our relationship, but I'll talk."

"Good. I know we only met because of the tattoo, but I'd like to see you happy."

He couldn't help it; Cam grinned wide. "Thanks. I wasn't really sure about the move here. I didn't know anyone and all, but I've met some great new people—you included."

"Yeah, Asheville is a pretty cool place with some great people. Not everyone is, though, so be careful when you're out. But for the most part, I love it here."

"Uh-huh. And you're going to settle down when? I mean, you're being all 'little old lady' butting into my love life, so I figure it's fair trade to butt into yours."

Raven sighed and looked away. "When I find the right boy, I'll know. It's been a long time since I've found one I've wanted for more than a scene, but who knows… maybe my Mr. Right-sub is out there waiting for me."

"I'm sure he is. Now be good while I finish shading in the work on the underside of your wrist, and then you'll be done."

"I hate that part," Raven grumbled so low Cameron almost missed it.

"Yeah, I don't like that part, either, but hey, it's going to look fabulous when done, so hush up and focus on the outcome, not the discomfort of the now."

"Easy for you to say, you're on the other side of the gun," Raven quipped, but his voice was more normal and the tension was gone.

"I'll let you see what Bass and I have been working on on my shoulder and arm if you want when we're done. You saw my back already, so I don't want to hear it. Tattooing along my vertebrae and shoulder blades wasn't what I would call comfy, though I did tend to kind of zone out after a while and stop noticing anything."

"I've heard of people doing that. I would like to see, just because I love your work. I'm assuming it's your own design as I can't imagine you letting anyone else draw on you."

"Well, Bass has been doing the parts I can't—angles and reach, ya know. But it's all my design, yeah."

"Cool. So finish torturing me so I can check you out before I have to get to work."

Cam shook his head. At least he wasn't the only one that got tat work done before work. Raven would be sore. Probably. Maybe.

"No checking out my Cam without permission" came Liam's voice from the doorway.

When Cameron paused and looked over, Liam was leaning against the doorjamb, a soft smile on his lips as he watched every move Cam made. He didn't seem to even notice Raven even though he'd spoken to him.

"Hi, Lee."

"Hi, beautiful. You trying to replace me already?" Liam winked, the smile turning into a smirk.

Making sure to let Liam see his eyes roll, Cam snorted. "Hardly. Lee, this is Raven. Raven, this is Liam, who apparently thinks you need permission to look at my tattoos."

"Well, if he's your boyfriend, then I probably do," Raven replied, looking Liam over. The odd thing in Cameron's opinion was that it seemed more like a friend or parent checking a guy out to make sure he was good enough, not another guy *checking* Liam out.

"Considering it would require you to take off part of your clothes, I'd prefer it, yeah." Liam didn't move into the room, though he did twitch a few times as if he wanted to.

"I'm almost done here. Why don't you go out to the front and I'll let you know when I'm done."

"No, he can come in and stay," Raven countered. "As long as it won't mess with your concentration and work, I don't mind."

"Cool." Liam sauntered over and took up residence on Cam's stool at his drafting table, turning so he could watch Cam work. He didn't talk much as Cam finished up, and Raven was pretty quiet, but Cameron didn't sense any tension between the two men.

"Okay, done. What do you think?" Cam gathered his supplies so he could clean off the tattoo and then cover it before sending Raven out.

Raven turned his arm left and right, looking it over and smiling wider all the while. "Looks great, Cam. I knew you were the right man for the job." It didn't take long to have it treated and wrapped. But before he led Raven out, Raven asked to see Cam's sleeve.

Cam took off his long-sleeved T-shirt and turned. "Damn! Now that's hot. The knots and feathers. The ink work is amazing, as is the artwork. I love how you incorporated the shape of your muscles and all into the form of the design."

"Thanks. It's not done, as you can see, but…."

"It's something to be proud of," Liam said, stepping beside Cam and sliding one arm around his waist.

"That it is. Well, let's go settle up and I'll get out of your hair."

After a moment Cam asked, "Um, settle up? You already paid in full."

"Tip, my dear man. Never correct a customer when they want to give you more money. Now, come along and maybe you can also sell me a couple of new pieces of body jewelry before I get out of here. Then go spend some time with your hottie."

"I am not a hottie." Liam almost sounded insulted. Almost.

Raven cocked his head and stared at Liam a moment, then turned to Cameron again. "Oh, and use some of your pay to get his eyes fixed or to buy him a mirror, because he must not have seen himself lately. Now, come along and be good boys."

Cam giggled the whole way out to the front as Liam grumbled about not being a boy, though Cam knew Liam liked hearing that someone thought he was hot. Who didn't? By the time Raven left, he'd bought five new jewelry bits and given Cam a tip for how much he'd liked the tattoo work. All in all, it had been a very productive sale, and the talk they'd had had helped Cam decide on what to do next. Now he just had to hope Liam would be good with what he wanted and with his worries and fears. Stupid as it was, Cam was truly freaked out by how much real sex and dream sex felt the same.

CHAPTER 15

LIAM WALKED with Cam back into Cameron's workspace after his friend and customer, Raven, left. Raven was handsome, but he was just a little too familiar and commanding for Liam's taste when it came to Cam. He shook off his worry as best he could, not wanting to let jealousy get a foothold. He knew firsthand how much damage that little monster could cause and wasn't about to let it interfere with his hoped-for future with Cameron. Besides, Cam was not cheating on him. No way.

"Hope you don't mind me stopping by, but I wanted to see you."

Cam's face lit up as he smiled. He bounded up onto his toes and gave Liam an all-too-brief kiss on the lips. "Of course not, hon. I just didn't expect to see you yet is all."

"Well, I know we're supposed to go out tomorrow night, but—" He shrugged. Liam didn't know why this was so hard, but it was. He swallowed hard and met Cam's gaze. "I didn't want to wait that long. I know I can visit your dreams and all, but I wanted the waking you, not just the dream you," he continued as he cupped Cameron's cheek. He then bent and took Cam's lips in a soft but firm kiss. He didn't want chaste, he wanted to taste and feel his lover.

Cam let out a soft moan and wrapped his arms around Liam's neck. Liam teased his tongue along Cameron's bottom lip, tracing and licking before pushing inside to taste and claim his love. Cam didn't take any time in tangling his slick muscle with Liam's, tasting and driving Liam crazy, much to his delight. Unfortunately, before they could get into things too far, a bang startled them apart. When Liam looked around to see what had happened, the door to Cam's room was still closed and there was no one but them in the room.

"Take a break, Cam," boomed through the closed door, making Cam jump against Liam. Liam wrapped his arms around Cameron tighter as he grinned. Yeah, Cam wasn't very quiet with his moans and groans, but Liam didn't really want him to be. He loved hearing how much pleasure he gave Cameron, but yeah, Cam's workplace probably wasn't the best place to make out. *At least not while they're open....*

"Yes, sir," Cam squeaked, then buried his face in Liam's shoulder.

"Relax, beautiful." Liam stroked his hands up and down Cameron's back, hoping to sooth Cam enough to get him out of the room and maybe out for a walk or to the coffee shop. Either of their apartments was a little far for just a "break," though they could have a lot more fun there.

When Cam finally looked up and met Liam's gaze, he gave a tentative smile. "Sorry about Bass."

"I'm sure he's not actually upset. But for propriety's sake, how about we go for a walk?" Liam wanted to kiss Cam again but knew that would only lead them back to the reason they needed to leave. Instead, Liam opened the door and noted that no one was nearby. He threaded his fingers with Cameron's and tugged him out the door, through the lobby—where Bass and the blue-haired girl he could never remember the name of heckled them—and then outside and onto the sidewalk. "Come on. Let's go get a coffee since I'm really not into PDA."

Cameron giggled and nodded. "Yeah, that would be more my thing than yours, I think. Not that I'm into public stuff either, but people wouldn't be as shocked, I think."

"Well, since you're with me… no public anything. And I'm never giving you back."

Before Liam knew what happened, Cam was wrapped around him, peppering his face with kisses. It took a few minutes to get Cameron under control and calmed down enough to make any sense. Arms tight around Cam, Liam leaned back enough to look into Cameron's eyes. "Much as I love the lovin', beautiful, what brought that on?"

"Sorry." Cam's gaze darted away as a pink flush spread up his cheeks and down his neck.

"No, no need for sorries. I just want to know why the kiss attack." Liam leaned in and whispered, "Though I'm always in the mood for your kisses." He nipped Cameron's lobe quickly, then pulled back before Cam could catch him. "For your passion. But why now?"

"Just, you said you wanted to keep me," he said, his voice a cross between a mumble and a moan. He didn't look up at Liam.

It took a moment for the words to fully register, but when they did, Liam hugged Cameron tighter. "Of course I want to keep you, beautiful. I've come back to you via dreams for how many years? Somehow, I just don't see you getting rid of me now."

"I...." Cameron looked down and kicked at the ground with those beat-to-hell Converse of his. "Well, no. I don't know. This all still seems so...."

"Like a dream?"

Cam nodded but didn't look up. "Can we go get that coffee now?"

"Sure, but maybe we can talk about this worry a bit too." The dream versus reality hadn't been a concern for Liam, not for Cam at least. For himself, sure. Sometimes he wondered how real reality really was, but then it wasn't hard to tell the difference. It was more the concept for him than the actuality of it. Still, the thought that Cameron was struggling tore at him, though he wasn't sure what to do for Cam. He wasn't sure how to make things seem more real for Cam when it wasn't Cam that played with dreams. *How…?*

"Yeah, okay." Liam released Cameron, and they walked hand in hand down the street.

When they went inside the little shop, the scents of coffee, chocolate, and baking muffins nearly knocked Liam over. He loved the smell of the place and the taste of damn near everything he'd ever tasted of theirs. The line was short, so it didn't take long to get to the barista.

"Hey, Cammy. Whatcha having today?" the tall, willowy boy with the green hair and the usually mopey attitude asked as he batted his lashes at Cameron and leaned forward a little.

Liam would have been annoyed, but Cam's hand tightened around his in a sort of hand hug, he guessed he'd call it. Whatever it was, he liked it. "Hi, Steve. I'd like a white chocolate with peppermint mocha, large, and a double fudge brownie." Cameron then looked up at Liam with wide eyes. It was almost a doe-eyed expression—not one he'd known Cam could even make. "What'll you have, love?"

It was hard for Liam not to smirk—or crow—as Steve's gaze whipped between Cam and him repeatedly, a frown becoming more and more pronounced. "But...."

"I think I'll have the dark chocolate mocha and the blackberry scone," Liam answered Cameron, ignoring Steve. When the man didn't make the notes for their drinks or move to get out their snacks, Liam cleared his throat loudly. "Is there a problem?"

"Um... n-no?" Steve managed. "I'll have that right up." He scampered off to make their drinks. Liam didn't step back, as he wasn't entirely sure his food and drink would be safe now the fact he was with

Cam was public—and was obviously not making Steve very happy. Not that he really cared. He couldn't be happier about finally having Cam, the real, live, *waking* Cameron Danu as his beloved partner. Now to figure out how to make him that permanently and how to get him past his worries and fears of what Liam's unusual abilities meant.

Thankfully it didn't take long for their drinks to be ready and their treats to be plated. Soon they were seated in the far corner, sipping on their drinks. "Want to tell me what's going on in that head of yours, beautiful?"

"Not really," Cam replied but then flashed Liam a bright smile. "Actually, Raven had just talked me into talking to you when you showed up, so I guess I kinda have to now."

"Don't sound so put out about it." Liam laughed at the sourpuss face Cam pulled. "What's so bad that your customer had to talk you into talking to me? Damn that's a lot of talking going on in there."

"I know, right?" Cam nodded rapidly before taking a nibble of his brownie. "Well… it's just that…. God, this is going to sound stupid or weird or something."

"Hey, just tell me what's got you so bothered, okay? I can't help fix it if I don't know what the problem is, right?"

"Yeah." Cam took another sip of his mocha, then sighed. "Look, the problem is in my head, and I know it. It's just that when you're not around, all this—" Cam waved one hand between them. "—seems like it's just part of one of my dreams. When we're really together, it feels real, but later, the doubts and worries creep in. I mean, the other night was perfect, but that's actually part of the problem."

Liam thought about that for a moment, then thought some more, not sure what Cameron meant. Perfect was somehow wrong and not being around made things seem like part of a dream? Yeah, that didn't make any more sense the third or fourth time he tried thinking it through than it had the first time.

"Beautiful, I don't understand. You're happy about the other night. You're happy with me. In fact, you kiss-attacked me for wanting to keep you, but when I'm not around, the fact we met in dreams becomes a problem?"

"Yes. No. Well, sorta. It's more that our relationship seems more like one of the dreams than something real sometimes. I know that doesn't make sense. I mean, I'm the one that came to your house and all. Kinda pushed you into dating even in a backward sort of way, but this all seems…."

"Okay, maybe if we talk about things one at a time this will make more sense. What about the other night seems unreal? You said it was perfect, but that seems to be a problem."

Cameron rolled his neck, his eyes closed as he hummed softly. When he finally looked up, he smiled tenderly. "Every touch was how it is in the dreams: knowing, perfect, wonderful. There was no fumbling, no learning curve like with a new partner. It didn't seem 'real' if that makes sense. I mean, I know it was. My body told me just how real—by the way, you're bigger in real life," he added with a little giggle.

Liam couldn't help but preen a little at the compliment, but the initial comment bugged him. "Of course I knew your body already, Cam. We're not new lovers. Not really. I mean, we are while awake, but really, we had sex the first time when I was what… seventeen or so?"

"Yeah, about that. I was fifteen, I think. Even back then you made a hell of an impression and the dreams were too real. I mean, I remember wishing the boys in school were as hot and as sexy as my 'dream boy.'"

"Thanks." Liam grinned, loving that Cam had thought of him outside of their shared dreams even back then. He knew he had thought of Cam often, to the point it had cost him a lover or two over the years. "I'm thirty-two now, so while being with you while awake is wonderful—and something I want to repeat regularly and *soon*!—it's not something I haven't done before. Just as you touched me and kissed me like you've known me forever."

"When we're together, that all makes sense. It's when we aren't that the doubts start messing with my head. Like I said, it's stupid."

Cameron looked so miserable, Liam tugged on Cam's hand until he got up and finally consented to sit on Liam's lap. Liam wrapped one arm around Cameron's waist but made sure not to do anything inappropriate.

"What did your friend suggest since you said you two talked out the issue? Oh, and does that mean you discussed my dream walking and dream weaving?"

"No, I didn't tell him that. I'm not ashamed of your ability, but I don't know how others would react, so I left it to more generic concerns and worries. But, um, he suggested a token. Well, more of a collar or cuff, really, but he's a Dom, so that's how his mind works," Cam explained, his lips twisting up on one side in a sort of half grin, half smirk. "But the idea was for me to have something from you that shows us as a couple, I think." He shrugged and looked away. "Something I could see and be reminded that we are true and real and all."

That made perfect sense. But Liam didn't think a collar would be right, not with the fact they weren't into the kink lifestyle. And he didn't think Cam was ready for rings yet, though Liam had definitely thought about those already. When he'd said he was keeping Cameron, he meant it. "What if we go shopping tomorrow, while we're out on our date, and see what we can find? I know most guys probably don't think of shopping as a good date, but—" Liam shrugged. "—in this case, I think it makes the most sense. Besides, you need new shoes."

Cam pulled away and gaped at Liam. "New shoes? Heathen! There's nothing wrong with my Chucks!"

"They're so beat up I'm not sure how they're still on your feet. I mean, you're hot in or out of anything, you know that, but really. I'll even buy you new Converse." Liam threw in a pleading pout for good measure. Why Cameron wore shoes like that was beyond him. Cam was not some malnourished, starving college student who couldn't afford better. The man could, he simply didn't, which needed a damn good explanation or some serious shopping—and Liam wasn't the shopping whore; that was Di.

"But, Sarah gave them to me," Cam mumbled as he looked away.

"Oh." *Damn, open mouth, insert foot.* "I'm sorry, beautiful. Then I won't rag on them again. We can still go look for something for you tomorrow, and maybe soon she can come up to visit?"

"Yeah, I want you to meet her. She, well, and Dan of course, are all the family I have left. She knows about you and wants to meet you so bad I'm surprised she hasn't just up and appeared at either your store or my door, demanding to meet you."

Liam grinned. "Let me guess, getting her and Dianne into the same room will be dangerous for us both?"

The peals of laughter were good to hear after the sadness of moments before. "You know it. Between the two of them, none of us will be safe. Though...." Cam paused and cocked his head as if listening to something only he could hear. "Maybe Sarah could get your aunt to stop this nonsense about not dating her priest. Sarah is a born matchmaker, I swear, and I've never seen her not want to meddle, especially if the couple is that obvious."

"Then maybe we ought to invite them up just for that reason alone. I want her happy, and the way she's going, neither one of them is, or is likely to be anytime soon."

"Oh, thinking of Raven before… I was wondering, what kind of Dom is your one friend looking for?"

"Nate?"

"Yeah, him. You mentioned him and I'm supposed to get to meet him, soon hopefully, but I know Raven is without a boy at the moment, and…."

"And you want to play matchmaker? I thought that was Sarah's specialty."

"Just answer the question." Cameron pouted and batted his lashes. "He told me about this sub friend of his—guy's in a wheelchair—and then it made me think about Nate. You said he had something odd about his legs. Maybe Raven could be the right Dom or at least introduce him to Doms that would see the guy, not the disability?"

They spent the next little while chatting about what little Liam knew about Nate's likes and dislikes as far as BDSM went. Since Liam wasn't into the lifestyle, he didn't know everything, of course, but by the time they were done, they decided they had to find a way to get the two men into the same room and see if they could at least get them talking.

"But, that's neither here nor there on our date issues," Liam said. "I have to return you to work before your big, scary boss comes looking for you. That's one man I do *not* want to be on the wrong side of."

"Me either, but really, he's nothing like the badass he likes to portray."

"I know, but still. You have work, and I do too. My part-timer is running things for now, but I have to go in. I told you how Di informed me I was going to hire someone? Well, today is the interview."

Cam hopped up and dusted a few crumbs off his clothes. "Then we should go. And yeah, we can go shopping some. It's not like Asheville doesn't have a ton of cool shops, malls, and such to hit."

It didn't take long to collect their things back up and to make their way back to the Indigo Dragon, where Liam left Cameron. He didn't want to, but he wanted to seem clingy even less. With one last "bye, beautiful," Liam strode away, heading back to work, back to life without Cam's soothing yet exciting presence. Tomorrow couldn't get there fast enough. Thankfully, he had lots to keep him busy. Now to just survive hiring someone new and dealing with his—he was sure—gloating aunt and best friend.

CHAPTER 16

"WE'RE COMING up next weekend, Cammy, so you need to figure out where you're going to put us," Sarah said when Cam hit Answer and said "Hey" into his cell the next afternoon.

"Um, hi to you too, little sis. You know you're always welcome. My place isn't big like yours, but y'all will all fit, no problem. Actually, Liam and I were just talking about having you up so he could meet you. You know, the 'meet the family' thing and all."

"Liam wants to meet us? What did you have to do to get him to agree to that?"

"Brat woman, I don't have to bribe my man. He wants to meet my family, not that I know why. Especially not when that means you. But... for some unknown reason he does, and you want to come up, so perfect timing! Now quit being a meanie and give me the deets on your arrival."

Huff! "I am so not being mean. But as for arrival, I'll have to let you know in a couple of days exactly when that'll be. I'm just calling to let you know we're coming so you can get the apartment ready. You know, hide the porn, clean up the bodies, cancel the freak shows... those kinds of things. Oh, well, and to warn your new boyfriend, of course. And I promise Dan and I won't give him too hard of a time. Maybe. Perhaps. We'll try, at least."

The fact she was willing to tease and wanting to meet Liam meant more to him than he had the words to express. It'd been so long since he'd had anyone in his life who he really wanted to have meet his family, even if his family wasn't that big anymore. Sarah and Dan might be the only family he had still, but they were also the only family that mattered, and he couldn't wait to introduce them to Liam.

Now to hope that Sarah liked Liam and that Liam liked Sarah. He didn't want to imagine how things would go if they didn't like each other. How horrible it would be if the man he wanted to keep forever and his sister didn't get along. He was pretty sure that wouldn't happen, though. Not with how friendly and easygoing Liam tended to be and how much Sarah wanted Cam to be happy.

He knew it was silly to worry about it right then, though. They wouldn't meet until she arrived, so there was no use fussing about it now. Instead, he turned his focus to visiting with her and getting ready for his date later.

"Ha-ha-ha. You're hysterical, sis. I'm pretty sure anything you dish out Liam can handle. After meeting his aunt and best friend, Dianne, I'm pretty certain you're outclassed and outranked in all shapes, forms, and fashions in the nosy, pushy, and bitchy parades."

"Pest!" Sarah managed while giggling. "I am absolutely none of those things. I'm a good, kind, and sweet sister. Now be a good brother and let your boyfriend know your sister is coming to visit. By the way, what is it he does again?"

"He owns and runs The Feathered Quill. It's a quirky little bookshop not too far away from where I work. He specializes in hard-to-find books. He also happens to have a large section of gay romance, trans books, bi books, pretty much anything to do with the rainbow, really. But no, it's *not* word porn."

"So we've got the Indigo Dragon and The Feathered Quill. And is he of good Irish descent?"

"His name is Liam Grady. What kind of heritage do you think he has? Goofy woman. Not that it really matters. I'd like him no matter what he was or where his family came from. By the way, his aunt is a witch."

Cam could have never told his parents, or most of the people he grew up with, about such things as Dianne being a witch or her coven or the fact Liam's family, other than his parents, were hereditary witches. He definitely couldn't have told them about Liam's dream walking or dream weaving abilities, or so many other things for that matter. But Sarah had always been interested in other things, things the conservative, controlled religious and political right they'd grown up with didn't approve of. Because of that, though, he knew it was safe for her to know about Liam, even if he hadn't gotten the guts up to explain it all to her yet. He wanted to, but half the time he couldn't believe it all and he'd lived it, and continued to live it every time Liam visited him in dreams—dreams he cherished and eagerly awaited like he had since he was a teen.

The squeal through the phone nearly ruptured Cam's eardrum. "Like a real witch or one of those fake, poser types? Please say a real witch. Like with an athame and a coven and all the really cool stuff."

"Yes, that kind of witch."

"Yes!"

Cameron couldn't help the chuckle that slipped out. "You can meet Dianne when you come up too. I know she'll want to meet you. Now let's discuss what I'll need to get for your visit before I have to go so I can get ready for my date. And that's a very, very important thing, you know? And I'm sorry—not really—but date trumps sister *every* time."

She made him swear not to do a bunch of grocery shopping before they got there. He hated agreeing, mainly because he hated the thought of her having to shop and cook when she arrived. She did that all the time at home, so he didn't want her to have to do it when she was supposedly taking vacation time. But he also knew how much she loved to cook, so he ungraciously agreed.

By the time he got off the phone with Sarah, having had to also speak with Dan twice to verify his address and to state that the following weekend *was* actually okay with Cameron—Dan refused to allow Sarah to force Cam into the visit, much to her annoyance—it was time to get ready to go out with Liam. Well, it was time to shower and shave and try to do something with his mop of hair. And just to completely tweak Liam, while he was going to dress fun and funky, he was also going to wear his beat-to-hell Converse.

Dressing was actually the part that stalled Cameron in his preparations. He wanted to look good but not like he was trying. He also wished to show enough skin that the tattoos were visible but not so much Liam would be uncomfortable. Unfortunately, he still wasn't quite confident in where that line was. Liam dressed much more conservatively than Cam and acted it too—outside of bed, at least. No tattoos, body piercings, colors added to his hair… nothing. And while Cam loved how Liam looked, just as he was, he worried Liam would be bothered by how tatted up and pierced Cam both was and intended to be.

He selected a slim-fitted button-down shirt in dark blue that had mesh sleeves instead of the usual solid material like the body of the shirt was made of. The mesh was a silvery color that was light enough to allow his colorful tattoos to show through well. There was a shirt pocket on the left breast made of the mesh material, and the collar was silver, though it was the same kind of material as the rest of the shirt. Cam figured he was covered enough that nowhere they might go would give him too much trouble—he hated how so many people assumed that tattoos meant you were a troublemaker or violent ex-con. He was neither, thank you oh so very much.

By the time he had his skinny jeans and his Converse on, he was thankful he'd put his kohl on when he'd done his hair, as there was a knock on his door. Cam sprinted from his bedroom area to his front door and wrenched it open, pasting on a wide smile. "Hi, Lee."

"Hey, Cam. Happy to see me?" Liam's answering smile was just as bright, which drew a sigh from him. Liam was dressed as he usually was—dark dress slacks, a loose silk shirt in a light jade-green, and what looked like Doc Martin shoes, if he wasn't mistaken.

"Always."

"I'm glad, and don't you look yum. So, you ready?"

Cam stepped back into the apartment to grab his wallet, keys, and phone, then pounced Liam. He pulled Liam down so his lips were at a more reasonable level, then licked and teased the seam until Lee gasped, parting them. Taking advantage of the opening, Cam thrust his tongue into Liam's mouth, tasting the cinnamon of toothpaste, mint of mouthwash, and the underlying sexiness of Lee that never failed to drive Cam crazy and make him hunger for more.

Liam didn't respond at first, worrying Cam, but just as he started to pull back, Liam's arms wrapped around Cam, and instead of them standing in the doorway, Cam found himself pushed back into his apartment, and that instead of being the aggressor, he was now the one being ravaged. *God, but I love how aggressive and in charge Lee is! Mmmmm....*

Liam ripped his mouth away and growled, "I love all the sounds you make, beautiful. Wonder how many I can get you to make?"

Before Cam could manage to think up any form of reply, Liam dipped his head down and latched on to Cam's neck, at his pulse point, licking even as he nibbled and sucked on the flesh under his lips. Cam tugged at Liam's buttons, not wanting to rip the shirt but wanting the damn thing off. *Now!*

Instead, Liam stepped back, leaving Cam so quickly he nearly fell. "Wha...?"

"If I keep at this, both our shirts are going to be in tatters, beautiful. I don't think we want that. Now, bed. Strip and I'll do the same for me."

"Huh" was all his lust-addled brain could manage.

"Get naked and to your bed, Cam. Hurry." Liam started stripping as soon as he stopped talking.

Bed. Right. Cam scrambled out of his clothes, only giving a moment's thought to how long it had taken him to decide what to wear and to actually get ready. More important things were happening, like getting naked with his Lee! It only took moments and they were both naked, beside Cam's bed. It wasn't as big as Liam's, but it would do.

When Liam's member slid against Cam's, he thought his head might explode, or he might come—neither was acceptable just then as he wanted more, dammit!

"Tell me you have supplies here, Cam."

Cam nodded and managed a strangled yes as he ground his hips against Liam's. "Drawer. Just for you."

"Better be," Liam snapped back before he bent and nipped down Cam's neck. He hefted Cam into his arms and set him on the bed. Cam didn't even flail that time—a point he was rather proud of—though he was annoyed he had lost his hold on Liam.

"Lee," he whined. "Get back over here."

"Patience." But he didn't make Cameron wait long. He prowled up the bed, between Cam's thighs, until he loomed over Cameron with a wicked smirk that made Cam want to beg and his dick throb at the same time. "Now, I need to know the truth, Cameron," Liam said, sounding more serious than he had since he'd arrived. The tone pulled Cam back from the edge of lust he'd been riding. "Do you like being fucked after you come as much in real life as you do in dreams, or is that a dream thing only?"

Oh. My. God! Cam whimpered. He knew he did and didn't even care. Not even a little bit. "Oh please, Lee. Oh God, *please* take me like that." Damn how he loved that, not that most of his exes believed him. Or were any good at keeping him excited after he came—which was the real secret to making that work, at least for him.

"Damn but you're perfect, beautiful." Liam scooted over enough to rummage in Cam's nightstand drawer, returning with a still-sealed box of condoms and the half-used bottle of lube he kept in there. Lee tossed them on the bed beside Cam, then returned to his assault on Cam, but this time he zeroed in on Cam's hypersensitive nipples. He licked and sucked until they were little pebbles. Liam then proceeded to nip and pull on them, forcing Cam to moan, yell, and writhe beneath him.

"God! Please! More! Need! Lee! Ungh!" Over and over again in random order. When Liam wrapped one hand around Cam's aching cock and started to slowly stroke, starting with light touches that moved to a tight, near-brutal grip, then back to the light, almost teasing touches, he was certain he would die before he came and that Liam was both wonderful and beyond evil. Whatever was worse than evil, that was Liam!

Eventually the speed of the stroking increased and the teasing touches stopped—the tight grip didn't, but it wasn't quite as brutal. With every stroke, Liam twisted right at the end, adding an excruciating zing of pleasure. Liam suddenly sat back and grasped Cam's sac with his other hand even as he continued stroking and teasing just the way Cam loved. No pain, just sweet, sweet pleasure. That, coupled with what Liam was already doing, sent Cam over the razor's edge he'd been living on for so long—he had no sense of time or anything outside of Liam and the need to come, really.

He screamed as the white-hot pleasure ripped from his body, blinding him to anything else in that moment. Cam had no idea how long he was out of it, but when he managed to pry his eyes open, Liam was licking Cam's spend from his chest.

"Um...."

Liam sat up and smiled. "Welcome back, beautiful."

"Hi."

The laugh was joyous and welcome. "Hi to you too. Now, my turn."

Before Cam could ask what Liam intended, Liam moved over, then flipped Cam onto his stomach. "Um, what are you doing?"

Liam ignored him. He pulled Cam up to his knees, forcing them apart, exposing his hole. Well... he did agree to sex after coming, so he guessed that's what Liam intended. He usually did more before that part in the dreams but—

The first swipe of Liam's tongue across Cam's tight pucker made him yelp and twitch forward. Liam simply tugged him back into place and continued, licking and nibbling, sucking and probing with his slick muscle as Cam writhed and moaned, unable to form words again. He loved being rimmed. Especially after coming! And damn but the man was amazing at it.

Cam wasn't hard again, but he was horny and wanting in no time. "Lee, please. I want to feel you in me. Please, baby."

"Your wish," he mumbled against Cam's right cheek at the same time there was a crinkle and tearing of a condom wrapper, "my command," he continued as the lube cap popped.

"Oh God," he gasped when Liam petted Cam's hips.

"Calm down, beautiful. I won't do anything until you're ready." Liam's voice was raspy and low, and his hands trembled against Cam's skin slightly. "I want to feel you wrapped around me, but I would never hurt you."

"I know. Just want." He wondered if Liam would last long enough to not only finish getting him hard again but also to get him off again too.

"Me too. Now, try to stay open for me. I don't want to wait, but I don't want to hurt you, either."

"'Kay." He could do that. Though if Liam didn't hurry up, he couldn't be held responsible for his actions. His thoughts derailed when a slick finger probed his opening before plunging in. Liam immediately removed it but then thankfully returned quickly. This time, two fingers stretched and rubbed him inside, teasing and giving him a taste of what was to come. But it wasn't enough. Not nearly enough. "Dammit, Lee. Get your fuckin' cock in me *now*, or I'll fuck myself and leave you to deal with your own damn dick," he snapped as he thrust his ass back toward Liam.

The chuckle from behind him wasn't quite what he was aiming for, but when it was immediately followed with pressure as Liam slowly breached him in one long, frustratingly slow thrust, his planned complaint died a swift death. Instead, a low moan left his lips as he fought to stay still. Damn but he loved feeling how Liam filled and took him—and it was so much better in real life. How full and stretched he felt. How Liam's cock seemed to touch everywhere as he moved in and out.

They found their rhythm almost immediately, the in and out, thrust and withdraw, the drag across Cam's hypersensitive nerves driving him insane even as he begged for it not to stop. For Liam to never stop. He was always more on edge if he'd already come once before he had sex, but God! What the hell was Liam doing?

Liam's fingers dug into Cam's hips as he continued his assault, the bit of pain adding to the swirling pleasure until Cam's screaming orgasm was right there. He was right at the edge again, but somehow he wasn't able to go over. He needed…. But he didn't know what, just that he needed.

"Shhh, Cam. It's okay."

Cam couldn't even find the words to ask what was okay. A moment later, Liam's hand wrapped around Cam's desperate cock, and two strokes later, the need boiling in his sac came screaming out, shorting out his brain and whiting out the world.

CHAPTER 17

LIAM LAY beside Cam for a while, just breathing in his sandalwood-and-musk scent, now heavily tinged with sex, loving it more and more every time he smelled him. The joy of finally being with Cameron. Of knowing this sweet, quirky, impossibly wonderful man was his threw his mind into a spin every time he let himself think on it too long.

He wasn't altogether certain if he should be smug or worried that Cam had effectively blacked out twice during sex. Liam hadn't known Cameron could even make a few of those noises, but he had every intention of getting him to make them again—soon. However, as soon as they were both cleaned up, Cam had crawled back into bed, under the covers, and tugged Liam down with him, all while grumbling that he now needed a teeny, tiny nap before they could go shopping. Liam had laughed but agreed.

Unfortunately, he hadn't been able to doze off like Cam had. Instead, his mind raced and his worries tumbled through it. Would Cam want to make them permanent? Could two so very different men truly make a lasting relationship? Would Cam be satisfied with Liam? It was the last one that got to him the most. He didn't doubt his ability to satisfy Cameron—he'd just proven that to them both—but rather his history of failed relationships nudged at his happy hopes, trying to shove them away as always.

All it took was looking down at the man in his arms to chase those shadows away. Liam hadn't come up with a way to show Cam what he meant to him in the waking world yet, though. Of course, that was the whole point of the shopping expedition, but he'd hoped to have a plan of some form in place before they left, and sadly, nothing he could think up fit when he thought it through in connection to his beautiful Cameron.

Still, he'd take Cam out and let him pick where they went to look for the "token," whatever that wound up being. He'd even corralled Di into watching the store until closing for the rest of the night so he didn't have to worry. Though he'd had to sit through a minilecture about how if he had already hired and trained someone, this wouldn't be an issue. He pointed out he had a part-time worker. Of course, she countered with how said worker couldn't close, which was true. Every time Saul closed, Di had to go over to the store and help. Thankfully, she was good about helping—and Liam had done as she'd wanted and hired Chell. She seemed bright and knowledgeable about a wide assortment of genres and fields. The fact she loved books was a huge plus as far as he was concerned. He still had to train her, but he had hopes she would allow him to have a more normal life now that he had a partner—even if that partner was nuzzling and snuffling into his ear at that moment.

"Cam, beautiful?" Liam murmured as he stroked his fingers up Cam's pale cheek.

"Huh? Time to get up?" Cam stretch, groaning as he did, random pops sounding from his joints.

"Yeah. If we want anything to still be open, we should get going. That and I'd like to eat tonight."

"I have to put out *and* I have to feed you too?" Cam fake pouted. "You're so damn high-maintenance."

Liam sat up, flipping his pillow over onto Cam's head as he did. "Yeah, that's me, always the greedy, drama boy. Seriously, hon, I'm all for a good derailing—and this was an epic one!—but I can't buy you your pretty if I'm trapped in your bed. Besides, that was only a box of three condoms. How long do you really think that will hold us?"

Cam blinked up at Liam owlishly. "Um, but I didn't think I'd need much here as you seem to prefer your place and all. And well, I mean, I only bought them for you."

"Which was good planning, apparently, at least until we can get tested and all." Would he even want that? Just the thought of going bare with Cam had Liam fighting his sudden need to be back inside Cameron again, but attacking him just then didn't seem the best idea. His libido disagreed, but then, it often did.

"You'd want that, with me, I mean?" Cam asked, his voice so small it was nearly lost thanks to Liam's own heart beating so damn loud.

He'd heard though and nodded even as he said, "Yes! Of course I would. I told you, I want to keep you. I meant it. Now get up and dressed. We're going to go get your token thingy, get some food, hang out like a normal couple, and make plans for when the clinic is open and we're both off." There was no question of his status—of any of his statuses, actually. He'd been tested so many times it was beyond not funny. Being gay meant his doctors thought he needed to be tested, his friends and aunt thought he needed to be tested. Hell, he'd gone to an LGBT picnic during the summer and had come to find out that it was sponsored by one of the STD clinics in town and they'd set up a free and confidential testing area right there. And of course, he'd been dragged over and shoved into line.

If Di ever found out about this, she'd go nuts. She knew he'd never agreed to go without before, no matter what. He'd never trusted any of his previous partners, even his longer-term ones. But then, none of them had been Cam, and none had been with him as long as Cameron had been. Not really. Besides, there was something special about Cam, something that had captivated Liam even when he'd thought Cam nothing more than a dream.

Of course, Nosha insisted that was because their souls were connected on a deeper level, that the divine had gifted them with each other, and that was why they'd found each other via dream sharing to begin with. Liam wasn't ready to agree, but he wasn't going to disagree either, as saying it was all just random did seem a bit beyond ridiculous at this point. Besides, if the Gods, Fates, Guides, or whatever had led him to Cam, he would thank them and hold on tight.

"'Kay. Let me see if I can't put myself back into some semblance of order and we can go." Cameron crawled out of bed, scooped his clothes up, and padded into the bathroom naked, giving Liam an excellent view of his sweet ass and the bruises he'd left. But considering how wild, loud, and amazing Cam had been, Liam couldn't find it in himself to regret even the bruise marks left behind on his lover's body.

While he waited, Liam hopped back into his own clothes and finger-combed his hair—thankful that with how short he kept it, it wouldn't look too bad even without being able to fix it properly.

LIAM WASN'T sure how it happened, but he was again sitting in the passenger side of Cameron's VW Bug as Cam whipped through the streets of Asheville. At least he'd let Liam punch in the address for Kress Emporium over on Patton Avenue, where they had decided to start their shopping expedition. Liam had been there many a time with Dianne, looking for some new and unique piece of jewelry or art. It was really a showcase for many artists and types of art, so he hoped something would resonate with Cam. Well, and it was a hotbed of local artists, so Liam kind of wanted to show off some of the talent of Cam's new—and hopefully permanent—home. During the summer, he intended to drag Cam to some of the festivals too. He *would* make Cameron fall in love with Asheville so he never wanted to move again! Well, and hopefully fall in love with him in the process.

"You know those red octagonal objects at the side of the road? Yeah, those aren't suggestions, Cam."

"Tell that to the asshat riding my bumper that wasn't stopping either. This is a Bug, not some big 1960s all-metal car that can handle having a huge SUV ram into it from behind." Cam's voice was higher than he'd expected, so Liam turned in his seat and realized that, yes, there was a Lincoln Navigator right on their bumper even now.

"Beautiful, pull into the next business. Don't care what it is. Just get out from in front of this nut, then when you're ready, get back on the road and we can finish getting where we're going."

Cam nodded, and the next thing Liam knew, he was jammed against the door as Cam took a hard right into an empty parking lot, the SUV not slowing in the least as it kept going past.

It took a couple of minutes of Cam glaring out the windshield, but eventually he took a deep breath, held it a moment, then let it out slowly. He then turned and gave Liam a small smile. "Sorry about that. I don't mind traffic. I used to drive into Atlanta to go clubbing and all, seeing as home didn't have any kind of 'gay scene,' but I don't like uber-aggressive drivers like that. Especially not when I have others in the car."

"I'm all right, as are you. Just get out from in front of assholes like that. Don't let them get to you. Now—" Liam leaned over and drew Cam into a soft but lingering kiss, not pulling away until Cam moaned and pushed into it. "—do you need me to drive or…?"

"No, I'm fine, hon. And we need to hurry or they'll be closed and we won't get to start where you wanted." Cam looked away but not fast enough for Liam to miss the pink creeping along his cheeks. "I, um, didn't really mean to delay us so long. Or at all," he added in a whisper.

"So you hadn't intended to pounce me? Even though you'd stocked up…." He had to admit, Cameron had looked ready to go when he'd arrived. Cam had even grabbed his keys, wallet, and all. But then the kiss and what came after? It was hard to imagine Cam hadn't intended to ravage him—not that Liam minded even a little.

"No." Cam shook his head, his silver eyes wide. "You just looked so sexy and all, and well, sex sorta kinda happened."

Liam couldn't help it though he knew he'd likely upset Cam, but he burst out laughing so hard his eyes teared up a little and he near doubled over. "Sex happened? Like you don't know how? Oh my God! Love it," he gasped between his cackling.

Cameron sat in his seat glaring at Liam, which did nothing to help him gain control of himself. When he finally did, Cam snapped, "All done now? Maybe I should make you go without since you seem to think it's so funny."

It should have been a question, but the tone said it wasn't. However, the smile in his eyes gave the lie to his tone and words. "Uh-huh. That would require you to go without too, so I'm thinking I'm pretty safe there."

With that, Cam's frown cracked and turned into a small smile. "Yeah, I don't think so, either. I mean, you were so evil. Got me going at work, then just took me for coffee. Then were surprised when I jumped you. Crazy man." Cam faced forward and put the car in gear again. "Back to our trip before they close?"

"Let's."

It didn't take long to get to Kress's, thankfully. They wouldn't have nearly as long as he'd have liked, but since they lived there, Liam figured he could always bring Cameron back another time to see more.

Eventually, they made their way up Patton Avenue where they pulled off the road and parked in the lot across the street. There was still a lot of foot traffic out, but then there usually was downtown until the early hours—it would just change from those out shopping and dining out to those out clubbing and partying.

Liam hurried around the car. When he reached Cameron, he slipped his hand into Cam's and laced their fingers together. "Ready, beautiful?"

"For you to spend money on me? Sure." Cam hip-bumped Liam, and they walked across the parking lot. "Seriously, I'm not even sure what I want or if this will help. If anything but time will. I don't even know why this is such a thing with me. I mean, I know you're real, that *we're* real, but...."

"Hey," Liam said and pulled Cam to a stop at the curb. He cupped Cameron's face and waited until Cam looked up at him before he continued. "I don't mind. If this will help, then I'm happy to have part of our day be spent here, or somewhere else for that matter, shopping. It took too much to get to this point to let something like your fears or worries stop us, so I'm willing to do whatever it takes to help you get what you need to feel secure."

Cam sighed and leaned into Liam's hand. "I know you will, that's what makes this whole thing with me so stupid. You nearly killed yourself trying to protect me from yourself. You started working and training with your now-friend Nosha to learn things you didn't even believe in because you thought you'd seen me in a club. I don't doubt you're here or that you're real. Well, not usually."

"Hey, instead of worrying about the cause of the trip, just enjoy getting to see some of the local artistry, maybe get inspired for some new designs to ink on your customers, and just have a little fun. Now, come on before they decide we aren't going to go in and close on us."

Instead of replying, Cam chuckled, but he nodded before he turned and, once he'd checked traffic, darted across the street. When he reached the other sidewalk, he stopped and looked at the storefront. "You know, from the outside I wouldn't think to go in. It's just a plainish white building with a little red for a background where the name is in gold. The upper floors are edged kinda cute, but you said this is an artisan thing, right? I mean, it looks kinda stuffy."

"Plainish?"

"So -ish. Now answer me."

"Don't be a snob, Cam. You don't like when people misjudge you based on your tattoos, so don't prejudge what's inside because it doesn't look artsy enough for you on the outside."

The gasp that escaped Cam, mixed with the slight pink flush, told Liam Cam had received and understood his point. He hated when people prejudged and misjudged like that. Of course, he'd always thought Cam's tattoos were sexy, even though he still didn't have any of his own. He thought about it a lot lately, though. He had decided to get one, but then that had led him to meeting Cameron in real life and he'd never gotten around to getting inked.

Shaking off his thoughts of ink and Cam's hands on him before he ended up hard and not in the mood to be around people, he opened the front door and dragged Cameron inside. He loved how quickly the look of doubt was replaced with excitement and curiosity. Watching as Cam darted around from vendor to vendor let Liam know he'd made the right choice in choosing to bring Cameron there. He dutifully followed along, smiling at Cam's excitement for the local artwork. Of course, going to local artisan fairs probably wasn't unusual for the Georgia boy. Still, when Cam bolted into the handmade-soap shop and started debating which bars he needed to get for himself and for his sister—Liam wasn't even sure what some of the scents and scent mixes there were—Liam couldn't hold it in any longer and began laughing softly. He didn't want to embarrass or discourage Cameron, but it was like taking a little kid shopping instead of a thirty-year-old man. Still, he wouldn't have traded a moment of it for anything.

Liam allowed the distracted shopping for a little bit, but as the shops were near closing time, he wanted to move things along. "Cam, beautiful? We need to head over to the jewelry area if you still want something to wear for your token. We can come back for you to buy more stuff from the other vendors, I promise."

CHAPTER 18

"FINE, FINE. Take all the fun out of it." Honestly, after seeing everything else, Cameron was terribly curious about the jewelry. He couldn't wait to see what they had to offer. It didn't take long to find the right area. The vast store area contained various display cases, jewelers, craftsmen, and mini shops.

"Oh, Liam, look at this." Liam had wandered away and was currently staring at a wall case of various necklaces and chokers. Cam tugged on his arm and pulled him over to a display case full of cuffs of different kinds. While he'd balked when Raven had first mentioned a cuff, because of its connection to BDSM and collaring really, the idea had grown on him. He'd always thought they looked nice, just hadn't ever found the right one for him. Well, until now, maybe. "What do you think?"

Cam pointed to a cuff in the center of a long, dark wood tabletop and glass display case. It was made of distressed brown leather and had a tree at the center, which was made from an unusual sort of beaten metal as the center focus piece. He couldn't put his finger on why it seemed *different*, but it was and it… just seemed right for him somehow. The tree was fixed to the cuff so it would always be on the top. The cuff was wide enough that it had two buckles to clasp it together—both of which were silver in color, though they didn't look weathered like the tree did.

"That's hand-tooled leather and hand-beaten silver, sir," said a little wisp of a woman as she approached them from the side. "Would you like to try it on? Oh, and I'm Angelina by the way."

"Is it the kind of thing you're looking for, beautiful?" The look Liam gave him made Cam's heart hurt even as it made his hopes soar.

"Can I see it first, Angelina?"

"Sure thing, sweetie." She unlocked the case and carefully pulled the cuff out before she presented it to Cameron. "Which wrist you going to wear it on? I'm assuming not the one with all the tattoos. Don't want to cover up all that pretty ink, right?"

He grinned, thrilled that she liked his in-progress tattoo sleeve, especially since it was 100 percent his own design work—even if Bass had done a lot of the upper inking. "Exactly! Don't want to cover it, but I definitely want a cute little cuff like this. What kind of tree is it, by the way? I like the look of it, but I want to make sure it's not going to be the wrong fit that way too."

"That makes sense. As far as what it is, it would be a Celtic Tree of Life. Well, a stylized one, of course. If you notice, the roots are actually an alloy and have been deliberately tarnished while the trunk and the branches have been kept bright. The metal has been treated so it won't change over time."

Oh, that would be so perfect! Wonder if she'd alter it just a tiny bit....

"May I see it?" Liam asked, holding out his hand. "Please."

Cameron took another long look but then did as Liam asked. He turned back to Angelina as he debated how to make his request. "I do love the cuff, though I'll want to try it on before I decide if I want to buy or not. Of course, I'll have to get it back from Liam first to do that." He chuckled softly to himself, as did she. "Are you the craftsman or is that person here? Because I'd really like to have a slight alteration made to the design before I take it with me... if we decide to buy it, that is."

Angelina cocked her head to the side and frowned slightly. "What kind of alteration are you wanting to make, exactly?"

"Nothing major, I promise." He looked over to where Liam was still testing the cuff, then turned back to Angelina and bent down to make sure Liam wouldn't overhear him. "You see how it has little leather band pieces to hold the tree on? Well, at least in part. I was wondering if a couple of unique, at least to the item in question, charms could be added to that. I'd want a feather and well... something that represents dreams, if possible." He twisted enough to make sure his sleeve was exposed, then pointed to his tattoo through the mesh and winked.

Her face brightened, and the smile returned double what it had been before. "That would be very easy to do. I have plenty of charms of different types for the necklaces and bracelets and such that I make. You would just have to pick which ones you want, and I can add anything you needed of that kind. But—" She nibbled her bottom lip and seemed to stare at nothing for a moment. "—what would you use for sleep and why?"

Cam took a moment to look her over and noted her pentagram choker. He just hoped it meant in her case what he thought it did. He leaned just a little closer and lowered his voice a bit more before he said, "My partner's a dream walker, and I'd really like a way to represent him. It's a sort of weird complement to my tattoo sleeve really, which is mainly all him too."

"That's so sweet." Her eyes went wide, and the little sip of air she took made Cam smile. "Does he know Reverend Nosha?"

"That's his mentor," Cam replied as he nodded.

"What's this about Nosha? And does it have anything to do with Dianne?" Liam was directly behind Cam. He hadn't even heard Lee sneak up behind them. *Damn.*

"Nothing bad, sir. I was just asking if you knew Nosha, that's all. He said you were a dream walker. Wait, you know Dianne too?"

Cam couldn't help it, he started giggling so hard that had he been holding the cuff, he was pretty certain he would have dropped it. "I think we just found more of your coven people, Lee."

Angelina just nodded, her startled, wide-eyed gaze not changing one bit.

"Dianne is my aunt and best friend. I'm Liam" was all the explanation Liam gave, but the obvious realization dawning in Angelina's eyes indicated she knew exactly who Liam was already. It seemed strange to Cam, with how big the city of Asheville was, that they would run into people who knew Liam so easily through such a random event as going shopping. Not that he minded as long as she could fix up the cuff how he wanted, though. Still, it was weird.

"Oh my Goddess! You're that Liam and Cam! I know all about you two and the dreams and stuff. How wonderful to meet you. And of course I'll fix the cuff up however you want. You just go right on over, Cam, and pick whatever you need to make the cuff exactly how you need. Go on. Go on." She shooed him over to an area nearby where she had charms, pendants, and the like. She then took the cuff from Liam and headed directly back to a worktable at the edge of her shop area and began tinkering with the cuff while talking excitedly to herself—or so he assumed since it obviously wasn't to either one of them.

Liam only gave Cam a couple of minutes before he joined him. He wrapped one arm around Cam's waist but didn't say anything. He merely held Cameron as he continued sorting through the different items. There was a series of little charms that Cameron couldn't remember the names of but knew he'd seen before. Something about ancient Celtic writing or divination or something. But they caught his attention nonetheless. "Angelina? Can I borrow you for a sec?"

She set the cuff and pair of funky pliers-like things down, then came over to where Cam and Liam were. "Sure, what do you need?" Angelina looked at what he had in his hand and smiled. "If you really want one of those—do you even know what those are?—you'd want the one for *Ur*. It's the one that looks like a line with three evenly spaced horizontal hash lines through it. Its tree is heather, and its meanings are dreams, romance, and feelings, mainly. I mean, that is what you're going for, right?"

"Um, well yeah, actually… that sounds about perfect. Can that be added?"

"What are you having her do to your cuff, beautiful?" Liam looked back and forth between Cameron and Angelina, his brows pulled together and a slight frown on his face. "And why are you messing with oghams?"

He snapped his fingers. *That's their name!* Cam grinned but then sobered. "I'm not. I just wanted something that represented dreams. Well, that represented you, really." He turned back to Angelina and asked, "How long will it take you to fix it? Can you attach it all tonight, or will I need to come back?"

"It's a real simple fix, sweetie. Give me ten minutes and you can have it back, then you and your partner here can take your new cuff for a spin."

Cam was so excited that by the time he had the cuff on and Liam had paid for it, he didn't even notice that Angelina charged less than the price tag, even before the additions. That didn't register until they were at dinner over an hour later.

"It was really nice of your new friend to give you the discount she gives to her coven members just because you brought up Nosha and Dianne. I tried to tell her we weren't actually members, but she said that I was sorta since I was a student of her priest and all. But you know, you didn't have to have things added just to represent what I am to it. Though… it does look fantastic on you."

Cam only half paid attention to the compliment at the end, as he was too busy with the initial information. "She did? Why'd you let her do that?"

"Yeah, and because she insisted, beautiful. What was I supposed to do, argue with her with other customers nearby to make me pay more while you were bouncing around on cloud nine?"

"Well, no, but if you aren't really a member...." Cam knew he was frowning, but he couldn't help it. "Um, not to nitpick, hon, but why aren't you? I mean, you train with him, you do ritual and circle stuff with him, you dream walk and all. Why aren't you actually a member of that coven or grove or whatever they are?" He'd not thought about it until then really, but it seemed odd to him that Liam would learn and train and talk about possibly learning to use his energy and ability to heal somehow—not that Cameron understood how that all worked—but that he didn't join the coven or the faith. There was something he was obviously missing—not that he knew what, though.

"I was raised agnostic, well, atheist really. My grandparents were pagan, Wiccan really, just like Dianne is. But my mom rejected that as false and later married a man that felt the same way. For a long time, I guess I figured there was something out there but didn't give it much thought beyond that and never really paid Di much mind. Well, not when it came to religion. Her gods and goddesses were no more real to me than the Christian god was. It was all just stories and make-believe."

"But you said you'd talked to a spirit guide and you'd worked with some kind of guiding spirit or energy. That you felt stuff when Nosha or you called quarters or circle, right? So then.... Sorry, I guess I don't get how you can practice parts of a spiritual path without embracing the rest of the path."

The waiter saved Liam from having to reply by bringing their meals just then. *Mmm.... Grilled shrimp skewers with garlic asparagus and roasted potatoes and carrots on the side. So good!* Cam looked over at Liam's plate, but the beef tips with mushroom gravy over peppers, steamed broccoli, julienned orange, yellow, and purple carrots, and button portabella mushrooms just didn't look quite as good as his food did. Though he figured Liam probably thought the same only in reverse.

He let Liam get a couple of bites in—A1 sauce added, of course—before he prompted him. "Lee?"

Liam sighed and set down his fork. "It's nothing Di hasn't said a million times recently to me already, Cam. Joining a coven isn't a quick or simple thing. It takes a long time and a lot of study. Well, if I want to be formally initiated into it, that is. I'm still finding my way spiritually, but do I believe in the gods and goddesses, the spirit guides and ancestors? Yes. Kind of hard not to now. But since you're not Wiccan, isn't this a strange argument for you to be having with me?"

"Not really. I believe that whatever you do, you should do it fully. Be what you really are or don't do it at all, right?"

"Well, yeah, but I wasn't really sure how much of the spiritual part of this you were okay with. I'm glad you're not going to be upset if I do decide to study and join."

"If that's what you decide to do, then I'll support you. Don't think I won't." The idea Liam would hold back on his account was too weird. No one had even cared that much about what he thought or believed before. "But only do it if it's what's right for you. I wanted you to train with him because you were so lost and hurting. That sad, angry, scared, drunk man Dianne convinced me to have dinner with was not someone I could ignore. If Nosha could help you, then of course I was going to encourage you to go to him. But if that's changed.... Or if it's not changed...." Cam paused, not sure if he was making any sense. "You get my point?"

"Yeah, Cameron, I do. Do what's right for me now, not what I think you or Dianne or Nosha want me to do."

"Good. Now dig in before it gets cold."

As they ate and chatted, Cam couldn't help but stop every so often to look over his cuff with the feather and ogham added. He decided to talk to Dianne, and maybe Nosha, not that he knew the man, and to maybe add one or two of the ogham symbols into the sleeve on his other arm. There was a lot he needed to find out about that first, though, as he wasn't about to put letters that were also magical symbols onto his flesh without a lot of thought and research beforehand.

Eventually, they made their way back to Liam's apartment and tumbled into bed together. And even though he was a tiny bit sore, Cam urged Liam on in every way he could until they both toppled over the edge of pleasure together, spent and exhausted, and he drifted to sleep with his head on Liam's chest and his arms draped around Liam.

Well, until sometime very early in the morning, before the black had even begun to lighten to grayish-indigo, when Liam began thrashing and screaming hard enough to not only wake Cameron but to land him on the floor next to the bed.

CHAPTER 19

THE SWIRLING darkness seemed to seethe and pulse around Liam as he tried to find his way out. He didn't know how he'd landed in this nightmare. He'd intended to visit Dianne, actually, but instead he wound up…. Well, he didn't really know where he was, which was a state of things he liked less and less with every second that passed. The fact he couldn't simply will himself out or to wake up was alarming, but that he couldn't even figure out where *here* was, was even more so.

The other thing that had him worried was that the dark felt as if it were watching him. Not that he could figure out why. Sadly, that didn't change the sense of dread welling up inside.

He tried to will his nerves to behave as he continued to attempt to use the skills he'd been practicing all this time with Nosha. Unfortunately, the darkness only seemed to get thicker and the pulsing only increased in strength and speed, as if it were a rising heart rate.

Something brushed his right arm, but when he spun around, nothing was there as far as he could tell. Again he was bumped, this time on his left calf, and again nothing was there. This continued until he was so disoriented and panicked, the pulse so fast it was almost a strobe only without light, he felt certain he would have a heart attack inside the dream and die if he didn't escape. The fact people claimed you always woke before you would actually die did nothing to help just then, as he knew more than most about how dreams worked and how you could actually be hurt and killed while within one.

The pain that blossomed just after that thought terrified him. Who the hell had trapped him? And what did they want? He was now certain someone was truly out to hurt him. He had not accidentally stumbled into someone's nightmare and gotten himself caught within it.

"Release me," he demanded, doing his best to keep his voice steady.

"Interloper." Searing pain as he felt wetness slowly trickle down his left cheek. "You have no right!" Another slam to his right shoulder, this time not a shove or a thump, but a bone-jarring hit that he was afraid to see the bruises left behind by. "I'll teach you to try to take my place!" With each increasingly insane rant, he was hit with new pain and injuries.

Liam tried to fight back, tried to get out of the dream, but he didn't know how. He couldn't wake up!

Until he did.

That was as confusing and painful as the rest had been, though, so right at first he wasn't sure he really was out of the nightmare.

"Liam," Dianne yelled into his face as Cameron held his arms down and Nosha knelt to the side, his eyes closed, his face pinched in what appeared to be pain. "Stop."

"Stop fighting us, baby. Please," Cam added over her. "Please."

He did as they ordered, his body going slack as he collapsed back on the bed. It was then he realized how painfully bright the lights were and how much his body still hurt. "Hurts," he slurred.

"I know it does, Lee." Cameron sat beside him, only wearing a loose pair of sleep pants—a pair of Liam's, actually—and draped the sheet over Liam enough to cover his bits. Unfortunately, even that caused pain. "Dianne. We need to take him to the hospital, not that I know how we're going to explain his injuries to anyone without us all landing in jail and him out at Mission Copestone.

"I'll call Dr. Aisling. She's one of our members, so she'll understand better than anyone else when we explain what just happened. Of course," Dianne continued as she turned and looked over to Nosha—Liam couldn't seem to do more than follow along with what they were saying. He hurt too much and was far too confused. "I have no idea what to tell her just happened."

Nosha frowned, then opened his eyes and blinked a few times. "I'm not sure who, but someone built a dream trap, well, a nightmare trap really, and used it to beat Liam half to death before Cameron here could get to us. Thank the Goddess he thought to call you so fast." Nosha shook his head and blinked hard again. "Nasty piece of evil it was too. I'm sorry it took us so long to get you out, my boy."

Liam reached up to touch his face where he knew there had been a bad cut in the dream, but Cam caught his wrist. "Don't touch it, hon. Dianne? Please. Hospital or your doctor witch, I don't care, but he needs care. Just *do something*."

"He's right, Di," Nosha added as he stood and joined them.

She sighed but finally pulled out her phone as she stepped away. A moment later her muffled voice was all Liam heard from her as she paced in the next room.

"Liam?" Nosha said.

He slowly turned his head as Cam hovered. He didn't seem to know where to touch, but Liam didn't know where was safe, either. He hurt everywhere all at once.

"Yesh?"

"I don't know who attacked you or why, but with your permission, I will put up protections to make sure nothing like this can happen again. Also, protective and defensive work obviously need to be added to your weaving skills. I hate that someone has perverted dream weaving and done this to you!"

"Hey," Liam forced out, not liking the anger and hurt in both Nosha's voice and face. "Not your fault. Bad people are not your responsibility."

"No, but you're one of mine, so I take it personal that someone attacked you. Did they say anything we could use to find them?"

"Don't know." He explained to Cam and Nosha what had been said, but it hadn't made sense to him, and Nosha didn't immediately jump up and announce any names, so he figured that was a dead end.

"Right now, I am much more interested in this damn doctor than in finding who did it. You," Cam snapped at Nosha. "Don't care if you're the damned pope, go make this place safe for him. And Dianne," he suddenly bellowed. "Where the fuck is the doctor?"

Just then the doorbell rang, and if Liam thought he could have laughed at Cam and not hurt worse, he would have.

"Right the fuck here," she snarled back, and a moment later Dianne led in a tall redheaded woman who looked more like she should be at a club than standing at his bedside ready to doctor him.

"I thought it was me who was supposed to have the bad bedside manner?" Dr. Aisling said." Now why don't you go be useful, Di, and take the two men with you so I can do what I need to without the three of you in the way?"

Nosha immediately got up and headed out the bedroom door with Dianne in tow. Cameron, however, didn't move an inch. "I'm not going anywhere, so don't ask again, lady."

She sighed but then nodded. "You're the partner, right?"

"Yeah. Cameron, and this is Liam."

"Got it. Fine. You can stay. Don't suppose you want to play nurse? I could use a helper, really." Once that was decided, to Liam's relief as he didn't want to be alone with a stranger just then, he relaxed and let her do her thing.

Unfortunately, things like the cut on his cheek required surgical glue—she told him it would scar less than stitches but that he needed something for a cut that bad. A lot of the other injuries were just bad bruises and some abrasions. And while he'd known dream injuries could translate to real-world ones… it hadn't been all that "real" to him until then. It was one lesson he'd have been happy to have never received.

"So this all happened in the dream?"

"Yeah, some kind of nightmare trap, Nosha said." She'd given him something for pain, and while he was a little loopy, it wasn't all that bad. "I don't know what I did to piss whoever this is off, though, and I hope never to gain their notice again. But… um… have you ever treated someone for dream injuries before?"

"I've heard a few doctors say drunks or druggies complain of such things sometimes. Once, I knew of someone being sent for a psych referral over something like this. But no, I've never personally treated anything like this that wasn't a mugging or domestic abuse case. Personally, I hope not to. I prefer the abuser to be someone you can call the cops on and have them go and pick the asshat up. We can't exactly do that in this case, even if we knew who it was. But, make no mistake, you are the victim of abuse or battery or however you want to think of it. Someone broke into your home and attacked you. The fact they did it via dreams makes it even more insidious, not less."

"I…."

"Have to agree," Cam said when Liam couldn't think of anything to say. He knew he felt as though his home had been violated, and he worried about what they could have done to Cam if they were capable of doing something like this to him. He also worried about them going after Cameron next and a million other things, none of which he could know the answers to. "Nosha is making it safe for you to sleep, and I'll be right here to make sure that if something were to happen, that they get called again so they can fix it again. I can't do whatever he did, but I can speed-dial like a mother!"

Dr. Aisling giggled, then patted Cam on the head even though he thought she couldn't be but maybe in her early forties at the most. "I'll give you all the instructions, as he'll probably forget by the time he sleeps off the meds."

"Hey, I'm all right."

She smiled and nodded. "You will be, but pain meds tend to make people's memories a little like swiss cheese, so humor me if I want to tell your cute partner here all about checking on you and making sure you do okay."

"Oh, be that way. But, um, will everything really heal okay?"

"You'll be right as rain in just a few days, hon. Don't worry. I'd be more worried if I were the person that did this if I were you. The whole coven is going to want their head for this. We don't take kindly to those who hurt our own."

"Told you they claimed you," Cam teased as he took Liam's hand. Dr. Aisling had assured them the hand was only bruised, that nothing was broken or even sprained.

"We do. I know you've been training with Nosha, but eventually, you're going to have to start attending things with the rest of us. Di and Nosha can't keep you all to themselves."

"This will make more sense eventually, I hope. How you can be so sure I'll join when I've not been is beyond me, but thank you so much for helping tonight. I'm sorry for Di calling you out like this."

"I'll check on you later today, Liam. For now, rest. I know that will be hard, but try. And Cameron, don't forget to do all the things we talked about. I'm going to check on them and make sure everything's in place before I go home and crash. I was actually on my way there when she called."

Moments later it was just the two of them again. "I was so scared, baby. I didn't know what to do."

"You did fine, it seems. Just, don't leave." *Ever.*

"I won't."

Nosha poked his head inside the bedroom. "I've warded the whole apartment, so it's fine for you to sleep, Liam. I'm going to stay out on the couch too, just as an added precaution so you can sleep. Know you're safe, okay? Both of you."

Liam couldn't talk for a moment, truly touched Nosha would be willing to even stay just to make him feel safer. When he could, he managed to choke out a small thank-you. It wasn't much longer until the mix of meds, injuries, and everything else caught up with him and he dozed off, Cam sitting up with his back against the headboard and Liam's head on his chest for a change.

CAM STOOD in the middle of Liam's kitchen sipping his coffee as he debated whether he wanted to make something to eat or just grab something via the drive-through. Or if he could even stomach anything after the events of early that morning.

"You need to eat something, you know."

He turned to find Dianne in the doorway dressed in a nice business skirt-suit and low heels. It wasn't what she'd had on when she'd arrived after he'd called her in a panic. No, after he'd woken up on the floor with Liam screaming and flailing, Cam had tried to wake him. Unfortunately, that hadn't worked so well. Cam had a black eye and a sore spot or three for his effort. So instead he had done the only thing he could think to do: he'd swiped Liam's cell and called Dianne for help.

"If you don't eat and don't sleep, how will you work and be safe for your customers that trust their skin to your hands, and then come back here and take care of Liam?"

"I'm more worried about his bookstore and about him right now. Both the attack and his healing. He didn't sleep well, though I know that was the pain and such, not another attack, but it still worries me." What would happen when Dianne and Nosha left? Would the person try again? And even if they didn't, how would Liam feel about his abilities now? Cam didn't want Liam to go back to hating his dream walking. The scary drinking was not a place he wanted Liam to ever go again!

"Liam's store will run as always, just without him there, don't you worry. I won't let it stay closed just because he's out for a few days. And someone will be with him from now until he's better and we know more. Honestly, I think you should stay here for now too." Cameron opened his mouth to argue, but she held up a hand and talked right over him. "Not that I believe for a moment that you would leave him alone given what just happened, but I'm not sure if they wouldn't go after you since we don't know what's really going on yet. Nosha's sleeping right now, but when he's up, he's going to do some digging and see what he can find out. We won't quit 'til Liam is safe again."

She scowled up at him hard. "And whoever's doing this better hope it's Nosha that finds them and not me. I'm not sure I'll remember the 'an it harm none' rule right about now."

"They better hope it's not me, either," Cameron grumbled. He knew about the Rede she mentioned, and while he liked it, right then he wanted nothing to do with the concept. Anyone who would trap his lover, hurt him in both dream and waking, and would leave him bloody, bruised, and shaken... yeah, they better hope it was Nosha who would deal with them, because Cam was pretty sure he would end up in prison right then if he found the culprit.

"You two need to get to work and stop plotting the death of someone you don't even know," Nosha grumbled as he thumped into the kitchen. For such a thin man, he could make a lot of noise when he walked.

"I have every right." Cam glared at Nosha, daring him to argue.

"As do I," Dianne added, hands on her hips as she stood next to Cam.

"I'm not arguing with either of you, but what Liam needs is positivity, not negativity in his space. And while Cameron may not know better, you do, Di."

She shifted, her shoulders drooping as her hands slid down to dangle at her sides. "Sorry, but.... You saw the same thing I did, Noshie. They could have killed him." Her voice tore at Cam, not that he hadn't thought the same more than once since it had all started. "And he's not just my friend, he's my nephew. My family."

"I know, Di, but he needs support, positive energy, and love, not anger and negativity. Actually, right now he needs you to get whoever you have on call to run the store so he doesn't have to worry while he heals, and Cameron here needs to get to work. And before you argue with me, Cameron, if he thinks this is damaging your life, it will make things harder on him. The drinking should have shown you what he's willing to do to protect you, misguided and stupid as it was."

He didn't like it, but he knew Nosha was right. *Dammit!* "Fine. I'll head out, but only if you promise someone will be here with him at all times. He's in no condition to be alone right now. I wish we could have taken him to the hospital, but...."

"I promise I'll still be here when you return later. I have some calls to make and some checking around to do to see if I can't track down who is behind this. But for now, go, both of you."

It didn't take long to gather his things, so he was ready quickly, but not as fast as Dianne, who stood waiting at the front door for him with her purse, a laptop bag, and a sour expression on her face.

"What?"

"I just don't like being managed." She sighed but then pasted on a small smile. "But since it's usually me doing that to others, I guess I'll live. Come on. You can walk me out."

"'Kay." As they exited the building, he finally asked, "By the way, where did all your clothes and stuff come from? You didn't have all that with you when you got here."

Dianne giggled, her smile hitting her eyes for the first time that day. "I called a friend to stop by my place and pick some stuff up for me. One day you'll get to meet everyone, don't worry. For now, have a safe day and be careful out there, sweetie."

"You too, hon."

The one warm spot—which he clung to with both hands—was how she seemed so sure he'd be a permanent fixture in Liam's life. Now if they could never have a repeat of the previous night. It wasn't until later that it dawned on him that he could have called in, and he wondered why no one thought of it. By then he was in the middle of a tattoo on a biker's back, so he couldn't cut out. Then he determined that as soon as he could clear his schedule, he would be back with Liam and stay there.

CHAPTER 20

LIAM SAT on his couch, his elbows resting on his knees and his chin sitting lightly on his hands. His cheek hurt a little, but the pain wasn't nearly what it had been, though he figured that was mostly the über-strength ibuprofen and the sleep. Waking when Cam got up for work hadn't been too bad, and he'd quickly fallen back to sleep, the bed soft, warm, and still smelling of Cam. But now he was up, and Nosha sat in the overstuffed chair directly across from him, intent on figuring out what had happened. The problem was…

"I have no clue what happened. It was dark and it seemed like the dark pulsed. Whoever controlled it was angry and blamed me for the loss of something. I have no clue what, though. I mean, what the hell have I ever taken from anyone? Oh right, *nothing*!"

"Hey, calm down," Nosha said, his voice annoying in how quiet and low it was. Why couldn't the man have the decency to be irate too? "Anger won't help here, and am I really who you're upset with?"

Dammit! "No, sorry. I hurt and that scared the life out of me. And… I saw the bruises on Cam before he left this morning. I did that to him, didn't I?" he managed to force out, though how Nosha heard him, he wasn't sure. He'd barely heard himself. Liam had seen the black eye on Cam, and there was only one way he could imagine it getting there since last night.

"No, Liam, you didn't. The fault for that lies at the feet of the person that hurt you. We just need to figure out who that is. I couldn't trace it last night. It was hard enough to get you out and then to deal with the real-life aftermath. I couldn't chase them down on the dream plane. I'm sorry."

"Not your fault. I just—"

"Want that to never happen again?"

"Yeah," he grumbled, then sighed. "Why couldn't I get out? I mean, I did everything you taught me, but nothing worked."

"Liam, you've been dream walking and to a point dream weaving since you were a teen. But, and it's a huge one here, you only just started studying and training to use your abilities. If you were a martial artist and had dabbled in scrapping and such but only just begun formal karate or jujitsu training and then wound up set upon by someone with a black belt and lost, would you be surprised? Or would you realize it was logical that you lost because of the difference in ability?"

"Well yeah, but this isn't combat training."

"Sometimes it is. And energy can be used to heal, to divine, to help, or, like in this case, to harm."

"Then teach me to fight back, to defend myself, to be able to stop whoever this is. Please." He never wanted to go through that again, but even more, he never wanted to put Cam through anything like the night before again. But he also wasn't willing to give Cameron up. He'd finally found the other half of his heart and soul. He was sure of it! No way was some nightmare asshole going to take that from him.

Nosha agreed, though he didn't seem overly happy about it. Thankfully, Cam arrived home shortly after, and his attempts at nursing were sweet and involved a lot of things Liam was sure would not be approved by any doctor or nursing-review board.

Over the next week things at home were good. Cam slept over every night, only running home before work to shower and change. No more nightmares or injuries happened. Unfortunately, that couldn't be said for when Liam strayed from his apartment.

After two days, he was stir-crazy and demanded Dianne get out of his way and let him get back to work. The temp she had helping at his store could stay, but he could run the register and talk to his own damn customers *thank you oh so very much! Ugh....* However, on the third day back, when he went into the back of the store to work on the books and dozed off, he woke screaming and with a few new bruises and a small cut above his left brow. A little butterfly bandage was all it needed, but that wasn't the point as far as anyone seemed to want to tell him. Again and again and again.

This happened a total of three times, where he drifted for a few moments and wound up injured and screaming, though not trapped, thankfully. But his patience was nearly gone, he was jumping at everything, and everyone was starting to look suspicious to him.

"CAM... CAM... Cameron!"

Cam jerked away from the blow to his right cheek at the same time he felt fingernails gouge down his left forearm with what burned like fire in their wake. The next thing he knew he was sprawled on the floor of his workroom at the Indigo Dragon with Bass and Jason standing over him, Jason looking more than a little pale.

"Cammy?"

"What the hell?" Cam groaned and he tried to focus and figure out what happened. He'd been working on a new tat design for a customer and then he was.... Where had he been? He couldn't remember what had happened, just that he'd been terrified of... something and that he'd been hurt. Actually, he still hurt, if he was honest.

"Um, Bass, we need to tend to the bleeding," Jason mumbled then darted out of the room.

"Bleeding?"

"Yeah, your arm's bleeding, Cam. Let's get you upright and figure out how bad you're hurt."

Cam nodded, but his head still felt as though it was filled with cotton. Bass helped him into a sitting position against the wall—no way was he going to try to sit in a chair or on his stool right then, figuring he'd probably just wind up on the floor again if he tried.

Jason came back as he settled with the shop's first aid kit, which was actually a huge medical rolling unit. Considering they did tattoos and body piercings, they had more than just Band-Aids and aspirin in their stock. As Cam took in his bloodied arm, he only managed to become more confused, though. He reached out to touch the bloodied streaks, but Bass caught his arm and held him.

"Uh-uh. Let me get this cleaned up. You know we can't have blood just lying around like this. I need to treat you, then we have to sterilize your area. You'll need to have them properly seen to too. We can't have health code violations and you know it."

Yeah, the last thing any of them needed was someone getting pissy and trying to claim Bass wasn't protecting the customers, especially since Cam was known to be gay. He was neurotically careful, tested regularly, had the papers to prove it—as did Bass—but his blood was on the floor, the drafting table, the stool, his pants, and now on Bass too. Yeah, he'd have to go in for testing again, at the very least, just for appearances if nothing else. God how he hated stupid prejudice and assumptions.

"I'll go by the clinic today, all right?"

"Fine, but what the hell happened?" Bass didn't pause in his cleaning and care of the four gouge wounds down Cam's arm. "It kinda looks like someone tried to rip your new wrist cuff off and took your skin instead, but you were screaming and whimpering in some dream, not out fighting with someone. What happened?"

Cam closed his eyes and tried to focus on the nightmare they'd woken him from. He vaguely remembered someone yelling at him, but not the words. There had been something on his wrist where his cuff normally was, but in the dream, it wasn't the same. What was it…? "I don't remember. There was something on my arm someone wanted to take from me and then you woke me. Thank you, by the way."

"Um, dreams can't really hurt you," Jason said from beside Bass.

Without thinking, Cam starting laughing though there was no humor in it. "If only you knew, Jason. If only you knew."

Bass and Jason both looked at Cameron askance but shrugged after a moment. Bass looked up at Jason and said, "Could you go get Cam's day planner and see about clearing his schedule. We need to have him properly looked out. I can butterfly these okay, but one of these is pretty deep and I think needs to be looked at professionally."

It didn't take long for Jason to leave, Cam's book clutched in his hands.

"Well, you got rid of him, what did you want to say to me?" Cam knew there was more to it than just the rescheduling of his appointments, though one of the gouges really didn't want to stop bleeding, continuing to seep even with the butterfly bandage and pressure.

"Don't bullshit me, Cammy. Are you saying you were hurt in the dream and it really hurt you out here?"

He debated answering but knew if he lied Bass wouldn't likely forgive him. Not with how he was staring him down right them, almost daring him to lie.

"Don't ask me to explain, because I can't really, but yes. That's exactly what I'm saying. There was a shield thingy on my wrist where my cuff normally is that… someone… tried to take but I can't remember anything else. Right now I really need to get the one cut tended too and then go talk to Reverend Nosha and Liam. I promise I'll explain better if I ever understand myself."

Bass nodded slowly. "Okay. Let's get this wrapped and then you can go to outpatient, but I'm holding you to that explanation later."

"Thanks, Bass."

By the time Cameron made it back to Liam's he was exhausted. They'd used surgical glue like the doctor lady had on Liam's cheek, and they had taken blood for testing since he'd bled all over work and his boss. Bass hadn't mentioned the bruises, and though Cam obviously had a bruised cheek, Bass hadn't called him on it. It surprised him. Cam chalked it up to Bass being distracted by the blood.

When Cam walked into the living room, Liam and Nosha were the only two there, thankfully. He raised his left hand and gave a brief wave, not thinking about the bandage wrapped around his arm.

"What the hell, Cam?" Liam jumped up from the couch and hurried over.

"Calm down, hon. Actually, I'm kinda glad it's the two of you here as I wanted to talk to the both of you about what happened."

"Why?" Nosha asked as Liam pulled Cam into his arms and held on tight. "What's going on that requires you to be bandaged?"

"Lee? Can you let go long enough for us to settle on the couch? I'll explain it all then, I promise."

Liam grumbled under his breath but complied. Once they were all sitting, Liam again asked what was going on, and that time, Cam explained everything he remembered: the pain, the yelling, the weird glowing treelike shield thingy where his cuff should have been. The fact he couldn't remember anything else frustrated him more than it did Nosha or Liam, though, it seemed. They began talking about dream constructs and energy things and he wasn't sure what all else. It made no sense to him.

"Um, guys… much as I love listening to you two babble—and since I don't know half of what you just said… yeah, babble—could you please make some sense to the non–dream walker in the room? Please?"

Nosha gave a deep chuckle as Lee huffed and turned back to face Cameron.

"Sorry, Cam." Nosha shrugged. "Before I explain, could I see your cuff a moment? I promise to give it right back."

"It's a good thing, I think, Cam. Please?" Liam turned his big beautiful gaze on Cam and before he thought about it, he'd unbuckled the cuff and handed it over. What wouldn't he do for Lee?

Nosha closed his eyes and hummed, seeming to go into some kind of trance. Cam wasn't sure what he was doing but when he turned to ask Liam, Lee put his fingers to Cam's lips and shook his head, mouthing *quiet*. Not knowing what else to do, Cam sat quietly and waited.

Cam felt odd without his cuff, even though Lee had only just gotten it for him. Still, any time he got to cuddle with his man was good with him, even if it did begin with a nightmare. Thankfully, it didn't take long for Nosha to do whatever he was doing.

"I'm not sure how you did it, Liam, but you turned Cameron's cuff into a protection charm on the dream plane." Nosha turned the cuff over again before he shook his head. He handed it back and Cam put it back on as Nosha continued talking. "Honestly, whoever did this, had to have expended a huge amount of energy to have hurt you, Cam, to have gotten past the charm enough to leave the bruises and the cuts. I don't want to imagine what would have happened if you hadn't had it. Maybe once all this calms down, we can teach you to use the charm correctly, Cam. For right now, though, I think figuring out who's doing this is even more important. The attacks aren't only coming at Liam now, they're coming at you too, and you're not a walker, much less a dream weaver."

"I—"

"And before you say it, Cam," Liam said right over his objection. "In dreams, you don't know how to take control, much less fight."

Cam slumped back against the couch. "Fine, but I don't like it. I'm not some helpless damsel in distress."

"No, you're his partner who was just assaulted by a monster on a plane that you don't have the ability to fight on. Don't let your pride get him or you injured." Nosha squinted at Cam then asked, "If it had to do with art or tattooing, would you let him do it?"

Cam stared at Nosha, wondering if the man had lost his mind. "What do you mean?"

"If what we needed right now was someone to draw and then ink a tattoo on someone, would you let Liam do it? Trust him to permanently modify someone's body like that?"

His snort slipped out before he thought to stop it. "Of course not. Love him dearly, but no way would I let him ink someone! He's a scholar and a dream guy, *not* a tattoo artist."

"Exactly my point. We each have things we excel at, and things we leave others to do. This is one of those times. You need to leave the dream combat and figuring out how to find whoever is doing this to us. What he needs from you are your strength and love."

"He has that. He has since we were kids, really, even if we neither realized it at the time."

CAM PACED in his work room as he thought through his rather bizarre— in his own opinion—relationship with Lee. They had been together since he was fifteen, yet they'd only met in person since Cam had moved to Asheville. The issues with the dream walking and the attacks had Cam both scared and pissed off. How dare someone hurt his Liam! What if things like this kept happening? Would they ever be safe?

The worries and questions kept going round and round as Cam did laps in his work space. He wished the area were bigger. He'd been chewing on what Nosha had said to him and couldn't get the words out of his head. The idea that Lee would need him, that Nosha would doubt that Cam would be there to support Lee....

How much support was he, though, really? He was living with Liam, for now. He loved Lee, and he knew it was for the long haul. He was pretty certain that Liam felt the same and would stay with him. They'd been together all that time, always came back together even when they'd thought the other wasn't real, so staying together in the real, waking world had to be possible. Right? Not easy, necessarily, but possible.

Ugh! Why does figuring things out have to be so hard?

"Cam?" Bass asked, the door only cracked open enough to allow him to poke his head inside.

"Yeah?"

"You okay in here?"

Cam sighed. "Yeah. Just trying to figure some stuff out. I don't have anyone due yet. Did you need me?" *Please say no. Please say no.*

"No." Bass stepped inside and closed the door gently. "Look, you've seemed off lately. Happy, but worried, and then there are other *things* that are odd. If something's up, you know you can talk to me, right?"

"I know, and I still need to explain a shit ton of stuff to you, I know. But not yet, okay?"

"Fine, for now. But what's got you wearing a hole in the floor tonight?"

Cam looked at Bass hard for a moment before he stared at his scuffed shoes. "How do you know when to make something permanent? That it's more than enough and that scary is okay?"

Bass rumbled and stroked his beard for a few moments as he seemed to mull over his answer. Cameron wasn't going to push. He couldn't believe he'd even asked.

"If this is about your little scholar slash dream boyfriend, I think it's too late to ask about permanent, Cam. You tattooed him onto your body and he's worked his way into your life and heart. The real question is, can you handle the scary parts, the dream stuff and all? I can't see you letting that stop you from being with him. You're no quitter and not so delicate that a few bruises and scratches will scare you off." He held up his hands when Cam tried to argue about it being a few, considering it wasn't a fair attack. Wasn't like Cam could fight back! "If you love someone, you find a way. We men aren't supposed to talk about feelings and such, but it's that simple, really. You love him?"

"Very much so, yes."

"Then that's your answer."

"You're kinda scary."

Bass grinned wide. "You say the nicest things."

They both laughed as Cam thought about what he wanted to do next.

CAM NEVER faltered, never backed off, and the night after the last set of injuries Liam received, Cam showed up at Liam's with flowers, a bottle of wine, and a large box. Instead of coming in as he had been, he rang the bell and waited.

Liam stood in the doorway confused, but he smiled at Cameron. "Um, why are you out here, beautiful? Come inside."

"Because this is important, hon. These are for you." Cam handed over the dozen purple roses and smiled shyly. "I brought you that wine you liked the other night at the restaurant. The one you had with the beef tips you said were so good. And the chocolate divinity cake too."

Cake, wine, and flowers? Um, okay.... "And to what to do I owe all this?"

Liam took the flowers into the kitchen and searched until he found one of the vases Di had insisted he'd need and filled it partway with water. He then cut off the bottom tips of the stems and placed the flowers in the water. When he turned, Cam had set the cake and wine on the table. If anything, he seemed even shyer and more nervous.

"Love? What's going on?"

"Well, I wanted to ask you something, so I got you all this, but I don't think I'm doing this right. Maybe I should just wait and ask you later."

"Cameron, it's fine. Whatever it is, it's perfect because it's from you. Now, is it something to do with your sister? I know she and her husband arrive tomorrow. If you need to go back to your place, I'll understand."

"No! No, it's nothing like that. I mean, yeah, Sarah and Dan'll be here, but, um...."

"What is it, Cam? Just tell me." What could he want that had him so worried?

"You know how we met for real when you came into the shop because you wished to get a little tattoo to represent mine because of how you felt about me even though you thought I wasn't real?"

Liam nodded, not sure where Cam was going but happy he was at least talking. "Yeah, but I never did get that tattoo."

"Well, um... and you know how you've mentioned permanency and forever and keeping me and all?"

"Yes, Cam. I've told you. I'm not giving you back. You're stuck with me unless this"—Liam lightly traced the newest Band-Aid—"is too much for you and you really want out. I mean, I love you and want forever, but I would never make you stay."

"I know that. But that's not what I want. The out part, I mean. See, I told you I'd mess this all up."

"Cam, love, you've totally lost me. What is it you're trying to ask?"

"Marry me and let me tattoo that mini version of the wings on you as part of the bonding?" The words rushed out so fast it took a moment for Liam to decipher them, as they had started out as one long string of sounds, not separate words.

"Wait what? M-marry you?"

Cameron stared at Liam, his usually pale face draining of what little color it had as he twitched and bit his lip, hard. He nodded, but it was more a flop than anything.

"You want to marry me? Really? Even with all this mess going on?"

"I talked to Nosha, and he said he'd perform it if you said yes."

Well, he guessed that was a definite yes if Cam had already lined up the clergy. "Yes! When? And what does this have to do with your sister?"

"I want them at the wedding. They're my only real family, but we don't have to rush the wedding just because they'll be in town. Just, yes? Really? Yes?"

"Of course, yes!" Liam wrapped his arms around Cam tight and pulled him in, taking his lips in a kiss he was determined to make sure Cam never forgot. He licked and nibbled, sucked and sampled, and when their tongues met, the flavor that was uniquely Cam's nearly overwhelmed Liam as the love and want mixed with the *yes* ringing through his head.

"Excuse me," intruded a loud voice, one Liam didn't know, and being he was in his own kitchen with his... fiancé?... trying to climb inside him kiss first, he was less than amused.

Liam pulled back and spun to face the intruder, pushing Cam behind him. "Who the hell are you and why are you in my house?" he barked.

"Um," the man squeaked and took a step back. "I'm Drew."

"And you're in my kitchen why?"

"Di and Nosha asked me to stay with you? Um, until they got back to explain what they were setting up to help you."

The poor man's voice cracked half a dozen times and he stayed back across the room, looking as if he expected an attack from Liam any moment.

"Sorry, Drew. Things have just been a little, um, stressful, and then you interrupted something important."

"Very," Cam added with a snort.

"Yeah, I could tell, but I didn't think having your aunt and priest walk in on you having sex sounded like a good plan, so I just...."

"Thought to warn us," Cam finished for Drew. "We get it. But, um, how'd you get in? We didn't let you in."

Drew held up a key. "Dianne gave it to me. It's how all of us have been coming and going to help out since the attack on Liam. I was so sorry to hear about that, by the way," he said, looking back at Liam. "I don't know who would do that, but none of us will put up with it. Especially not when it happens to blood family of Dianne's."

"Why Dianne's blood relations, specifically?" Cam asked. "I mean, why's he so special to y'all?"

"Not blood that way. It's... we protect our own. Wouldn't you if it were your sister or perhaps someone she was very close to? Like how some churches have prayer circles or crisis trees. She's a member, a friend, part of our family. Therefore, Liam is part of that chain. Plus, he's Reverend Nosha's student, so he's sorta one of ours, anyway."

"Oh, huh." Cam looked from Drew to Liam and back. "Now you have to join them, hon." He giggled. "I mean, they already have the keys to your place, so why not, right?"

"Your logic seems flawed, beautiful, but we'll see. Right now, how about if we deal with Drew, talk about when to get married, and maybe find a way to stop these nightmare attacks? That's what would make life perfect."

"Yeah." Cam sighed and wrapped an arm around Liam's waist. "It would."

"Did I hear you say you're getting married?" Drew asked as they walked back to the living room.

"Yeah, Cam here just popped the question, and I, of course, said *yes*."

"Of course. So when? Where? What kind of service? How big?"

"Hey, hey, hey. We've had all of thirty seconds to figure this out. We don't know yet," Liam countered as Cam chuckled.

"I'm new here and I don't have much family, so it only has to be as big as Liam wants." Cam didn't let go even once they sat down. "I talked to your priest, so I'm guessing whatever Wiccans call a wedding is the kind. And, um...." Cam turned his big, silver eyes on Liam and blinked.

"Don't look at me like that. We could go down to the courthouse and get the license today if you wanted. As long and you and Di are there, and an officiant, I'll be happy. I just want to get to the 'I do' part." Liam grinned. "Because I really, really *do*."

"I'd recommend you wait 'til at least tomorrow." Drew flashed a wide grin. "They might frown on you showing up after they closed and demanding they issue it."

Cam sighed with his whole body and rolled his eyes. "If I must."

"Yeah, ya really should. But you could plan things in the meantime. I'm a caterer, so we could plan you a big party instead of a big wedding.

That way, the 'I do' part is personal, but you still get to do the eating-and-dancing part with everyone, right?"

That actually sounded about perfect to Liam. Once Cam was on board, the three men put their heads together and in no time had things planned. Drew started making calls and finally left Liam and Cam alone, though he was still in the apartment.

"What about the tattoo, beautiful?" Liam asked once they were mostly alone. "Will you do the work yourself? I don't like the idea of anyone else putting something so permanent on me."

"Of course. No one else is allowed to mark your skin ever again. Not if I can help it!" Cam touched the still-healing cuts so softly, it tickled slightly. "But do you really want the tattoo? I mean, you only wanted it because you though I wasn't real."

"Well, sort of. Remember, by that point I was mostly convinced you were real, but yes, I want it. And having it be a wedding present of sorts is perfect. I want a ring too, though. I've always wanted to be a husband, including rings. The fact I would have a husband instead of a wife never fazed me a bit. I want what my grandparents had, just with a guy. With my guy." He bent and took Cam's lips in a soft press, eventually shifting so his forehead rested against Cam's. "Will you wear my ring?"

"Only if you wear mine."

"Deal. You know, with all the talk of weddings, I almost forgot why Drew was here. But I can hear Dianne in the hall talking, which just reminds me again. And we still don't know what to do."

"Hey." Cam pulled Liam into a hug and held him tight for a few moments before he let go enough that he could meet Liam's gaze. "We'll figure it out, even if it takes time. They won't quit and neither will I. You're not alone, hon."

Not alone. No, that he wasn't. Not anymore. It was something he was still trying hard to come to terms with. Honestly, that was half of his hang-ups with joining Dianne's coven. He knew the deities and spirits were real. He knew magic and all was real—he wore the proof of when it was used for harm right then, in fact. But the idea of joining the coven-church-group made him nervous. What if they decided to turn on him like so many others had in his past? What if…? He knew it was probably stupid, but his past pains definitely colored his feelings in cases such as these.

However, their rallying around him like this put paid to his fears. He was pretty sure he not only ought to, but needed to... apply? He wasn't sure of the right way to do it, but he determined in that moment that he would find out and go through with whatever he needed to do. They had done more for him than his parents ever had. Only Di and her coven-slash-friends had ever rallied when he needed help.

CHAPTER 21

"IT'S PAT." Nosha spoke, but the name meant nothing to Liam, or from the blankness on Cameron's face, to him, either. However, the gasps from Dianne, Drew, and a few others in the room who they had met over the week—Kane, Jeb, Robbie, Matt, and Brittany—told him plenty. This was obviously a known and not beloved person. Of course, the bruises, cuts, and injuries Liam had suffered—and shared with Cam twice now—told him that much.

"What's that, and is this someone we can stop? I'm really sick of this crap and with it interfering with our lives. Cam and I want to get married, not have to constantly guard against the nightmare king wannabe."

"That's actually not a bad description, Liam," Nosha said. "We actually warlocked him about a year ago because he's a predator and abuser." More than one of those gathered shivered and crossed their arms over their chests when Nosha continued. "He used his abilities to hurt others. I did what I could to protect the others, inside the coven and outside it, from him, and when he moved away, I made sure to talk to the local covens in his new home base that I had contacts with before he turned on them and pulled a repeat of what he did here."

"And he decided to target me why?"

"He had a fascination with me. Not sexual as far as I know, but he had tried repeatedly to get me to train him, and I'd refused each time." Liam remembered Di mentioning that Nosha had had issues with someone who had wanted Nosha to train him, but no one had mentioned that the guy was that bad. No wonder Nosha had been so strict and grumpy about Liam proving he was serious and would use his ability the right way. "Before I knew what he was about, I always got a nasty feeling from him, so I said no. Later I was very glad for it. All I can guess is that he found out I'm training you and still holds a grudge for my refusal. If that's the case, I'm sorry. In Cam's case, I think he probably caught you dream sharing and figured out hurting Cam would hurt you."

"If that's the case, then he's a sick fuck," Cam countered. "Unfortunately this isn't the kind of thing we can go to the cops with, so how do we make him stop?"

"Binding," Di said, her voice strong as she stared at Nosha. Liam knew that look and was glad it wasn't turned on him.

"That's not something to be done lightly, Dianne. We can't just take someone's free will like that without just cause *and* without Karma debt."

"I know that, but it's time. You didn't do it before for those very reasons, but look at what he's doing to Liam. To Cam."

"Binding someone is not a simple thing or something to do—"

"We talked it all through before and decided not to. I agreed, as did all your inner council. Things have changed, and not just because Liam is my nephew. This has to stop. Plus, now you have another dream weaver so you can do it in a dream, so it will be more powerful on that plane." She looked down and swallowed hard before she looked up again slowly. "Please, Noshie. I'm afraid of what he'll do to Liam and Cam if this isn't stopped. Of what he will do to the next person."

Nosha looked at the others, but they all nodded along with Dianne. After a long moment, he seemed to fold in on himself as he nodded. "All right, Dianne." He then looked to Liam. "Will you agree to help? I'll walk you through it, but mainly what I'll need from you is for you to enter the waking-dream trance state you've practiced and link with me. With Pat being the aggressor, he may try to attack you or trick you into thinking you're not with me, but don't believe it. I won't let go. Even if you can't see me in the dream, you won't be alone."

"If it means stopping this psycho, then I'm in. I want my life back."

"What can I do to help?" Cam asked.

PLANS FOR the binding were mixed with the preparations for the handfasting—Liam and Cam had learned that was the proper name for a Wiccan wedding—and with Cam's sister Sarah and Dan's arrival, things were further complicated by the fact they couldn't tell Sarah and Dan about the dream attacks. Sarah knew a little about the dream walking and thought that was cool, but Cam was afraid she would either think Liam was crazy and dragging Cam into it, or that the dream stuff was too dangerous, and then she would want Cam away from Liam. Either way, it would be bad. So Cam juggled his sister, Liam, Liam's family-slash-coven, work, and wedding plans. And he had to prepare and finalize the design for Liam's tattoo, but Liam had done most of the work before they met in real life, so fleshing out the design and tidying it up wasn't that hard.

The fun part had been the actual inking. Liam had been a good sport about it, but Cam doubted that Liam would ever agree to another. Even though the tattoo was over muscle, not bone, Lee obviously hurt and hated the sensation and sound. However, when he'd seen the little version of Cam's back tattoo on his arm, the smile he'd given Cam made his heart hurt and his groin tighten. Cam had gotten the tat covered and then dropped to his knees and blown Lee right there, not caring if anyone heard. Thankfully, Bass hadn't noticed—or had chosen to ignore them for once.

Really, the wedding was the easy part. He needed the license, the grooms, the priest, the service decided on—they'd done that the night before—and the rings—they had picked them up the night before also, before going over to Nosha's. He loved the intricately engraved tree on each band. One band was gold, where the tree was inlaid in silver, and the other was a titanium band—Cam was hard on his hands, after all— with the tree inlaid in gold. They could be held together to make the Celtic Tree of Life.

"Cammy! You need to pay attention." Sarah stood in his bedroom, beside his made bed that hadn't been slept in in over a week, pointing to his closet and frowning. Well, at what had been his mostly filled closet, anyway; the contents were now mostly piled on the bed. "You don't own anything appropriate to get married in. Nothing!"

"I have lots of nice clothes, you Heffalump. And why the hell are all my clothes on my bed?"

"But not for a wedding," she explained, not answering his questions. "Men wear tuxes and such. Not club clothes or jeans or, hell, I'm not even sure what a few of those things are in there." She sniffed as she pointed at a pair of leggings. He was pretty sure she would completely lose it if he explained what else he owned that went along with them.

"Dan," Cam called, hoping for some support. He wasn't going to wear a damn monkey suit. He knew Liam wasn't, either, so Sarah needed to stop. "A little help in here, please."

"Oh no. You do not call for the hubby like he'll protect you or something." How a woman no bigger than she was could figuratively tower over him as she was doing, he never had figured out, but Sarah, unfortunately, excelled at it.

"Sarah, dial it down a notch. I think the neighbors back home can probably hear you. Now, why are you terrorizing Cam, and why are all his clothes on the bed?"

"Thank you!" Cam threw up his hands.

"Because he's getting married and doesn't own anything to do it in, *but* he doesn't want to go to the formal shop. Help."

He nearly whimpered as she batted her lashes up at Dan.

"But, love, did you ask him what kind of wedding it was yet? I mean, your brother just doesn't strike me as the super-formal type, even for a wedding. Not for his own." Dan turned and faced Cam as he slid one arm around Sarah's waist. "What's the theme or colors or whatever? That might help more than that mess there," he added with a nod to the pile of clothing.

Cameron sighed, thankful for Dan's influence on his sister. "Thanks, man. It's a small private handfasting. Silver and blue. And nothing formal. Liam said he didn't care if I was dressed any more formally than I would for a date. He just wanted me there. Which is about what I told him, by the way."

"Oh." Sarah sighed and stared up at Cam, the near panic gone from her face that fast. "Then why don't we get you something really nice but that still says 'you'? Not a tux, then, but maybe something more artistic. Maybe that would even show off your sleeve since it was inspired by your fascination and desire for Liam, even before you knew he was real."

"See, I like that idea. Plus, that means I can show off some of the cool, funky little shops tucked all over Asheville that I've found."

As they got ready to go out, Cam again looked at the mess on his bed and shook his head. He'd fix it later. Right then, he needed to shop and then get ready for the dream thingy that night. He still wasn't sure about that, either, but whatever it took to help and protect Liam was good with him.

Hours later, he had not one, but three new outfits, plus wedding-night attire—he was still certain it should be against the sibling code to have his sister take him to a sex shop to get naughties!—and outfits for both Sarah and Dan for the wedding and reception. He'd taken them out to dinner, and while they'd had a lot of fun, Cameron's nerves were about to fray if he didn't get back to Liam.

"Cammy? Why don't you go on and spend time with your guy tonight? Dan and I can entertain ourselves here. Don't worry." She pulled him down into a hug. "You're getting married tomorrow, but it's okay. You can go over now."

"Thanks."

"I know his coven is doing something special tonight for y'all. So go do whatever and have fun, 'kay?"

Fun? If only she knew. He pasted on a smile for her. "Will do, sissy. I'll be back in the morning, and then we'll meet up with him and his people for the handfasting."

"Sounds good."

Dan got out of the car, then grabbed Cam's bags as well as theirs. "I'll leave your bags on your bed."

"No, I'll hang it all up so there's no wrinkles. So, go have fun on your last night of freedom."

By the time he made it to Liam's, his stomach was a huge knot and he was sweating even though it wasn't hot out. The sight of so many extra people in Liam's place didn't help any. "Lee?"

"In here, beautiful," Liam said, appearing in the doorway to the dining room. He was in a pair of light sweatpants and a plain T-shirt. Simple, but on Liam, it managed to still look good. "Things go okay with your sister?"

"Yeah, it did. We have the shopping done. Finally. Um...." Cameron looked around at all the people again. "I know you were supposed to have a group over to help with this ritual thingy, but this many?"

Liam nodded and frowned slightly. "Yeah, I know. It's a lot, but Nosha and Di insist it's needed. Thirteen for the circle around us, plus Nosha, you, and me. I'm still not comfortable with you being part of this." Liam cupped Cam's cheek and traced his thumb back and forth against Cam's bottom lip. "I don't want you hurt again, beautiful."

"And I don't want you hurt. Nosha thinks having me with you will help you somehow. I won't claim to understand a damn thing other than I'm not letting you go through this without me. Now, what can I do? I want this over with so we can get married tomorrow without this hanging over our heads."

"Me too, baby. Me too."

"You two are so sweet you're going to give me cavities," said a bubbly voice behind them. "And it's a horrible thing for a dental hygienist to get those!"

Liam turned and smiled at the woman. "I would imagine. Bad form and all that. But since this is my fiancé, sweet is allowed." He beamed when he said *fiancé*, making Cam chuckle. Cam couldn't wait to see how Lee preened when he got to use *husband*. Of course, Cameron figured he'd been pretty horrible about it too.

"Well, then I guess it's allowed." She thrust out her hand. "It's good to meet you. I'm Mandy, and you *must* be Cameron. I've heard so much about you from Dianne."

"Di's been telling them since before we met how you were perfect for me and how I'd better not mess it up, it seems. I didn't even know these people, but it seems they all knew tons about me."

"Sounds like something my sister would do."

"Then she's a good sister," Mandy pronounced and smirked.

"She is. So, how's this work tonight?"

"Antsy to begin? Well, I've never helped with one of these, exactly, so I'll let Reverend Nosha do all the important talking. I just wanted to meet you. I know he said it was almost time to start and that we should all start getting into out meditative positions and make sure we're all grounded and centered. If you need help with that," she continued, looking at Cam, "I can help."

"It's okay. Nosha and I helped him practice last night. And I'll do so again tonight. But thank you."

Once it was just them, Liam bent and brushed his lips back and forth across Cam's lips again and again, the sensations one of comfort, not passion for once. "You ready, Cam?" he asked when he finally pulled back a little.

"For our future to begin? Yes. This is just one part, and we're not alone."

NOT ALONE. No, they weren't alone. Liam held Cam's hand as they walked into the living room, now devoid of its usual furniture. Instead, there was a circle of thirteen men and women sitting on the floor. Beyond them were candles and quartz points at the four quarters. The center was left open instead of having an altar as one would expect for a ritual. Liam hadn't been to any of their big holy day rituals, but he still knew how things worked. However, this time he knew that was where he, Cam, and Nosha were to be—holding hands as they went into the dream space together. Dianne also had ribbon and a few other things Liam didn't really understand that had to do with part of the binding, but he knew most of it would actually happen in the dream realm by breaking through the nightmare and taking back control. In that way, the attacker would be weakened for a time, and in that time Dianne would do the binding back in the waking world.

Liam had tried to follow it all, but it had gotten overly complicated and magicky, so he'd given up and focused on the part he had to do: break through the nightmare and not let Cameron get hurt in the process.

"Liam, Cameron, please take your places." Nosha stepped up behind them. "I know this is scary for you both, but we won't let anything happen to you. Either of you. And Cameron, thank you for wanting to help Liam like this."

"Of course I wish to help him."

Liam was torn between wanting to kiss the indignant look off Cam's face and hug him. "Thank you, beautiful."

"You two ready?" Nosha asked, ignoring Cam's outburst.

It didn't take long for everyone to be settled and things to be ready. Incense lit, candles burning, the thirteen chanted "Ohm" until the sound began to resonate through Liam, and he found himself sinking into his state of lucid dreaming or something similar. He wasn't quite sure, but this time felt different as he was aware of not only Nosha's presence, but of Cam's as well. The other thing he was aware of almost immediately was the wall of black magma at the edge of his area. His dream space didn't have the same spatial limits as his apartment, but for once it felt that definitive.

As he looked around, he noticed the large spirit panther and spirit eagle that often accompanied him since he'd gotten better at dream weaving thanks to Nosha. He wished his dream or spirit guide, Angus, was there, but he didn't see him. Not that he'd expected he would. Nosha had told him things like this were outside the purview of the guides to interfere in, so by rights, Angus would have to stay out of it. Still... he would have felt a lot better had the redheaded imp been there.

"You ready for the walls to drop?" Nosha's dream-self was the same as his conscious self, oddly. The only difference was the clothing.

But that was fine with Liam. He assumed that meant the man was just that comfortable in his own skin.

"As I'm going to be."

"Good man. Just don't forget. You don't need to protect Cameron. He is here to boost you, but he's in no real danger. He won't let go, nor will I, but he won't see or feel what we do. He's not a walker, much less a weaver. In this, it's a blessing for him."

"Right. Good. Okay...." Liam took a deep breath, even though he knew he probably wasn't really in his real body. "Let's deal with this. And Nosha? Thank you."

"Nothing to thank me for, but you're welcome."

A moment later, the barrier that had been keeping the black at bay fell, and the magma-like nightmare surged forward. Even as prepared as he'd thought he'd been, the cold desolation that wrapped around Liam stole his breath and clouded his thoughts within moments. Remembering how to combat the fear, the pain, the hollow despair that wasn't his own was beyond him. The twitch of fingers in the hand that held Cam's reminded him to fight and that he wasn't alone. That he could do this. That he had to.

Yanking at the threads of the nightmare surrounding him, he worked to unravel it. Just as he thought he'd gotten it, it morphed and changed, the threads slipping from his fingers. When that happened, a new pain surfaced and surrounded him. Instead of the nothingness, it morphed into his father's condescending tone and scowl as he again berated Liam for never working his way up in academia and "settling" for "working in" a bookstore. Liam had always dreamed of owning his own bookstore, of sharing the written word with others. He'd never wanted to be a professor or librarian like his father had demanded.

Beside Liam's father stood his mother. She took her turn snipping about how he was too like Dianne and his freakish grandparents. Her pinched faced twisted as she pointed out it was his failures and weaknesses that made men cheat on him and use him… and that it was his own fault. She'd told him that more than once. He remembered now.

No! This was all wrong. His parents were like that in many ways—which was why he had nothing to do with them if he could help it—but they weren't that bad, and it didn't matter. He had Dianne. He had Cameron. He had friends who cared about him for him, not for any other reason. And with that realization, he again broke free and began unraveling the magic used to trap and harm him—though so far, the only pains had been emotional, thankfully.

Things shifted and swirled, but then it was Cam lying broken at his feet, bloody and weeping, that drew his attention from his work with the threads of the dream around him. On the ground near Cam lay the cuff that Nosha had said was a protection charm, but it was torn in half and no longer doing its job, obviously.

Just then Cam lifted his head and cried out, "Please stop. It... hurts…. Please…." He twitched and fell to the ground in what resembled a seizure to Liam.

Liam was torn between fighting the strands of the dream weaver they were here to confront and stopping to help Cam. What if that was really Cam and he'd been pulled into the fight somehow?

"Cammy?"

"Please," he begged again. Cam stopped twitching and he turned his head enough to look up at Liam, but when he did, Liam found brown eyes. Brown? *No, that's wrong!* With that realization, he again managed to shake off the trap and knowing that this Pat person would not only hurt Cam but would mimic him within the nightmare fight only served to piss Liam off more. He channeled that energy into his fighting, determined to make things safe for Cam in the waking and sleep world.

This twisted type of attack—the ripping out of his fears and past pains and making them real before him—repeated four or five more times, with Liam sometimes seeing Nosha, yet at other times feeling as if he were completely alone until a vague sense, what he thought was Cam in the waking world, made its presence known. It helped keep him grounded and fighting no matter how he felt, what he saw, or how much he hurt.

Eventually, Liam heard a horrific scream and the nightmare he was currently battling unwound around him, the colors spinning out into a strange vague nothingness. Suddenly he was back where he had been in the dreamscape before Nosha had first released the shields he'd put up after the first attack.

Liam looked around, confused. Did that mean it had worked? Or had the asshole run?

"Nosha?"

"Ow," Nosha groaned. "Remind me not to do that again if possible."

"No shit. Now are we done? And can we wake up now? Is it over?"

"Yeah, I think so. We still need to find where he is in the waking world as he probably needs medical attention and we need to make sure this can't happen again. That this binding sticks. That last was his nightmare backlashing on him when he tried to continue even after Dianne started the binding. I know that energy signature well."

"Good. I want to make sure Cam's okay."

Liam didn't wait for more instructions, he just chose to wake up. Unfortunately, things weren't as serene as he'd have liked when he opened his eyes. Cam was still holding his and Nosha's hands, just as Nosha was holding his and Cam's, but Dianne was dabbing a cloth to Nosha's face—an odd, tender look he couldn't quite place on her face as she worked—and someone, he couldn't remember the man's name, was doing the same to his. Cam clutched his hand so tight his fingers were numb, and his eyes were wide and glassy.

"Lee? Oh God, Liam? You're okay?"

"I'm fine, beautiful," he croaked. Damn, his throat was sore. "How long were we out and am I really hurt again?"

"Five hours, hon," Di answered instead of Cam. "And yeah, you and Noshie are both banged up again. You more so than him. But—" She flashed a wicked, if tired, grin. "—it's done. The asshole won't be doing anything to you again. I doubt he'll be able to use his ability to hurt anyone anymore. Thank the Goddess!" A round of tired *so mote it be*s went up around the room following her words.

"You'll be fine, but you both need rest. And we'll do our best to cover the bruises and such so no one notices at the handfasting or in the pictures. Don't worry."

"Okay. Why don't you take Nosha into the spare bedroom and let him rest in there? I thank everyone, but I'ma be a bad host and go crawl into bed once I have some Motrin and a few Band-Aids."

A spattering of chuckles sounded from around the room, but no one seemed to mind. Cam stood and pulled Liam into his room once the nice man—who he'd ask the name of once he was awake enough to remember—was done with his face. He didn't remember his head finding his pillow.

CHAPTER 22

"IT'S A woman thing," Cam growled as his cell rang at the same time Di knocked loudly on their bedroom door.

"Come on, you two. You have a wedding to get to, so get your lazy bones outta bed!"

Liam rolled over and watched as Cam silenced his phone and glared at where Di's voice came from at the same time. "You think they time it? Was that your sister you just rejected a call from?" he added with a small chuckle.

"It was, and yes, I do. Sarah has the excuse of not knowing what actually happened last night. She thinks we went out clubbing before probably having sex all night or something. Dianne"—Cam raised his voice to make sure he was heard—"fucking knows what hell you went through last night—what all of us went through—yet she still acts like this."

"Beautiful…." Liam tugged Cam into his arms and rolled so he could press their bodies tight together. "She's just excited for us, I think. She's wanted to marry me off since we were like ten. She's always had a fascination for gay boys. Seriously. Only one of her little girlfriends that wanted her Ken dolls married instead of her Barbie and Ken dolls together."

"Still." Cam pulled a face. "Can't she do it at a lower volume? And really?"

Liam shrugged. He was used to Dianne and knew the woman too well to ever expect that from her. "Not likely, and yes. Instead of pouting, why don't we get our showers and see about getting ready? You have to go back to your apartment for your clothes and your family, right?"

"Yeah. I still need to move everything over here and all. I have a little time left on my lease, sadly, but it was only a six month one to start."

"We've got time, hon. Let's get showers and food, then you can go spend some time with them before we meet up for our nuptials." Which felt surreal to say but perfect at the same time. "But afterward, you're staying with me, here, in our room."

"Of course! Where else?"

"With your sister and brother-in-law?"

"Nope. They can use the loft. I'm here with you."

"Love you too, beautiful."

Liam insisted on separate showers, certain that if he didn't, Cam would cause him to never be able to look Di in the eye again. Plus, he really did think Cameron needed to spend time with his sister while she was in town visiting. It would be good for them both.

By the time they made it out to the kitchen, the living room had been put to rights and someone had set out pastries and coffee. Dianne and Nosha were the only two people there, though.

"Morning."

"Morning, hon," Di said as she tugged him down and pecked him on the cheek. She touched his face and tsked softly. "I've got some stuff that should cover those marks up for you. I'm not happy you were hurt again. But then, I'm even less so that Nosha was injured."

In the light of day, Liam could see that Nosha had a few scratches on one cheek and a nice shiner too. "Bobbed when you should have weaved too, huh?"

"Yeah. But it's over, so all we have to do is heal now. This really isn't what I wanted you to see of dreams and magic, though. It's not all like this. In fact, it's almost never like this."

"I realize that, and this hasn't changed anything. Well, not in a bad way." Liam leaned forward and lowered his voice. "After we fell asleep, my spirit guide visited me, and we talked." Seeing Angus after the events of the attack and binding had done Liam a great deal of good. More than he'd expected, if he were honest. Being through so much, feeling and seeing so much, had scared him more than he'd wanted the others, especially Cam, to know. But having Angus's take on things had helped him put a lot of things into perspective. Finally, he was ready to listen! (Much to Angus's amusement.) "After things calm down a little, I want to talk to you about becoming more involved in your coven, but for now, I think food is the plan." Liam looked back at a still-pouting Dianne. "And makeup, I guess. For the both of us. She won't forgive either of us if we aren't presentable for her pictures."

"We'll talk later," Nosha said as Dianne smiled.

"I thought the pictures were for us," Cam said as he sat down and snagged an apple turnover.

"Ha! Pictures are always for the womenfolk, even when it's not their wedding or their child's wedding." Liam's thoughts strayed to his parents and the fact they wouldn't be there when he gave his vows to Cameron later. He had invited them to the reception later that week but knew they wouldn't show. "Our women are giving us away, so the least we can do is put up with pictures and prettifying for them."

Nosha chuckled in that deep way that still didn't seem to match his face and body. "The scholar uses prettifying and the pretty boy pouts? You two are funny. What I'd like to figure out right now is how we missed what was happening before so nothing like this ever happens again."

"Noshie," Di chastised. "It's their handfasting day. No more talk of nightmares or old grudges."

"No, it's okay, Di. I'd love to know that myself. I mean, I had a couple of disturbing dreams recently, but I easily took control and corrected them… until that night. And you know about everything since then. But I don't want to go through that again or risk exposing Cam to that kind of thing again."

"But handfasting… happy thoughts… positive energy…. Come on, Nosha. Don't bring that into today. Please." Di's eyes were huge as she pleaded. "I want them happy for however long they have on this earth, at the very least."

"One thing, and then I'll agree with you. You didn't mention any bad dreams before. When did those start?"

"Um, I don't know. A week or two before all this. It wasn't anything major, and they were easy to fix. Just a twisting of positive to negative that I put to right or woke up from. I didn't even think about it after and wouldn't think of it now except for what happened. I'm not even sure it has anything to do with what happened. I mean, everyone has bad dreams, even dream walkers."

"True, but considering what happened, I think it's more likely he was testing you before the attack. I'd go try to find out for certain, but I want nothing to do with him. He's dead to us, and now he can't harm anyone again."

Dianne cleared her throat and glared, her cold gaze flicking between Nosha and Liam.

"Yes, ma'am." Liam turned to Cam. "Eat up, beautiful. You need to get back to your sister, and I have to put up with Dianne and her Makeup of Doom."

"It's fine, hon. I don't mind you talking with Nosha about all this. I'd love to know about why and when and all that too, so feel free to ignore Dianne all you want…. But"—he looked at his watch—"I should get back to them soon."

"Let me walk you out, then."

"That's fine. I think Nosha and Dianne need time to talk anyway." Cam leaned in and whispered against Liam's ear, "I think seeing the injury to Nosha last night finally shook her up enough to maybe get her past her worries about him being her priest."

"We can but hope." And if not, he would just have to dedicate some of his time in the near future to making sure they corrected that problem and finally got together.

Another twenty minutes and it was just Dianne, Nosha, and Liam. And her makeup.

LIAM STOOD on the grass in the same clearing he'd brought Cameron to on their first real outing, but this time the Biltmore castle view was the backdrop for their handfasting, not a date-night picnic. He'd spent so much time planning his outfit and getting ready, especially with the makeup coverage Di had used to hide the damage from the attack, but at that point he couldn't have told what Cameron was wearing—even though he was staring right at him—much less what he was. The only thing that registered was that they were surrounded by Dianne, Nosha, Sarah, Dan, Nate, Angelina, and Bass.

"These are the Cords of Handfasting." Nosha held up a braided rope that was actually three cords in one. One in silver. One in blue. And one in red. "They will bind Cameron and Liam together with bonds of love, passion, and hope. For such bonds to be healthy, they need support—not only from the couple themselves, but from the Divine. But most of all, they will need the support of their community, family, and friends. When I bind their hands together, please focus on the cord and let your support flow as loving strength into them.

"Know now before you go further, that since your lives have crossed in this life you have formed ties between each other. As you seek to enter this state of matrimony, you should strive to make real the ideals which give meaning to both this ceremony and the institution of marriage. With full awareness, know that within this circle you are not only declaring your intent to be handfasted before your friends and family, but you speak that intent also to your creative higher power. The promises made today and the ties that are bound here strengthen your union; they will cross the years and lives of each soul's growth. Do you still seek to continue?"

"I do," Liam managed to get out past the lump in his throat.

"I do," Cameron repeated a moment later, an enormous, watery smile on his beautiful face.

Nosha looked between them and continued, "I bid you look into each other's eyes. Liam, will you cause Cameron pain?"

"I may."

"Is that your intent?"

"Never."

"Cameron, will you cause Liam pain?

"I may."

"Is that you intent?"

"Never."

"Will you share each other's pain and seek to ease it?"

"Always," they said together.

As the list of vows and promises continued, Liam's thoughts focused on nothing but Cam and their future. There was nothing and no one more important to him. Even if the night before hadn't worked the way it had, he would have married Cam that day. He was just glad he didn't have the nightmare waiting for him when he closed his eyes.

"By the power vested in me by the great state of North Carolina and with the blessings of the Goddess and the God, I pronounce you wed. You may kiss your husband."

Liam was careful not to pull the cord binding their wrist apart as he pulled Cam into his arms. He then bent and feathered his lips over Cameron's as he whispered, "I love you, my beautiful one. You truly are my heart and my hope." He swallowed so he could get the rest out before they were swarmed. "Thank you for becoming my other half." Liam then took Cam's lips in a hard plundering, dipping him back enough to make him have to hold on tight before standing him back up.

The clapping and laughter pulled Liam's thoughts from the startled flush on his husband's angelic face.

"Now that's a kiss!" boomed Bass's voice, making everyone laugh even harder.

LATER THAT night, Liam led Cam into their bedroom, a soft smile on his lips. "Welcome home, beautiful."

"Thanks, hon, but we've been home for a little bit now."

"True, but it's our home and this is officially our bedroom now. So...."

"You just love saying that, don't you?" Cam asked, knowing how much he loved every time Liam said it.

"I do." Liam chuckled. "Now, you ready for the start of our honeymoon?"

Cameron raised one brow at Liam, not sure what he meant. They weren't going anywhere but to bed—not that that wasn't a wonderful place to go with his lover turned husband, and would he ever grow tired of using that word for Liam? "Going?"

"Mmm.... Beautiful? We can go anywhere you want, every night for the rest of our lives together. So where is night one of our honeymoon to be?"

Oh damn! Cam hadn't thought of that.... "Surprise me?"

"Your wish... my command." Liam then sealed his mouth over Cam's and stole all thoughts but *more, please,* and *unghh* from Cam until the wee hours when he drifted to sleep and Liam then proceeded to show him again the wonders that could be had when one was in love with a dream walker and dream weaver.

Stay tuned for an excerpt from

Whiskers of a Chance

By Tempeste O'Riley

Jason Grant runs his own IT business from home, owns his own home, and has the best friend he could imagine. What he doesn't have, or believe he will ever have, is love. When Jason catches a glimpse of his new neighbor on moving day, his libido ignites and his fascination in piqued. He even manages to concoct an excuse to go over and meet the man who makes him hope and want for more than he has in years.

Keith Skyler is a shifter in a world where his kind is known only to a few, but they don't often mix and they never mate. Keith has been hoping for a mate since before he can remember, but gay lynx don't have true mates. As far as he knows, they don't have mates at all. However, while moving his little family across Seattle—and away from their tribe—his reality tips and spins more than he thought possible.

When these two men meet over a dish of five-cheese broccoli-noodle casserole, sparks fly. Who knew a welcome-to-the-neighborhood gift could give both of them their chance at love?

www.dreamspinnerpress.com

CHAPTER ONE

KEITH SKYLER sat in the hard, high-back wooden chair across from his father, Adam, fighting the desire to scowl at the ignorant male. It was bad enough to be called into his office like a recalcitrant child, but to have to sit in the uncomfortable chair while Adam sat in the plush office chair irked him even further. The positioning was deliberate, to remind Keith that his father had the power, as if he didn't know that already.

"What part of 'Taylor and I are moving to one of the outer areas of town' don't you understand? You insist that since Taylor is without a mate, she needs me to live with her. You also demand it so Zeke can have a male figure in his life, at least until Taylor or I mate. She wishes to move closer to her work, as do I."

Adam Skyler's expression was stoic, as always, but the energy pouring off him was bordering on violent. Keith waited for his father to respond, knowing Keith would get what he wanted, though not certain what the cost would be yet. One did not simply do things without the great and mighty Adam Skyler, Alpha of the Glacier Rim Tribe, giving his approval… except when he and Taylor did.

"Why are you only bringing this to me now, Keith? You know how I feel about your sister's wild ideas of living with the humans. It's dangerous!"

"Other tribes live—"

"Chain." Adam closed his eyes as he pinched the bridge of his nose. "A 'tribe' of lynx is called a chain, and you know it."

"That's a human term, one that isn't even agreed upon by the inter-*tribal* council. Other lynx call their groupings *tribes*, not *chains*." He hated the term *chain*. It made them sound like a stupid fence instead of the extended family and friends that make up a tribe. Well, that's what tribes ought to be. Theirs failed on many points to be that, mostly thanks to his father's extreme patriarchal methods. When he took over, if he ever did, he swore to make their tribe more egalitarian—though Adam did not know that yet.

"I will not debate this with you, nor do I approve of Taylor and you moving away from our area."

"Father, the house is already bought. We signed the papers yesterday and picked up the keys." Yeah, he knew their method of gaining a little independence was inappropriate, willful, and could easily backfire, but he was determined to give his sister all the freedom he could and hopefully teach Zeke to be a good man, as well as a good lynx.

"You already did *what*?" Adam bellowed, his stoic demeanor finally cracking.

"We bought the house."

"On whose authority?"

"Mine. I am the prince and heir, and well over the age of adulthood. I need room to live and breathe. Taylor needs room to raise Zeke without the other females in her space. I know they mean well, but Zeke is *her* son, not theirs."

"They are only trying to help your sister. She's all alone and trying to raise her child."

"No, she's not. She has me. I know her mate died, leaving her single and with kit, but I am there for both of them. Besides, with both of us working in town, this arrangement makes the most sense. And don't worry, the house abuts the woods, giving us plenty of room to hunt, roam, and live in both our skins."

"And if I forbid this move?" Adam asked, his tone dropping to one of resigned irritation—a sound Keith was well used to.

"We are locked into the mortgage, Father." Adam Skyler was never one to waste money, a fact Keith was exceptionally glad of right then. "We will have to pay for it either way, and it would be foolish to own a home and not use it."

The growl from his father was not unexpected. Still, were he in his feline skin rather than his human skin now, his fur would want to stand on end.

"Since you have made it difficult to argue against this nonsense, you and Taylor may move, *but* I will visit shortly after you are settled. If the residence does not meet with my wishes and standards, you will come home and find a way to sell the house."

Thank you! "Give it a chance, Father. You know Taylor's tastes. She wouldn't live anywhere unsuitable."

"Anywhere among humans is already unacceptable, but we shall see."

"Thank you, Father. I need to make sure things are ready for our move." Keith waited, hoping Adam would allow him his leave and not push further.

"You are excused, Keith. However, I do not appreciate being managed this way. Until you come of age, I am still the alpha of this chain."

Tribe, dammit! "Understood, Father."

Keith quickly stood and exited the room, then maneuvered through the house to find Taylor. He was itching to shift and go for a run. His lynx always wanted to be outside, in his fur, after he was called before his father—or the council for that matter. By the time he found Taylor, outside playing with Zeke, he was bordering on screaming. Seeing them playing in their lynx forms helped calm him, allowing him to breathe easier.

"Taylor?" He couldn't help the smile that tugged at his lips when she turned, her tufted ears swiveling before her gaze met his. "When you're ready, I need to pick up the U-Haul and get things loaded."

They had been packing, but as their father never came to their part of the house, even though it was just one floor up from his own suite, he hadn't noticed all the boxes or layout plans. Their father's home was more akin to two houses stacked one atop another. He and Taylor had their own kitchen, living room, dining space, and bedrooms, but they didn't have any freedom or real space to be themselves. Not with their father and his advisers always underfoot and snooping into their lives.

Taylor hurried to where Keith stood, shifting as soon as she stopped in front of him—luckily her nudity no longer fazed him. When he was younger, her doing that had bothered him a great deal, but only because she was his sister. "He said yes?" she asked, her voice cracking on the last word.

Damn, she must have been more worried than she'd let on. "Of course. He insists upon checking on us once we've moved in, but that is to be expected," he explained, shrugging one shoulder. He didn't want to make a big thing about their move while they were outside. He never knew who might be within hearing range, after all.

Taylor grinned as she launched herself at Keith. "Thank you!" Without letting him go, she turned her head and called to Zeke, "Go make sure all your things are packed for Uncle Keith to take with him. I don't want you upset that something special left with him instead of being in your travel bag."

Laughing, Keith unwound his sister from around his body. "Go put something on, would ya? Like I want your girly bits on me."

Taylor swatted Keith's chest as she took off after Zeke—who had opted to stay in lynx form as he hurried inside and up the stairs.

By the time he'd caught up to them, Zeke was in his room, going through the special travel bag Keith had bought him the week prior. He'd been so proud of Zeke for not saying anything about their packing, not even to the other kittens in their tribe. Keith had been so careful when bringing boxes in and out of the house, making certain that neither his father nor his advisers were around to see what they were doing.

"Can't believe you managed to get his approval so quickly," Taylor said from behind him as he stood staring at the stacks of boxes ready to move.

"Hey, playing the money card usually works with him. Why do you think I wanted us to have signed the mortgage papers and all *before* I said anything to him? I'm not stupid, and moving away is the only way either of us will have any freedom to be who we are, instead of who he thinks we should be."

She sighed contentedly. "I know, and I can't wait to get going. Are you sure you want to do the move yourself? Zeke and I could help, instead of us only getting there after you have the house all set up?"

"Taylor, I know how you want everything set up. We've gone over the pictures and floor plan dozens of times already. This is safer for Zeke and will give me a chance to scope out the woods a little more before he gets there and wants to go run or climb."

"Yeah, I just hate for you to do all the work like this."

Her pout was adorable, but he had reasons, personal ones that he didn't want to tell her yet, for wanting to go ahead of them. When they'd gone over to view the house the second time—which was when they'd put in the bid—he'd caught a scent he never thought to find. The pull had been almost painful, and now he just needed to find out who it belonged to. Even though he needed more information, his mind kept yelling *mate*. Being gay, he hadn't believed he would have a mate, but he couldn't think of any other reason for the insta-hard-on, the driving need to mate, or the way his cat paced just under the skin after he refused to go back to the house early and find who the luscious scent belonged. Hell, he wasn't really certain he wanted to find the person. He didn't want a female! And though only Taylor knew that his heart and body only craved others of the same sex, he feared finding who Baast had chosen for him.

"I've got some friends that are going to help me unload in exchange for pizza and beer." He chuckled. "Seems that works for humans as well as cats."

"All right, Keith. But if you need help, you'll call me, right?" Her little upturned face always reminded him of her cat with its wide hazel eyes and tiny button nose, which she tended to wrinkle when annoyed. "Please."

"Of course, but it'll be fine. I promise. This time next week, you'll be in our new home and won't have anyone but me nosing into your business."

"Won't that be wonderful?" she chirped, bouncing on her toes. "Okay, go make sure you have your immediate-needs bag ready. When do you leave?"

"A little after lunch tomorrow. The cats helping on this end of the move will be here in the morning. The humans are, of course, meeting me at the house. It's all going to work out, sissy, I promise."

By the time Keith made it to bed that night, he was so anxious he barely managed to get any sleep. He wondered about the scent he'd caught, and the future, and hoped for freedom from his father's keen gaze and bigoted mouth.

THE DRIVE to their new home wasn't long, but loading everything into the U-Haul while his father looked on, scowling and making unhelpful comments, had Keith's nerves frayed and his temper short. The hope-slash-fear of finding his mate added extra layers to his stress. By the time he arrived at the Wendy's where he would meet the guys, he was in serious need of a drink—or three. Since that wasn't an option yet, he pigged out on Spicy Asiago Ranch Chicken Club sandwiches and Frosty treats. Carbs instead of booze....

"Dude," Dale groused. "How can you eat all that and still be as thin as you are?"

His eating habits drove his human friends crazy. If they ate like he did, they'd all be too big to get through the door. "Good genes," he quipped, same as always.

"So not fair," Ryan pouted. He struggled with his weight, wanting to be thin to attract guys at the club, but his body wanted to be slightly chubby no matter what he did.

Personally, Keith thought his friend needed to stop worrying about what shallow club-boys thought and focus instead on being happy and healthy for himself. "Sorry, didn't mean to make you feel bad, Ryan."

"You don't. Just wish I had your metabolism. Seriously, I can't figure out where you put it all."

If he just told them he was a lynx shifter and they even knew what that meant, they would know why—all shifters had overdeveloped metabolisms, a side effect of all the shifting they did. However, he was forbidden to reveal his species, and as often as he hated not being able to share that part of himself with his friends, he knew it was too dangerous for humans to know of their kind… or of any kind of shifter, for that matter.

Well, a few humans knew, but it was exceedingly rare and considered dangerous to their kind as a whole. What if the government or scientists wanted to collect them and experiment? A shiver tore through him at the thought. He pushed the morbid thought away and focused on his friends again.

"Ready to head out?" he asked. He didn't like depressing Ryan, so he usually didn't eat around him.

"Yeah, let's get this party started!" Dale crowed.

An hour later they were at his new home, with the U-Haul, and various cars filled with human and a few of his cat friends—the ones who didn't look down on humans—parked along the driveway and curb. As soon as he opened the truck door, the scent of his mate slammed into him, stealing his breath for a moment. Conscious of the other cats close by, he schooled his face and took a few slow breaths, trying to force down his desire and need. No way did he want others to know what was going on before he found the woman. *Woman*, he groaned internally. Why did he have to have a mate? Being gay was hard enough and not something he could let others know about, as it just wasn't done—not with how his father would react—and being mated on top of that would just be cruel.

By the time they were done with all the unloading, Keith decided that the Gods hated him. The scent of his mate constantly called to him—burning wood mixed with sandalwood and grass—teasing him mercilessly, and worse, he'd caught one of his neighbors watching him and his friends moving their things inside. The man pushed all his buttons—well, what of him he could see, thanks to the man being on the other side of a window from him—making him both thrilled that he'd moved and regretting it. His neighbor hadn't come out to meet him yet, but if the man didn't stop by soon, Keith decided he would just have to go over and say hello—if this whole *mate* thing didn't interfere. If he mated, he'd be screwed… or rather, he'd never be screwed again. That depressing thought wound through him, helping him keep his hormones in check and his focus off sex.

Once all the unloading was done, they broke out the beers and called for pizza. That done, Keith cranked up his stereo so it could be heard outside, though not too loudly, not wanting the cops called, then joined his friends for food, booze, and relaxing. Though it would have been more relaxing if the two couples—both gay couples, no less—hadn't been determined to dirty-dance and make out so much. Jealousy was ugly, he knew that, but right then it was a hard fact to remember.

Going to sleep the first night in his home, one that his father had nothing to do with, should have been an exciting and freeing event. Instead he tossed and turned, dreading the next day more than he had anything since his mother's passing when he was a boy. He had nowhere to be, and the house was mostly put together. He'd been up half the night after his friends finally left, putting books on shelves, dishes in cupboards, and trying to convince himself that his mystery mate would be a male. The last item was his only failure of the night.

TEMPESTE O'RILEY is an out and proud pansexual genderfluid whose best friend growing up had the courage to do what they couldn't—defy the hate and come out. He has been their hero ever since.

Tempe is a hopeless romantic who loves strong relationships and happily ever afters. Though they love writing M/M—they have done many things in their life—writing has always drawn them back (no matter what else life has thrown their way). They count their friends, family, and Muse as their greatest blessings in life. They live in Wisconsin with their children, reading, writing, and enjoying life.

Tempe is also a proud PAN member of Romance Writers of America®, WisRWA, and Rainbow Romance Writers. Tempe's preferred pronouns are they/them/their/theirs/themselves. To learn more about Tempeste and their writing, visit tempesteoriley.com.

TEMPESTE O'RILEY

DESIGNS
of
DESIRE

Desires Entwined: Book One

Artist James Bryant has forearm crutches in every color from rainbow for fun to sleek black for business. He even has a pair with more paint splatters than metal. After his family's rejection and abuse from a man he thought loved him, James only just gets through the day by painting. He lives in constant fear that he's not worthy of anything, let alone love.

As CEO of his company, Carrington Enterprises, Seth Burns is a take-charge kind of guy, and he is instantly smitten by the artist helping with his newest project. When he witnesses James suffer a panic attack, a protective instinct he never knew he had kicks in. He truly believes nothing is unobtainable—including James—if he's willing to put in the time and effort.

James is shy and confused by Seth's interest in him as a person. With Seth's support, can he work through his fears to finally find the true love he deserves, or will someone finally land the crushing blow he won't survive?

www.dreamspinnerpress.com

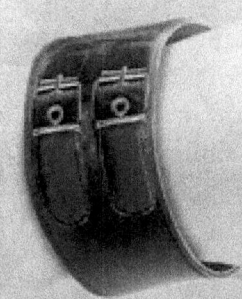

TEMPESTE O'RILEY

Desires' Guardian

DESIRES ENTWINED SERIES

Desires Entwined: Book Two

Most people see Chase Manning as the party-boy twink he seems on the surface. Only James, Chase's BFF, knows the depth of his loyalty and the extent of the wounds Chase carries inside. When Chase meets Rhys Sayer, things don't go well, but he can't shake his attraction to the huge, sexy man.

Rhys is a man of contradictions and fear—a strange combination for a PI and bodyguard. He's in a bad place emotionally when he sets eyes on Chase for the first time. When Chase puts the moves on him, Rhys insults him, thwarting any possibility of a relationship. Rhys doesn't see himself as a complicated man, but he dreads the very kind of connection he desires.

Just as they're trying to overcome their uncertainties, Chase is put in harm's way. Luckily Rhys and their friends have all the right talents to help Rhys save the man of his dreams.

TEMPESTE O'RILEY

TEMPTATIONS
of
DESIRE

DESIRES ENTWINED SERIES

Desires Entwined: Book Three

Alexander James Noble is a gender fluid gay man who gave up on finding Mister Right a long time ago. He's not asking for much, though. He just wants a guy who loves all of him and appreciates his feminine form too.

At the local LGBTQ center where Alex regularly volunteers, he meets Dal Sayer, an officer of the Milwaukee PD. Because he's been rejected one too many times, Alex doesn't trust the huge cop and the interest he shows in him, but once Dal sets his mind on something, he goes all out. Pushing aside his preconceived notions, Alex opens up just a little and soon caves.

From their first date—while dealing with his father's failing health and his parents' demands for him to settle down and have children—Dal never takes his eyes off his goal of making Alex his. But proving to Alex he isn't like all the men who couldn't see him for who he truly was and only wanted to hide him away is harder than he thought.

www.dreamspinnerpress.com

www.ingramcontent.com/pod-product-compliance
Lightning Source LLC
Chambersburg PA
CBHW060058260626
47160CB00005B/1713